MARILLA

of Green Gables

Also by Sarah McCoy

The Mapmaker's Children

Grand Central

The Baker's Daughter

The Time It Snowed in Puerto Rico

MARILLA

of Green Gables

A Novel

Sarah McCoy

WILLIAM MORROW

An Imprint of HarperCollins*Publishers*

HarperCollins books may be purchased for educational, business, or sales promotional use. For information, please e-mail the Special Markets Department at SPsales@harpercollins.com.

FIRST EDITION

Designed by Leah Carlson-Stanisic

Library of Congress Cataloging-in-Publication Data has been applied for.

ISBN 978-0-06-269771-4 (hardcover)
ISBN 978-0-06-287015-5 (international edition)

18 19 20 21 22   LSC   10 9 8 7 6 5 4 3 2 1

To my mother, Dr. Eleane Norat McCoy,
for being beside me on the journey, start to finish, apple seed to fruit

The spring was abroad in the land and Marilla's sober, middle-aged step was lighter and swifter because of its deep, primal gladness.

Her eyes dwelt affectionately on Green Gables, peering through its network of trees and reflecting the sunlight back from its windows in several little coruscations of glory.

L. M. Montgomery, *Anne of Green Gables,* Chapter XXVII

CONTENTS

Part Three: Marilla's House of Dreams

MARILLA

of Green Gables

PROLOGUE

1876

It'd been a rain-chilled May that felt more winter than spring. The apple, cherry, and plum trees were far less jubilant than usual. Their blossoms confetti-ed the pitched roof and washed down the eaves of Green Gables without anybody noticing. Marilla and Matthew worked side by side like blinder-clad horses, plowing ahead as they'd always done. The steady momentum they shared carried them toward the future. The farm chores needed doing, a lost button needed sewing, a batch of bread dough needed kneading: today was full. Tomorrow would come unpredictably, as was predictable. No use worrying until it was staring you in the face.

On this day, that face happened to be one of a red fox.

"Must've been trying to find a warm spot out of the rains," said Matthew.

Marilla huffed and dabbed the split in his forehead with witch hazel. He winced at the sting. Matthew was too forgiving. That fox wasn't looking for a nap. It was looking for her chickens and would've gobbled them up tooth and claw had Matthew not come upon it. She told him so.

"We had a mink in our coop last month," agreed old Dr. Spencer. "It killed all but one of our laying hens."

"Scared the milkers," Matthew continued.

He was in his bed now. Marilla had found him knocked out cold on the barn floor, dairy cows milling around like prissy church ladies.

"Scared me half to death is what it did."

She'd had to leave Matthew slumped over in the stable while she ran to the Lyndes' farm for Thomas, who then rode to fetch Dr. Spencer in town. Such a process. It'd taken her nearly an hour to send word for help. In her youth, she'd had quick legs, but they had changed. When she returned, Matthew was tottering around the barn, head bleeding, but otherwise alive. What if it hadn't been so? Time was of the essence when it came to life and death. She'd learned that well enough by now.

"Hit my head against the beam. Could've happened to anyone."

"Could've . . . but it happened to *you*." Marilla put the damp rag in the basin.

The wound clotted in a crimson streak across his brow.

"Glad there's nothing broken. A hearty contusion, though." Dr. Spencer leaned over Marilla to pull one of Matthew's eyes wide. "Don't see any dilation. You're just scuffed up and needing rest."

Marilla rose to throw out the pink water. The men's voices carried down the hall to the kitchen.

"You aren't the young man you used to be, Matthew. Sixty is a hard age to run a farm by yourself. This is coming from a friend who's got some years on you. Trust me, it only gets harder. Ever think about hiring someone as a live-in?"

There was a long pause. Marilla stopped pouring the water to listen closer.

"I couldn't have another man living here," Matthew said finally. "Not with an unmarried sister. Wouldn't do."

"No, you're right, not a man. A farm boy? There are plenty of orphans in Nova Scotia looking to work for their keep. My daughter-in-law is going over next week to bring one back for herself. 'Twould be easy to bring two."

"I'd have to speak to Marilla about it first."

Marilla alighted on an old hope buried so deep that she'd almost convinced herself it had been a dream. Laughing little boys over checkerboards. A Christmas tree strung with berries. Mittens by the fire. Cocoa and gingersnaps. The smile of true love. Red *Abegweit*. Wishing stones and Izzy—dear Aunt Izzy.

Her eyes turned watery from the memory. She wiped them clear and finished washing out the basin.

Dr. Spencer came from Matthew's room.

"He's going to be fine, Marilla."

"Grateful it wasn't worse, like you said."

He nodded. "Keep him off his feet. After a night's sleep, he should be back to his old self."

She gave Dr. Spencer the angel cake she'd baked that morning and one of their last bottles of red currant wine. The new minister disapproved of fermenting spirits. All the Sunday school members had clucked in agreement. Marilla wondered if they'd have been so reproachful of Christ turning water into wine. Probably so, given Rachel's temperament these days. Marilla had stopped making her batches, but Dr. Spencer had been around too long to capitulate to the growing temperance. He'd been the young doctor at her mother's bedside and attended to their every bruise and cough for the last forty years. The Cuthbert wine was his favorite. It was the least she could do to pay him for the house call.

She could barely wait long enough to wish Dr. Spencer good-evening before taking up the subject with Matthew.

"I overheard Dr. Spencer."

He looked momentarily puzzled, then realized what she meant.

"Aye, so what's your opinion on the matter?"

"Dr. Spencer is a wise man and a friend." She crossed her arms with certainty. "A boy would be a great help. I wouldn't have to worry so much about you working out there alone. We'd have someone to help with the farm chores. Run errands. Chase away foxes, if need be."

He exhaled and gave a little grin. "I hoped you'd say that. Been too long since . . ."

She nodded quickly. "I'll bake Mother's biscuits. Sweet butter with a little preserves."

A Cuthbert welcome. The wishes made were finally coming true.

part one

Marilla of
Green Gables

I

A GUEST IS COMING

February 1837

The sun and moon shine alike during snowstorms. They cast similar shadows, soft-edged, like dandelion clocks in the breeze. Marilla noticed that when she saw the silhouette of her father's sleigh coming down their snowy lane. The *Farmer's Almanac* had forecasted a mild winter. But it was late February, and the snowbanks continued to grow, leaving thirteen-year-old Marilla to wonder if spring would ever return. It was hard to imagine the apple orchard alive and green under this blanket of white and shadows.

She was looking out the new parlor window. The biggest room in the house, it had previously been the bedroom for all four Cuthberts: Marilla, her mother Clara, father Hugh, and older brother Matthew, plus a skittish white cat with a black streak named Skunk. Clara had found him in a burlap sack on the bank of the brook that whirled through the woods behind their barn. Someone had tried to do away with the poor thing. But Marilla and Clara had nursed him with warm milk and sardines until his fur was shiny as ice. He was still distrustful of strangers, but then, Marilla couldn't blame him.

Just before the snows came, her father finished the last addition to their farmhouse: the gabled bedrooms and the hired hand's quarters on the second floor, though they had no hands to hire as of yet. At twenty-one, Matthew had worked for their father every day since before Marilla could recall. Since it was not much more than fields, a barn, and a one-room cabin, most folks in Avonlea simply referred to it as "that Cuthbert place down yonder." But all that was going to change when spring came and they saw the completed Gables—*if* they could see it.

Hugh had laid the foundations nearly a quarter-mile off the main road of Avonlea, much to Clara's chagrin.

"So we have ample time to bolt the door when any of the Pye clan comes to call," he'd teased. That had even earned a chuckle from Matthew, who was bashful to laugh on account of a crooked front tooth.

The Pyes were "proudly cantankerous," Marilla had overheard one of the church ladies say. Personally, she'd never seen more than old Widow Pye's cloak flapping behind her like a crow's wings. She was left to assume the worst.

"But what if I need to borrow a spool of thread or a jar of preserves?" Clara had fretted. "I'll have to walk a fair bit to reach a friend."

"Aye, best not to run out then."

Hugh was painfully shy, with strict religious beliefs. His home was a private sanctuary. He kept the Bible on the table in the parlor and read one verse aloud to the family every night before Clara brought him his tea and whiskey. He went to church begrudgingly—not because of the sermon, which he quite enjoyed, but because of the parishioners who gathered between him and his buggy afterward. Matthew took after his father in that regard, and the two had become comrades in disappearing during the fellowship hour. But that was Clara's favorite part.

Marilla enjoyed standing beside her mother, quietly listening to the women gossip over the weekly comings and goings. It was nearly as interesting as the *Godey's Lady's Book* stories that Mr. Blair who owned the general store gave her and she hid under her mattress. Her parents didn't abide idle time, and reading was idle in their estimation. If ever Marilla had a spare minute, Clara told her she ought to knit another pair of mittens—one could never have too many sets—or work on one of the prayer shawls that their Sunday school class sent annually to the orphans of Nova Scotia. "'That their hearts might be comforted, being knit together in love,'" Clara would quote, and Marilla couldn't argue with the biblical Colossians.

But sometimes Marilla didn't want to knit beside her mother or follow her brother to their garden by the pasture field. Sometimes, as sinful as she knew it was, Marilla wanted to idle the day away however she pleased. When she could steal time, she'd take to the balsam woods with her *Godey's* magazine leaflets and follow the brook until it cascaded to a little pool split in half by a maple growing right up through the center. She'd sit there on her island with the water bubbling around and read until the sun slanted thinly through the trees. Then she'd walk home, being sure to collect a basket of sorrel for soup on her way.

"Always tough to find a good patch," Marilla told her mother. Not untrue. The rabbits nibbled away most of it in the fields.

Now, thinking of the fresh lemony tang of herbs made her mouth water. They'd been eating cellar turnips and pickled vegetables for weeks.

The clouds gathered low, making noon look like midnight. Hugh's horse and sleigh trudged sluggishly against the wind.

"Mother," Marilla called. "Father's bringing her down the lane."

Clara was in the kitchen baking a pan of choux buns to welcome their guest. Hearing the news, she wiped the flour off her chin but had a hard time reaching around her prominent belly to untie the apron strings.

"Don't know how I got this on in the first place," she muttered, lumbering left and right in an attempt to grasp one of the strings. "Marilla!" she finally relented. "Come and help your mother untangle?"

Clara leaned herself against the kitchen window frame. The chill was a relief. Tiny beads of sweat had formed on her forehead from the effort. Dr. Spencer had warned her to be cautious. Before Marilla was born, she'd miscarried two—then another before this one took. The babies had gone so early in their development that they hadn't anything to bury but flowers of the season, always spring. Reverend Patterson said that God saw every heart, even the ones they didn't. So they'd planted memorial crosses behind the barn on a knoll that gave a glimpse of the sea. Dr. Spencer was a man of modern medicine. He had advised her to listen to her body—that perhaps two children was all it could do and that was two more blessings than came to many women he knew. But Clara remembered well when she and Hugh were courting. He said he'd like at least half as many sons as the biblical Abraham to work the farm. They'd been young and naive then, but dreams carried a lifetime. She felt a disappointment for delivering so much less. Hugh never said as much, but he was a man of few words.

Marilla was at her back in a flash, untying and then folding the apron neatly away.

Lightly toasted butter scented the air. The puffs were a minute away from crisping too far. Clara opened her mouth to say so, but Marilla was already at the stove, pulling the iron baking pan from the fire with the strength of a grown woman. It made Clara touch her swollen belly. How fast they grew.

"Should I fill these with plum or crab apple preserves?" asked Marilla.

It was the first time she'd met her Aunt Elizabeth—Izzy, as her mother called her. Or at least, it was the first time she could recall. Izzy had moved to Upper Canada when Marilla was four years old and hadn't set a boot heel on Prince Edward Island since. When Marilla asked why not, Clara had shrugged. "Everybody got busy doing life, I suppose." It seemed as honest a reason as any.

But now, with the baby on the way, Izzy was coming to help her sister through the birth. She'd done the same for the births of Matthew and Marilla.

"Just sweet butter," said Clara. "Your aunt appreciates a simple pastry done up right."

Marilla frowned to herself. What was a puff without some kind of fruit filling? An empty puff! She set the butter crock beside the plum preserves on a starched napkin. She was excited to meet Izzy, but nervous too. Blood kin or not, Izzy was a guest and a stranger.

"Do her children and husband mind that she's going to be away so long?" asked Marilla.

The Cuthberts hadn't discussed their coming guest much. Hugh and Clara were well familiar with her, and Matthew had grown up with his aunt until the year Izzy went to Upper Canada. So it seemed the topic needn't be talked over. Everyone already knew everything that needed knowing—except Marilla.

"She hasn't any husband or children. Remember, dear?"

That was right. Clara had told her once before. Still, Marilla had a hard time imagining any grown woman alone. She didn't know a woman her mother's age with no husband or children in all of Avonlea. Even the widows had children, and the childless had husbands. To not have either made her wonder if Izzy wasn't somehow defective.

"She's a very successful dressmaker in St. Catharines." Clara tugged at the gingham hanging askew over her shoulders. "Maybe she can help us make new ones for spring."

Clara's hand with the needle and thread left much to be desired. Marilla would never say as much. She took the dresses Clara made, rehemmed the skirts, rethreaded the buttonholes, and wore sashes to cinch the waists. Easy fixes and a small price to pay in comparison to hurting her mother's feelings.

Marilla imagined that if her mother were a part of nature, she'd be a butterfly, merrily going about its affable business in the fields, light and pretty. But the smallest hand could crush it. Marilla imagined herself as a caterpillar, long and thin and steadily in motion. Her father and Matthew would be apple trees. Strong providers, silently bearing the weight of each season. These were the daydreams she found herself giving in to more and more.

Her schoolteacher, Mr. Murdock, said an indulgent mind was a wicked one. But then, she'd once heard her father tell her mother in private that Mr. Murdock came from a hoity-toity academy in York and considered everyone in Avonlea beneath him. Hugh spoke so little. When he did, Marilla remembered well. She never entirely trusted Mr. Murdock after that. She wouldn't believe his $2 + 2 = 4$ until she'd proved it herself.

Just then, the kitchen door leading to the back porch opened. A bluster of snow raced in, hit the warmth, and melted straight to the floor.

"Father and Jericho are coming down the lane." Matthew carried an armful of dry wood. He stomped the frost off his boots. "Figured it was best to stoke the fire before I get Jericho stabled. Mighty cold out."

"Thank you, son." Clara stretched her back and pressed a hand to the side of her belly.

"The pains again?" Marilla asked. Though her mother wore a placid expression, Marilla could see the darkness in her eyes.

"Little twinge. It's the cold. I guess the baby doesn't like it."

Marilla bolted the door closed and stuck a poker in the stove to turn the coals bright. She'd make some black tea to go with the unplum puffs. It was only half past noon, but on days like this, teatime could be any hour. One could hardly tell by the light.

"Sit by the parlor fire," she told her mother. "I'll make the tea." Then she wondered aloud: "Does Aunt Izzy approve of tea?"

Mr. Murdock said that some people living on the Lower Canadian border of the U.S. had permanently given up the drink after the Boston Tea Party in America: 342 tea chests thrown into the harbor. Three hundred and forty-two—Marilla had a mind for figures. Tea had three letters in it, and so Marilla made up the mnemonic: tea for two. It helped her remember 342 when Mr. Murdock questioned them on their American history studies. She'd been going to school since she was seven years old, but now she was on home study. After the baby came, she hoped to return and finish. She only had two grades to go before taking the exit exam.

"Of course she approves of tea!" Clara laughed. "Marilla, you mustn't worry so much about perfectly pleasing people. Aunt Izzy loves you, and she'll love you even more once she sees how fine you've grown." She kissed Marilla's forehead, leaving a milky sweet smell behind.

Marilla hadn't meant to be perfectly pleasing. She'd only meant not to offend.

She filled the kettle from the kitchen cistern and set it on the stovetop with a slight clang. Clara looked over her shoulder at the sound but then continued into the parlor.

Alone with her thoughts, Marilla was unnerved that those closest to her knew this outsider better than she did. And now Izzy was coming into their home to live for months. They'd never had a guest that long. In fact, they'd never had a guest at all. The gable rooms had just been built. Only farmhands had ever stayed overnight, and only in the barn loft. Izzy was the first official non-Cuthbert to sleep under their roof, and Marilla seemed the only one not entirely thrilled about it.

II

AUNT IZZY IS A SURPRISE

Marilla heard the jingle of Jericho's harness bells a full minute before the door opened. That gave her just enough time to pour the steaming water over the tea leaves and set the pot on the tray to brew. From the kitchen, she *heard* her aunt before she saw her.

"Clara! Sister! Oh, look at you—round as a pumpkin!" The voice was loud with a jaunty clip, different from anything Marilla had ever heard and nothing like Avonlea people.

Clara laughed and muttered, "More like fat as a sow in mud!"

Marilla frowned to herself. A sow in mud was the last thing her mother resembled. Clara's arms and legs were so thin, they looked like stems off an acorn, and just as easily snapped.

"I'm so happy you're here, Iz."

"It took an eternity. The stagecoach was dreadful. I was stuck between a man who had a slug of cod liver oil every three hours and a woman with two babes in nappies. Imagine the stink of it all? By the time I reached the ferry for the island, the sea air was better than a bottle of Floris London perfume. If only this snowstorm had waited one more day. I felt awful that Hugh had to drive out in it."

"No trouble," said Hugh. "Glad to do it. Clara's been lonesome for a kinswoman. Gone a long while, Izzy."

Marilla was still standing in the kitchen, somehow unable to bring herself to interrupt the reunion. For the first time, she felt like the stranger.

"Too long." Izzy gave a sigh. A bit theatrical in Marilla's opinion. "But I'm here now. So where are my niece and nephew?"

At the mention, Marilla's face went hot. She smoothed the pleats of her dress and made sure the strands of her hair were smoothed back off her forehead.

But before she took a step forward, Izzy cooed, "My sweet little Matthew! Not so little anymore. A grown man and handsome as the devil!"

Fiddlesticks. Marilla may have never left Prince Edward Island before, but there were enough boys around for her to clearly see that her brother Matthew was neither handsome nor the devil. He was sensible-looking and went to church every Sunday just like the rest of them.

"Marilla?" The gentle lilt of her mother called. "Marilla dear, come here and let your Aunt Izzy have a look."

A look? What was she—a circus monkey? Not that she'd ever seen a circus monkey, but Mr. Murdock brought in as many newspapers as he could, including the *London Standard,* which once featured the Bartholomew Fair. They had dancing monkeys, wild beasts, men who walked on their hands, women who danced underwater, and real gaslights—inside too! Marilla thought it all terrifying and wonderful. She heard there were such things on every street in St. Catharines, so close to the fashionable American resort at Niagara Falls. Perhaps Izzy was accustomed to spectacles.

Marilla made up her mind right then to prove to her aunt that the girls of Prince Edward Island were as well mannered as the princesses of England. She pushed her shoulders back, held her head high, cupped her hands neatly at her waist, and strode forward as confidently as she dared.

The room that had comfortably held the four of them suddenly felt crowded. The hearth fire blazed to a roar, sending up a little too much smoke and making the parlor hazy.

"This is our Marilla," Clara said in welcome, then stepped aside to reveal Izzy, still wearing her bright blue cape. Seeing her niece, she pulled the hood off her head with a smile.

Marilla shrieked and jumped back, clutching her chest and accidentally kicking over the box of yarn where Skunk had been sleeping. He leapt away from her boot with a hiss and darted down the hall to an unoffending corner. Marilla wanted to follow him.

Clara frowned. "Marilla. Child, what's gotten into you?" She took Izzy's hand in solidarity. The two stood shoulder to shoulder, staring at Marilla.

Though Izzy's hair held a touch more butterscotch, and she wore it in a cascade of coils, her face was the mirror of Clara's—identical, if it weren't for the rouge and powder where her mother wore none.

Marilla lifted a finger, *tick-tocked* it between the two. "You—you."

The sisters looked at each other, scowling the same scowl, which made Marilla want to cry for terror.

Thankfully, Matthew cleared his throat. "Well now, I dunno if Marilla ever seen twins before."

No, in fact, she had not. Marilla had heard about twins. Mrs. Barry had a cousin in Kingsport with a set of twins. She wasn't a country bumpkin. Had someone told her that her mother was a twin, she would've been prepared for this moment.

Izzy and Clara simultaneously broke into laughter. Both eyes squinting bright and shining. Marilla might've taken the moment with indignation had she not noticed that while her mother's cheeks remained smooth, Izzy had a prominent right dimple that pulled inward when she laughed. It gave her great relief to find that one distinction.

"I suppose I never mentioned it. I assumed everyone knew!" said Clara.

Izzy tossed back a ringlet gone lopsided at her temple. "Poor thing. Quite a shock."

Marilla composed herself as best she could. Embarrassment flamed her cheeks.

Hugh nodded to Matthew. "Let's get Jericho into the barn. Reckon this snow will keep to piling. You ladies settle in."

"Tea and nibbles are waiting when you finish," said Clara.

Hugh winked at her, and it made Marilla blush. It was his way of loving.

With that, the men left.

"Take this off—you're staying a while." Clara peeled her sister's wet cloak away and hung it to dry by the fire.

Izzy wore a calico dress of a purple pansy pattern. Finely sewn, the bodice had cream gauze from the elbow to the wrist and a similar swath around the shoulders. Unlike Marilla's housedress, the gown was tailored to Izzy's petite waist and pleated down the back in a respectable bustle. It wasn't audacious or frivolous. Quite the contrary. Its seams were so geometrically executed that it reminded Marilla of a church steeple. Not one ounce of wasted fabric. Every bit had a purpose in the overall construction. By comparison, her mother's dress seemed an incredible excess of haphazard material. Granted, she was with child, so it had to allow for expansion.

"Are you hungry from the trip?" asked Clara.

"Famished."

"Oh good, because Marilla made you cream puffs."

Not entirely true. Marilla had dropped the dough for her mother, then put them in the oven and taken them out. That was all.

"Choux à la crème!" Izzy clapped.

"Made with sweet butter. From Avonlea's finest—our cow Darling." Clara went to the kitchen.

Marilla opened her mouth to say that she put the crock and teapot on the tray, so her mother needn't lift a finger. But her tongue was tied, alone in the company of this new person.

Izzy stretched her arms wide in front of the fire with a dainty yawn. "Is Darling the cow you wrote me about three springs ago? The one you got from the Blythes? Their stock really is the best on the island. Even back when we were children. Just goes to show, fruit takes after seed, seed takes after fruit."

Marilla hadn't a clue what Izzy was talking about—seed and fruit piffle. These were cows, not crops. Maybe she'd been in the city so long that she'd forgotten how nature worked. But the fact that she knew about Darling and the Blythes made Marilla wonder how much else her mother had told Izzy about their lives. Meanwhile, Marilla hadn't even known her mother was part of a matching pair!

Izzy spun round then.

"Mari-lla." She trilled the *l*'s, birdlike. "You turned out pretty. Tall and elegant. I swore to your mother—didn't I, Clara?" She yelled past Marilla's ear at a pitch no Cuthbert had used indoors and hardly out. "I said, 'Sister, don't you fret. She might be a dark, homely little thing now, but all babies are.' You should've seen Matthew! 'Just you wait,' I said. 'I can tell by the glint in this one's eye, she's going to be lovely.' And that's when your mother asked me what we ought to name you, and I said, 'Marilla.' It comes from Amaryllis, you know. A beguiling, bold flower."

It stung Marilla to be called a homely baby, but what shocked her more was that her aunt had named her. *Beguiling?* Certainly not. Everyone knew Marilla was a derivative of the holy mother Mary. *Bold?* The Cuthberts prided themselves on being faithful members of the "blessed are the meek" church. Presbyterian.

Izzy sat down on the sofa and patted the seat beside her. Marilla obeyed in quiet defiance of the beguiling, bold comment about her name. So close to her aunt, she could smell the powders on Izzy's skin. Lilac with a touch of copper from the cold.

"I'm sorry I frightened you."

"No one told me you and Mother were twins." Marilla spoke

coherently for the first time and made sure her voice didn't waver a fraction.

"Your mother is the sweeter and more gracious, always has been." Izzy winked. "You take after her."

Then, out of nowhere, Izzy kissed her cheek. Marilla stayed as still as possible during and after, afraid Izzy's lip rouge might smear on her and stain her skin.

A spoon fell in the kitchen. "Marilla!" Clara called.

Marilla jumped to her feet with Izzy beside. In the kitchen, they found Clara gently laughing as she tried to look around her belly to see where the spoon had dropped. She took two steps forward, then two steps back, leaned right and left, then circled round again like she was dancing the Scotch Reel. The spoon stayed expertly in her blind spot.

"I thought I could . . ." Clara started, then ran out of breath and leaned on Marilla while Izzy curtsied to retrieve the spoon.

"What was this for anyhow? You know I don't take sugar or milk in my tea. Just pour into a cup and drink."

"I know, but I thought you might've changed," said Clara.

"Not me, Sister. My wheres and hows may change, but my whos and whats are as constant as the seasons."

She pulled a puff off the baking tin, light as a cloud, and split the bottom from the top. Using the fallen spoon, she heaped butter into the hollow and popped it in her mouth.

"Delicious."

She did the same to another and handed it to Marilla. Then a third to Clara.

"I'm not a guest in this house, so don't handle me with kid gloves. I'm family and here to take care of *you*."

She pointed her finger at them, a bit of butter on the tip. Seeing it, she licked it clean, then went back to the tray.

"Tea for three?"

Clara had shifted more of her weight onto Marilla's shoulder, pinching her breastbone, but Marilla didn't move away.

"We're glad you're here." Clara exhaled and ate her butter puff.

Marilla nodded and did the same. She still didn't think it as good as a full plum puff, and she still wasn't sure about Izzy as a person. But she was glad to have the extra set of hands. Her mother struggled more and more each day, and secretly Marilla was terrified of what came next. Birth was not something the church ladies discussed. Not something in her magazine stories either. The only thing she knew about it was from helping her father deliver one of Darling's calves the prior spring, and that was only because Matthew was away in the field.

The newborn beast had been far too large for its mother. Its front feet were extended out of the womb, but the head could not make a way. To save both, Hugh had reached inside and pulled the thing into the world. Marilla was tasked with keeping Darling steady. She'd stroked her head and whispered lullaby songs as best she could, but even she was sent retching into the hay when she saw her father covered hands to waist in blood and tacky fluids. It didn't seem to bother him, though. The calf was out and healthy. Darling was happy and resting. The only one left ill was Marilla. Clara had chastised Hugh for showing Marilla nature's way too soon. But Hugh had no choice.

Nearly a year later, Marilla worried that someone would have to reach inside her mother and pull her baby sibling free. It was not an undertaking she desired, and she was glad Izzy was here to do the task if necessary.

III.

A FAMILY RECIPE

The next morning, the sun stretched sleepy flaxen arms over the Gulf of St. Lawrence and stirred Marilla alongside the sound of laughter and pots being banged as if gypsy minstrels had taken over the Gables. The Cuthberts were quiet people, especially in the mornings. Her father didn't speak in more than a whisper before noon, and her brother could go clear through supper without a peep.

Outside her window, Matthew was already leading the milking cows from the barn to pasture. She'd overslept. Her mother had not woken her to help prepare breakfast for the men. Alarmed by the disruption in their Cuthbert routine, Marilla kicked her bedcovers to the ground. With her nightgown twisted round her like a rose, she hurried down to the kitchen.

"Marilla," greeted Clara. "Good morning, love."

Still wearing her house robe, Clara sipped a cup of tea at the little wooden kitchen table that they used for chopping vegetables. At her elbow was the sack of dried red currants that they'd picked in July and left on a yard of cheesecloth under the sun until the whole batch wizened to a cure. They'd been saving them for Easter scones, but it seemed Marilla's aunt had other plans.

Izzy whirled about the kitchen in a housedress striped like a candy cane. Her hair was done in a bouffant of symmetrical curls circling her face. The likeness between the sisters was still strange, but there was no confusing the two. Clara was the soft moon while Izzy was the glaring sun.

Seeing her niece, Izzy lifted the iron pot in her hand and struck it with a wooden spoon. It rang like a bell and started a headache in Marilla.

"My pretty flower!"

Pretty flower, my foot, Marilla thought and stomped her own. Barefoot, it did little more than pat the cold floor. She found pet names patronizing. Her name was plain Marilla, and she was a girl, not a flower. So she respectfully ignored her aunt and went to Clara's side.

"Good morning, Mother." Marilla kissed her cheek. "Why didn't you wake me?"

"We thought you deserved the extra rest."

We who? And why would she need any more than every other morning?

"I always make Father and Matthew breakfast . . ."

There wasn't a day in her memory when she hadn't cracked an egg into the skillet before dawn.

"Your aunt is here to help now. She made the most delicious porridge with maple syrup. We saved the best bowl for you."

Izzy smiled and bowed at the compliment. Marilla didn't think it all too impressive. She would've made them porridge too if ever they had asked her.

"A young girl needs as much time to dream as possible," said Izzy. "Soon enough you'll be all grown up and there will be no time but the doing."

Marilla frowned. So far, Izzy was proving to be a person of rhymes, riddles, and fanciful poppycock. It made Marilla's headache sharpen, and she feared she might lose her mind completely by the time the baby came and her aunt left.

"I like doing," said Marilla.

Izzy put down the pot and smiled. "Well then, why are you standing there? Get dressed and come back ready for the *doing.*"

She turned without waiting for Marilla to reply and filled the pot from the water cistern.

Clara patted Marilla's hand. "Do as your auntie says."

It smarted to have to obey a woman she'd only just met and who had seemingly crowned herself the new queen of their gables. But Marilla vowed to herself to be better than whatever lowly expectations her aunt might've had. So she squared her shoulders, righted the cuffs of her nightgown, and marched back up to her bedroom. There she washed her face with cold water and put on her cleanest frock. She'd sternly ironed it herself so that the arms shunted out from her shoulders like ridgepoles. She twisted her hair, which she might've left down on a normal day, up high in a bun and secured it with her wedged horn comb. The pull at her temples helped to alleviate her head's throbbing.

Evaluating herself in the vanity mirror, she thought she could pass as a mature sixteen and not her rightful thirteen. This gave her great satisfaction as she came back down to the kitchen. But her mother and Izzy, busy debating the next step in their recipe, hardly noticed her.

"We've got to dissolve the sugar in boiling water, then add the currants," said Izzy.

"I seem to recall Mother mashing the berries," said Clara.

"Yes, but those were fresh. We're using dried. Mother didn't use dried, but Mamó Flora did."

"Ah yes, that's right. I'm awful forgetful these days. I'll walk upstairs to fetch something, but by the time I arrive, I've completely forgotten what it was!" Clara laughed and leaned her forehead to her sister's.

It seemed Clara was even forgetting her only daughter. Marilla cleared her throat to remind her, but it was Izzy whose attention was won.

"Oh good, Marilla. We need you. Take your breakfast and then we'll begin. You've got to learn the secret family recipe."

Clara brought the bowl of porridge to the table. Warm maple syrup pearled atop the oats. Marilla had to admit, if only to herself, it was delicious.

"What secret family recipe?" she asked between spoonfuls.

Clara cooked like she sewed—just well enough to get the job done. She'd taught Marilla every recipe she knew because invariably the fare would turn out twice as good when Marilla was at the stove. Marilla took naturally to the kitchen and couldn't explain why she excelled while her mother floundered. "She has a gift," Clara had told Hugh. Like the sun's ability to put color on an apple and pull it from the linen. Some things just were.

"The Johnsons' Red Currant Wine, of course." Izzy winked. "Passed down through the women of the family and a revered tradition at every new baby's baptism. It needs to keep in the pantry for three months or longer to be tasty."

"We have to make it now to be ready for the baby." Clara patted her belly.

While Hugh had a bit of whiskey every night, her mother only partook of wine at Christmas and on special Communion days after the minister had offered up the first cup. So Marilla had assumed wine was a sacramental drink. Too costly and ecclesiastical to be made in an everyday kitchen. It could only have been prepared by Reverend Patterson and his acolytes in the Presbyterian church cellar, then locked up tight in hallowed casks to receive the heavenly blessing. She figured the bottles in their pantry had been tapped from the church barrels.

Once again, in the wake of Izzy's arrival, what she'd thought were the facts of her world were being proven false.

"How old were we the first time we made red currant wine, Iz?" asked Clara.

"I reckon a little younger than Marilla." Izzy looked up at the ceiling while she did the math. "Eighteen hundred and seven or eight? I can't recall. It was the year little Jonah Tremblay was born . . ."

"The year of the junebug swarm."

"So what'd that make us?"

"Twelve—no, no, eleven."

"That's right, because we were two full numbers old—zero being zero, and not really a counting number—and Mother said that was grown enough given that we'd stay two counting numbers until we reached 111, which was a far ways off. It was for the Tremblays' christening gift. God bless 'em. That was possibly the worst batch of wine in all of creation! I remember taking a sip and spitting it right into the yard. I didn't have another until long after seventeen."

"I lost a thumbnail in that first mash," Clara confessed.

"Clara!" Izzy gasped.

In a giddy rush, Clara continued. "It accidentally pulled off in the masher. I never told anybody! I felt too terrible to say I ruined the lot after all the work we did. So I prayed every day during the fermenting that the good Lord would make it disappear somehow. And like a miracle, when Mother strained the wine into the cask, not a speck of nail was to be found."

All three erupted in laughter. Not even Marilla could hold hers back.

"I don't know how I remembered that when I can't recall where I put my sewing circular yesterday." Clara wiped the happy tear from the corner of her eye.

"If Hugh came in now, he might think us drunk on the fumes," said Izzy.

It was the word that slugged Marilla sober. *Drunk.* She'd only known it once before . . . when Matthew had come home late one evening. He'd gone to a barn dance with a group of school friends, and there'd been more than lemonade in their punch cups. The gables were only halfway built at the time. The Cuthberts shared the parlor room for sleeping, so Matthew couldn't hide his stumbling. He'd tried to light a kitchen lamp to see his way, but the oil had turned over and caught flame.

"Get him away—the boy's drunk," Hugh had hollered while beating out the flames.

It was one of the first times in Marilla's life that she'd felt danger, and it troubled her that it'd come at the hand of one of the people she trusted most. So she told herself that it hadn't been *her* Matthew that night; it had been "the drunk." In the end, a braided rug had to be thrown out, the floorboards were scorched in the spot, and a burn to Matthew's leg would leave the skin rippled like pond water. A scar he showed no one. The memory made her temple twitch, and she pushed a finger to the spasm until it abated.

"Does your head pain you?" Izzy had been watching and now stood close, frowning with concern.

"A little." Marilla wouldn't lie.

Izzy sprinkled salt in Marilla's porridge. "You need more minerals in your diet. You're too thin. Eat and you'll feel better."

Marilla finished her bowl and true to Izzy's word, her headache vanished. Just in time too. The sugar water was ready for the currants. The bag was too heavy for them to lift without spilling the currant-ettes onto the floor, so they each took a teacup and scooped the berries into the pot, counting off in turn.

"One," said Clara.

"Two," said Izzy.

"Three," said Marilla.

She liked being part of the cadence, like casting a spell.

"Four."

"Five."

"Six."

"I think we need one more for luck," said Izzy. "Would you do the honor, Marilla?"

Marilla scooped, leveled the cup precisely, then plunked the berries into the water. "Seven."

Clara stirred the pot, making a pinwheel of red. "I have a feeling this is going to be the best in years."

"The best ever, I'm willing to bet." Izzy turned to Marilla. "Put the lid on and let it steep for an hour before we strain and bottle. That's when the magic happens."

"Magic?"

"Yes, water into wine! Technically, fermentation. Without it, we'd have a pleasant currant cordial, which is well and good for everyday occasions, but a baby is not an everyday occasion. Would you agree?"

"I would." It was the first time Marilla had agreed with her aunt since she walked in the door yesterday.

They spent the next hour peeling potatoes and churning butter for supper. House chores went twice as fast with Izzy around. She saved the potato skins on account of a beauty tip from one of her dress shop customers—an American actress—who said she soaked the peelings in lemon juice before applying them to her face at night. The result was alabaster skin. Marilla had never been vain about her looks, but it seemed a good use of scraps that would otherwise go to waste. Clara thought it a brilliant remedy for the squiggling lines that stretched across her stomach, and Izzy promised to wallpaper her belly later.

Izzy had also brought a book of nursery rhymes by sisters Jane and Ann Taylor.

"Oh, Iz," exclaimed Clara, "I haven't seen that in ages!"

"Shall I read 'About the Little Girl That Beat Her Sister'?"

The sisters bowed into each other when they laughed.

Marilla had never heard the poem or any other from the book. Clara hadn't read nursery rhymes to her as a child, deferring to Hugh's scriptures over whimsy.

"How about 'The Star' instead?" Izzy cleared her throat. "'Twinkle, twinkle, little star, how I wonder what you are. Up above the world so high, like a diamond in the sky' . . ."

Clara gazed lovingly at Izzy and rubbed her belly, as if coaxing the baby to listen up.

"'Though I know not what you are. Twinkle, twinkle, little star,'" Izzy finished with a smile.

Marilla found herself smiling too, though she hadn't meant to. Izzy turned the page to read another, and the hour flew by. Soon they were three faces hovering over the cooled pot. Inside, the currants had plumped as fat as rubies.

"This being her official first red currant wine, I do believe the *chef de cuisine* gets the first taste?" Izzy ceremoniously handed Marilla a spoon, and she accepted.

Clara and Izzy stood on either side as she ladled the fruit into her mouth. The concoction was sweeter than any berry on the vine, with a tart kick that made her crave more.

"It's quite good," said Marilla. "Quite."

Izzy clapped while Clara took the spoon from Marilla and taste-tested to agreement. "I must say, this has turned out nicer than with fresh currants."

"Maybe it isn't the berry but the cook who's improved the family recipe." Izzy put a hand around Marilla's shoulder. "All that's left to do is wait and keep turning the bottles. The torch has been passed. The Johnsons' Red Currant Wine is now Marilla Cuthbert's Red Currant Wine!"

"We'll toast to that once this baby has come. And if it's a girl, we'll teach her the recipe too, in time," said Clara.

Marilla warmed at the idea. She had a brother, but she'd never known sisterhood. Standing between her aunt and her mother, Marilla couldn't help smiling at them both. She tried to imagine them as girls her age. She thought they would've all been friends. She hadn't any true girlfriends in Avonlea. Hadn't ever wanted one when she had her mother, brother, and father. But seeing the kinship between Clara and Izzy made her wonder . . . might it be nice to have a sister?

IV.

LEARNING AUNT IZZY'S HISTORY

The last of the sugar had gone into the red currant wine. The women had planned to go to the Blairs' store that Saturday to buy more, but Clara was feeling poorly. So Izzy said she'd run the errand. True to her word, Izzy was a doer. She made a list of the chores she intended to take on around the Gables, the preparations necessary for the baby's birth, and what she called her daily sewing practices. She was always stitching a design on her circular, knitting a skein of yarn, or tracing out the looping lacework from her pattern book.

"One must keep one's skills sharp!" she'd said while her knitting needles *clickity-clacked* during Hugh's nightly scripture readings.

She'd begun to instruct Marilla on dress sewing without asking if she wanted to learn.

"The women who come to my shop are educated and moneyed but helpless to dress themselves. I won't have our girl so incapable. Right, Clara?"

To Marilla's surprise, her mother had agreed.

"You've got to be able to take care of yourself, Marilla."

Marilla knew how to darn a sock better than new and her crocheting had produced many fine shawls for the orphans in Hopetown, but she had yet to make any substantial garment. She wore mostly hand-me-downs from Clara's church friends whose older daughters had grown out of them. The few items Clara had sewn herself were made of old bed linens and special sale fabric, mostly housedresses with jagged but solid seams. They were never meant to be worn in public. Marilla couldn't help being excited at the prospect of making a dress like Izzy's—so finely tailored and sensible. Izzy was going to pick up material at the Blairs' to make the baby a play gown for summer. They'd start with that before a full woman's dress, she said. Marilla envisioned a fabric of yellow and green like lady's slippers, Clara's favorite flower. The pink ones grew everywhere on the island, but only along their farm's fence did they blossom yellow as the sun.

"I hate to spoil the fun," said Clara from the parlor, where she sat with her swollen feet in a bowl of Epsom salts and water. "It's such a beautiful day too."

The sky was the clearest blue Marilla had seen in months. It matched the watery horizon so closely that sky and ocean seemed one seamless shade pulled down over the island. The trickle of melting icicles played like chimes. You could nearly hear spring whispering hello.

Marilla had been looking forward to going to town, but of course Izzy could buy the items just as easily without them. So she took up her basket of yarn and started where she'd stopped on her crocheting.

"It's best you rest, Sister," said Izzy. "Never you mind doing the errands. Marilla and I can manage." She pulled her scarf from the hook and tied it round her neck.

Marilla was equal parts elated and distressed. On the one hand, they were going! On the other, her mother wasn't. Marilla had never been a clingy child. She enjoyed an independent excursion. What made her nervous now was the idea of being alone with Izzy. While Izzy had grown more familiar to her in the week since her arrival, her aunt still felt like a stranger.

"Come, come," Izzy beckoned Marilla toward the coat stand. "Make sure to wear your warm mittens. They call this the Windy Island for good reason."

Marilla was well versed in the island winds and in how to dress herself. This was *her* home, after all, not Izzy's. She buttoned up her coat, put on her wool cap, and stepped into her fur-lined boots. It would be a long walk to Avonlea, and she had little faith in the fashion laces Izzy wore.

Before she pressed a soft footprint into the snowy yard, Izzy came round with the crack of a whip in the air. She'd harnessed Jericho to the cutter sled and sat in the driver's seat with reins at the ready.

"Jump in, girl! I promised your mother we'd be back before Hugh and Matthew return from Carmody."

The men had gone there to discuss the prices of spring seed. Hugh wanted to plant a new potato crop this year.

Jericho had just enough time to stomp the snow from his feet while Marilla slid in beside Izzy. She gave a flick to the reins, and off they went at a dash.

Marilla had only been in the sleigh with Hugh or Matthew driving at a measured pace. But now Izzy let the reins go slack so Jericho could gallop faster, at his own free will. When the hood of her blue cape fell back, Izzy didn't retrieve it. Instead, she let the wind blow her curls from their tight pins until all of her hair flew loose around her ears. Stray pieces from Marilla's own bun pulled across her vision like seaweed in the bay, and it felt quite like they were swimming—gliding on the current. She had to hold her breath and close her eyes against the icy undertow.

They stopped at the edge of Avonlea, where the first row house began and the snowy road turned to shoveled sidewalk.

"Slow there, boy," said Izzy. "I think we've given Jericho his daily exercise. He's earned himself a sugar lump." She kept him steady while his breathing calmed.

"When we were young, your mother and I used to steal away some winter days when there was nothing to do inside but watch our fingernails grow and wait for the snow to melt. We'd hitch up the cutter and ride as fast as we could. Once, we went clear out to the Stanleys' by Hope River. You know the place?"

Marilla nodded. There was a bridge there that she'd driven over many times.

"We left the horse and sleigh to climb onto the frozen banks. We decided it wasn't the bay, but an enchanted sea, teeming with whales of possibility. To catch one, you had to throw a magic stone. If it fell through the icecap, whatever you asked for your future would be. We spent an hour throwing rocks. They lined the ice like plums on a frosted cake. Then finally, we broke through."

"What did you ask for your future?"

Izzy smiled, pulled a ribbon from her pocket, and tied her wild curls back to reveal a quartz pendant around her neck. Not purple enough to be amethyst. The stone was so pale, it looked almost blue. She smoothed it between her fingers. "I asked the same thing with every stone—to go somewhere and do something very great. More than chopping wood in the winters, picking peas in the summers, and being maid to a husband and home. We only have one life to live, Marilla." Her eyes grazed the length of the town. Still, she kept Jericho at a halt. "It's selfish of a person to take what's given without knowing if it's even what they want. For as long as I can remember, I had an urge for *more*. Some called that selfishness. But I thought it only fair if I tried to fill that *more-ness* myself rather than expect someone else to fill it for me. Do you know what I mean?"

Marilla did, but she couldn't imagine anybody leaving the island *forever*. It was just about the most perfect place on earth. What *more* could a person want? True, she'd never been off it, but from all she read in the newspapers, the rest of the world was riddled with strife. War and death from Texas down to Brazil in the south. Crops dying and farmers' families starving in Canada from east to west.

So instead of answering, she cross-questioned: "Then your wishing came true, did it not?"

"In some ways it did, and in some ways it didn't."

"But you went away to St. Catharines?"

St. Catharines might as well have been Timbuktu as far as Marilla was concerned. Mr. Murdock had shown it to them on a world map stretched wide across the chalkboard. It was on the border of America beside Niagara Falls. He said he'd visited the Hotel St. Catharines, which gave you a gold door key and silk pillows to sleep on. Marilla couldn't conceive of using such luxuries. A gold key—why, when an iron one would do the job? Silk pillows that you weren't even awake to appreciate? Foolishness. But even as she condemned them in thought, her fingers tingled: what would it be like to hold a golden key or sleep on silken pillows? She wondered if Izzy had such things. Clara said Izzy dressed all the city ladies with peacock-feathered hats and pearl buttons. Such finery . . .

"St. Catharines isn't so much different from Avonlea," assured Izzy. "The older I get, the more I see the truth. Greatness can be found anywhere. It doesn't need grandeur. There's greatness in the ordinary. Maybe even more than elsewhere. You remember that, Marilla."

Izzy exhaled, and Marilla thought it a sad sound. Had Izzy found her greatness in St. Catharines? Or did she wear a wishing rock because she was still seeking it?

Izzy clicked her tongue, and Jericho trotted down the main thoroughfare. Old Mr. Fletcher sold roasted chestnuts in front of the Avonlea post office.

"Well, if it isn't Miss Elizabeth Johnson—I almost mistook ye for Clara!" greeted Mr. Fletcher.

"Not the first or the last time!" Izzy stopped Jericho.

"Welcome home! Have a scoop on me." Mr. Fletcher handed her a rolled-newspaper cone of nuts.

"Never tasted a sweeter bite."

Across the street, the five Cotton boys were just coming out of the barbershop, looking like freshly shorn ears of corn.

"Izzy Johnson, is that you?" asked Mrs. Cotton from behind her gaggle.

Mrs. Cotton had been in school with Izzy and Clara. Back when they were girls throwing wishing rocks in Hope River.

"Good to see you, old friend. Clara told me you married a Cotton son."

Mrs. Cotton nodded and stretched her arms over the five pomaded heads. "They do make 'em fine."

Izzy handed each boy a steaming chestnut. "Be good for your mother, lads. She helped me learn to spell 'Armageddon,' and I won first place in the regional spelling bee on account of it."

The youngest boy turned to his brother. "Arma-what?"

One of the older boys flicked the middle brother behind the ear, and the eldest told them both to "quiet before I make ya."

"A-R-M-A-G-E-D-D-O-N," Mrs. Cotton said loudly to reestablish order. "Oh, the irony!"

Izzy laughed, though Marilla couldn't understand why. She'd heard the Reverend talk of Armageddon with fiery passion, thumping the pulpit and sending the pigeons out from the rafters. It was obviously a thing to be avoided.

"Good to have you back with us," said Mrs. Cotton. Her eyes darted to the Blairs' store for a flicker but returned smiling. She waved good-bye, and her sons followed her, shortest to tallest.

Izzy tied Jericho to the post out front of the Blairs'. It was a small one-room depot that had originally been Mr. and Mrs. Blair's parlor. They hadn't meant to go into the mercantile business. They'd started by selling a handful of brooms, soaps, and handkerchiefs—save the local wives the trip to Carmody—but before long the Blairs were taking requests for everything from lace to cinnamon. So

Mr. Blair turned the floor level into a little shop, and they lived in the apartment above. They didn't carry many items, but it was enough to keep their shop bell ringing all hours of the day.

"Well, bless my stars, I've seen a ghost," said Mrs. Blair. She stood atop a stool, fetching a roll of batting down from the shelf for Mrs. Copp.

Mrs. Copp turned to look, then raised an eyebrow high and huffed, "Oh dear. Elizabeth Johnson."

Unlike the women, Mr. Blair came round from behind the counter, leaving his paying customer standing with the bill in hand. He embraced Izzy as a daughter returned.

"Izzy!"

Mrs. Blair joined him hesitantly. "Hello, Izzy. It's been a long while since we last saw you. Not since . . . well, who can remember exactly."

"Indeed, it has been. I'm sorry I hadn't the opportunity to come back sooner, but I thought it probably for the best."

"Probably so." Mrs. Blair pursed her lips.

The space between Izzy and Mrs. Blair felt icy, and Marilla couldn't hold the winter's day entirely responsible. While Mrs. Blair was a proper sort, she'd never been one for unfriendliness.

"I'm here to help with Clara's coming baby," Izzy explained.

Mr. Blair nodded knowingly. "I'm sure she's mighty glad to have ya. Did you see where they set up house?"

A welcome change of subject.

"Of course she has. She's got Marilla with her, don't she?" said Mrs. Blair.

Mr. Blair went back to tallying the accounts book for his customer, while Mrs. Blair continued.

"It's so *far* off the beaten path. Clara was always such a sociable spirit, and now we hardly ever see her since Hugh built that place."

Marilla's father had just finished the gables the month before, so

Marilla didn't see what all the fuss was about. Clara was too burdened with child to be in town, and it was winter! The snow and
wind kept most everybody by their home fires anyhow.

"It's a beauty of a croft, though," Mr. Blair said in defense. "Hugh
Cuthbert knew what he was getting when he bought that piece. I
always thought it the prettiest place on the island. You can see the
forest and the sea, all in one." He finished his sale.

The customer tipped his hat. "Welcome home, Miss Johnson."

"Thank you kindly, Hiram. Please tell your mother I've missed
her butter nut cakes."

"Will do. She's moved in with my cousin to help with the
lil'uns."

"Your baby cousin has little ones?" Izzy shook her head. "So
many changes since I left. Please give them my hellos."

The man nodded again, cleared his throat in good-bye to the
Blairs, and left.

It seemed Izzy knew just about everybody in Avonlea, and they
knew Izzy, even better than Marilla.

"So now, what can we get you? I doubt you came to pay a social
call," said Mrs. Blair.

"We've come for a pound of white sugar and to see about some
dress material." Izzy put her arm around Marilla's shoulders.

Mrs. Blair gestured for them to follow her to where she kept the
bolts of muslin and poplins.

"We don't have all the fancy frippery of the big city," she warned,
"but I try to keep at least a dozen sensible patterns in stock."

"No flounces necessary. It's for Marilla's brother or sister a-
coming."

"Have a particular color in mind?"

"I think yellow," answered Marilla. "That way it can be worn by
a girl or boy."

Izzy smiled. "A wise choice, my dear."

"Solid, floral, or tartan?" asked Mrs. Blair.

Marilla ran her fingers over one soft woven cotton: pale yellow dotted with green-leafed ivy. Like a tall pitcher of lemonade and floating mint, the fabric made her mouth water and her skin crave the warmth of summer.

"That's a beauty," said Izzy. "Three yards, please, Mrs. Blair. That should be enough for a baby gown and whatever else we might dream up." She winked at Marilla. "We'll take some of that ivory muslin too. Collars and cuffs to tea towels—we can make anything from that. So clean and new with possibilities."

Marilla hadn't ever stopped to consider colorless muslin as anything but . . . colorless muslin. Assessing it afresh with Izzy made her understand how a homely thing can become quite extraordinary if given the chance to prove itself.

Mr. Blair scooped and weighed the sugar while Mrs. Blair measured and cut the material. Together, the couple packaged everything in brown paper tied with twine.

"I haven't any new *Godey's* magazine stories, but I promise to set them aside for you when I do," Mr. Blair whispered when Mrs. Blair had moved on to a lady customer debating milled rye or oats. The oats were a half-cent cheaper, but she wasn't sure they would bake up the same.

"I just don't know. I'd hate to ruin my brown bread. But that's such a pleasing price for oats . . ." she muttered.

Marilla never could understand folks who said whatever was on their mind to whoever might be present in whatever location. The woman spoke as if she were the only one in the room and thus begged the question: just whom did she think she was speaking to? Hugh called it the malady of indiscretion. Some people couldn't help themselves any more than they could help a fever. They were sick with it. Involuntary or not, such unconscious ramblings made Marilla uncomfortable. So she turned her attention away to the jar of peppermints on the counter. She had fancied peppermint since her first bite. It wasn't an herb that grew in their garden, which made it even more prized.

Seeing her stare, Izzy opened the jar, handed Marilla a candy, and took another for herself.

"Don't mind if we do," she said. "Peppermint is such a wholesome treat. I close my eyes when I'm enjoying a piece. Makes you feel bright, like you've swallowed a winter star. Don't you think, Marilla?"

Marilla had never thought such a thing. But now she closed her eyes with the mint on her tongue and found that Izzy was right. She could've sworn she saw starbursts in the darkness.

"You can add those to our bill."

"No charge," said Mr. Blair. "Mrs. Blair makes them twice a week. William's favorite, you know." His voice caught on itself, and he shuffled paper wrappings nearby to conceal it.

Izzy fumbled with the clasp of her purse and cleared her throat. "How is William?"

Mr. Blair looked to his wife, engaged across the room, then replied quietly. "He's well. Married up now, you know. Lottie is her name. Came over from Scotland. They're moving to Carmody in the spring and expecting their first child any day."

With a click of coin on the counter, Izzy finished counting out the payment. "It seems children are as ubiquitous as snowflakes in Avonlea." She gave a strained grin. Her dimple, which usually made itself apparent, stayed hidden. "Please pass along my congratulations to William and Lottie. I heard she is a woman of remarkable kindness."

"A bonny girl, that she is." He put a reassuring hand on Izzy's. "All things work together for the good."

From Romans, Marilla recognized. It was one of Hugh's favorite Bible verses to read to them.

Mr. Blair gave Marilla the sugar bag and Izzy the wrapped parcel of fabrics.

"If you and Clara be of a sewing mind," he continued, "they've just inaugurated the Avonlea Ladies' Sewing Circle. Isn't it so, Mrs. Blair?" he called out to where Mrs. Blair was weighing the sale oats.

"What's that?"

"Telling Izzy and Marilla about the ladies' sewing circle meeting once a week at the Whites' place."

Mrs. Blair gave a mouselike sneeze at the oat dust. "Can't say that I know the particulars. It's mostly younger women and wives. The rest of us haven't the time for such diversions. But by the increase in thimble and thread purchases, I expect it's the latest fad cut straight from the pages of one of those frivolous ladies' magazines, no doubt."

Mr. Blair waved her off. "Mrs. White was just in here yesterday asking me to spread the word. Can't have a ladies' sewing circle without a circle of ladies. Then it'd just be a sewing line."

"Well, I don't know . . ." Izzy began, but Mr. Blair persisted.

"Reckon you'd be doing them a favor, teaching them the newest stitchery from the city. The Whites moved here from East Grafton and are still getting to know folks." He winked.

"It would be nice to practice," conceded Izzy. "I aim to teach Marilla all my best tricks."

While Marilla had mastered her crocheting needles, she was a far cry from adept enough to join a formal ladies' sewing circle.

"The Whites' girl Rachel is about Marilla's age," Mrs. Blair chimed in, "and she's already doing French knots, so I'm told."

Marilla cringed. She didn't even know what a French knot was.

"I'll write to Mrs. White promptly then," said Izzy. "Thank you, Mr. Blair. I'm sure Clara will join us if she's feeling well enough."

Marilla knew her mother was even worse with the needle and thread. She worried over it all the way home until finally resolving that she'd have to face the circle. There was no way out. She was so caught up in her own thoughts, it wasn't until they unhitched the harness from the sled that she remembered, "We forgot the sugar lump for Jericho!"

Izzy pulled the peppermint from her pocket. "He can have mine."

In a single chomp, Jericho swallowed the candy and gave a whinny of satisfaction. It made Marilla wonder if animals too dreamed of winter stars and things greater than themselves.

V.

INTRODUCING RACHEL WHITE

The following Tuesday, Matthew dropped Marilla and Izzy at the Whites' house on his way to Carmody to buy a new cheese press. Their old wooden one had split down the base, and Clara claimed the baby had a mighty hankering for cheese. After a week without, she'd begun dreaming of cheese mountains, pillows of curds, and streams of sweet creams, while the baby kicked her voraciously. She was convinced that she could not last another day without a new cheese press. So Matthew was dispatched.

That same morning, Clara awoke with a touch of a cough. "I couldn't trouble the ladies. I'd shake all the needles to wobbly stitches."

Izzy had offered to stay home with her, but Clara insisted, "I want Marilla to go. She's been holed up in this house too long. A young lady needs to get out in the world. Show her. Please, Sister."

So they packed up their sewing circulars, colored threads, and some of the red currant wine. They'd just rolled the wine bottles a half-turn clockwise.

"One must always bring a gift for the hostess," explained Izzy. She nestled the bottle carefully in her hamper, reminding Marilla of the biblical baby Moses about to float down the Nile.

Marilla was nervous as a bumblebee on a honeycomb when Matthew helped her down from the sleigh.

"You'll do fine, Marilla," he whispered in her ear. "Just take a deep breath and go on in there with your head held high. Look for good things and good things is what you'll find, right?"

It was from the proverb Hugh had read them the night before: "He who seeks good will surely find it."

She nodded to Matthew. Hard to argue with Gospel. Still, it frightened her to be under the critical eye of these women. She wanted to impress them. Matthew pulled away down the lane, and Izzy waited for her at the front gate.

"Come on, girl. They'll start without us."

The Whites lived in a shingled house with painted peach shutters and a giant hollyhock growing beside the drainpipe like Jack's beanstalk. So near to the center of town was it that when the church bells rang the hour, the porch swing swayed.

"How do you do, Miss Johnson, Miss Cuthbert," greeted Mrs. White at their knock. "So glad you could join us." She opened the door wide, and the smell of baked vanilla spilled out. "The ladies are just having tea and cake before we begin."

Despite her dainty lace and pearls, Mrs. White was a buxom woman with large brown eyes, solid hands, and a no-nonsense air to everything she did. "Let me take your coats. Go on in. Our maid Ella will pour you a cup. Wouldn't want a wet chill to get in the lungs. Keep hoping I'll wake up and spring will finally have the gumption to arrive." She led them into the parlor room, where eight women sat in a circle of ten chairs, all eating frosted wedges of cake off glass plates.

"Miss Elizabeth Johnson and Miss Marilla Cuthbert," she announced to the maid as she passed to put their things in the closet beneath the staircase.

Ella was a young French girl not much older than Marilla. "Can I get you something to eat or drink, mademoiselles?"

Marilla had never been in a house with a maid before. It was strange to imagine someone unfamiliar living under her roof. She didn't think she'd like it much. She could barely tolerate Izzy, and she was blood kin. A maid would be privy to all their family's comings and goings, all of their talk, all of their secrets. What would stop such a person from gossiping or stealing or any other kind of mischief?

No, Marilla would not like it one bit. Not even if the maid darned all the socks in the house and baked a hundred cakes. She'd just as soon do it herself.

"Sounds delicious! Have you ever seen so many sugar whippets on a confection? I do say, whoever made this is an artist," crowed Izzy while Ella blushed and gracefully presented the slice sideways so the layers of strawberry jam showed pink.

"The first one's for you, Marilla," Izzy insisted.

Marilla took her plate and stood uncomfortably to the side, not knowing if the seats were designated or not. Everyone was paired up, chatting merrily between forkfuls of vanilla frosting. Mrs. White returned with a managerial clap.

"Ladies, now that we are in full attendance, welcome to the official assembly of the Avonlea Ladies' Sewing Circle!"

Forks jangled against plates in attempted applause.

"Fill up on sustenance, and we'll take up our sewing at a quarter past the hour."

Mrs. White ran the meeting and her home like clockwork, without a moment's dillydallying. She immediately circled round to Marilla.

"Come here, child, you must meet my Rachel."

Though she didn't dare disobey, Marilla's feet were anchored to the ground. Izzy gave her a gentle push.

Under a grand fern with arms stretched wide as an eagle's wings, Rachel sat with her needle already threaded and stuck in the center of her circular. She was pretty in a fair and fashionable way. Braids of her flaxen hair looped back behind her ears with little curls dangling from her neck like lily of the valley blossoms. Her cheeks and arms were far more soft and plump than Marilla's. In that regard, she looked almost doll-like in her posture.

"Marilla, this is my girl Rachel. Rachel, this is Marilla Cuthbert, Miss Johnson's niece."

Rachel curtsied. "How do you do?"

They felt like two fish in a bowl, all eyes watching to see who swam away first.

"Just fine and you?"

"As well as one can be with a stomach full of cake and no ice cream to settle it down with," said Rachel.

Mrs. White exhaled loudly. "Next time you can forgo the cake altogether. There's prudence in abstinence, dear."

Rachel's plate was scraped clean. It was obvious she had a sweet tooth.

"Well . . . maybe some tea for digestion," she relented.

"A wise idea," said her mother. "Why don't you and Marilla fetch yourselves some before we begin? Marilla, set your plate down beside Rachel's. That seat is for you."

Marilla had assumed she'd be next to Izzy. She'd hoped then that no one would notice her loose knots and crooked lines. Not knowing what else to do, she obeyed Mrs. White. Rachel took her by the crook of the arm and led her back across the room to the tea table.

"Mother would have us all drinking tonics and eating carrots if she had her way. My Uncle Theodore took my Aunt Luanne to the thermal baths in Vichy—that's in France, in case you didn't know— and she came back looking like Lady Godiva. She said they put her on a strict diet of tonic water and vegetables to improve feminine circulation. Can you imagine? That sounds like torture, but Mother's been on a kick. She didn't have a bite of the cake Ella slaved all yesterday making. Father told her that Aunt Luanne's transformation had everything to do with the thermal baths and clean air, but

Mother is convinced otherwise." She *tsked* and took a breath. "Do you ever feel like you are the only one in the world who sees plain as day what others cannot?"

Too often Marilla felt quite the other way around: others seemed to see plain as day what she did not. She made no reply, but Rachel didn't seem to mind.

"The Cuthberts sit fourth row to the left at church," she continued. "My family sits seventh row to the right, so you can see how we'd miss each other. Unless you were turned around."

The numerical calculation appealed to Marilla. She was flattered that Rachel had noticed her.

"And you haven't seen me at Avonlea School. I came down with a grievous case of the chicken pox two winters ago. It put me dreadfully behind the rest of my grade. So Mother thought it best if I studied with a tutor until I caught up."

"And you haven't yet?"

Rachel poured the last bit of tea out of the pot, being careful to avoid the floating leaves. "I have a hard time with my letters. Sometimes"—she cleared her throat—"they get sort of mixed up between the page and my eyes. Dr. Spencer says I need reading spectacles, but I never saw anybody our age wearing spectacles. Lawful heart, no! Those are for old maids. If I start wearing them now, I might never get a husband. Here—" She handed the tea to Marilla. "You can have the last cup."

Marilla smiled. "Very kind." She was parched from just listening. Rachel could talk an ear off. It had to be the sugar in the cake, she decided.

The sewing circle ladies finished their nibbles and gathered in the center of the room to show off their projects and discuss new ones. There was a collective gasp when Izzy pulled her stitching out of the hamper.

"It's Venetian Gros Point for a dress collar," she explained.

"Such fancy needlework over in St. Catharines."

"It's ever so lovely."

"Can you teach us?"

They clucked one after the other.

"So your aunt has come back," Rachel whispered as Marilla sipped. "I overheard some of the Sunday school ladies saying that she's only able to set a toe back on the island because Mr. William Blair is married now. They were engaged, you know, but before you could say Jack Robinson, she changed her mind and was on a train for St. Catharines without an explanation to anybody. Audacious without remorse! But Mrs. Blair told Mrs. Barry who told my mother that, while shocking, Mrs. Blair hadn't been surprised. Of the two Johnson girls, they could see plain as day that your mother was the more reliable. Elizabeth had a wild oat to sow, and Mrs. Blair had warned William from the beginning that she'd not settle into wifehood like her sister. So it was really for the good that she left sooner rather than later. William found a better marriage match for it, so they say."

Marilla sputtered on her tea and recalled what Izzy had told her before they went to the Blairs'. She realized now that Izzy had meant much more in the *more* that she spoke of. In Marilla's estimation, it took great courage to become engaged and even greater courage to dissolve an engagement. Izzy was already proving to be greater than Marilla had originally thought.

"Gracious, are you all right?" Rachel handed Marilla a napkin with concern. "Please don't die when we're just getting to be friends . . ."

Friends. Marilla hadn't any friends. She didn't want Rachel to know that, so she gulped down the knot in her throat and pressed the napkin to her lips.

"I—I hadn't heard about Aunt Izzy and Mr. Blair."

Rachel's countenance softened. "I'm sorry. Please, you mustn't mind me. Mother says I'm too outspoken a person. Maybe it's because I don't have much of anybody to talk to around here. So when I do, whatever's on my mind pops out. I shouldn't have said that about your aunt."

"She came back to help with the baby."

Rachel nodded. "A'course she did. I don't believe a word of those old crows' gossiping."

Mrs. White clapped again to gain the room's attention. "To your seats, ladies! The time is nigh!"

Rachel led Marilla back to their chairs. "I'm so glad to have someone my age to talk to while we stitch. I've got a box of threads—all colors of the rainbow—you can use them too. I may not be so good at reading letters, but my eyes are just fine for sewing. Aunt Luanne gave me a pattern book from France. There's one I've been dying to try. A spray of red amaryllis. It could go on a bodice or a sleeve. But then we'd need to make two so the right and left sides were alike. Maybe you could make one and I could make the other. Or are you working on something already?"

"I'm making a baby gown with Aunt Izzy, but we haven't started yet. We just bought the fabric from Mrs. Blair."

Marilla thought of the peppermints and Mr. Blair's mention of William. How strange to think Izzy might've been part of their family: Izzy Blair. Marilla frowned. It sounded like something an apothecary would treat.

"Might you be able to do both? We can take turns wearing the dress when it's finished." Rachel wrung her hands in earnest. "I'd greatly appreciate the help and company."

Marilla was more than glad to do it. She liked Rachel. It was refreshing to be around someone who didn't make you guess their mind. For better or for worse, Marilla appreciated that.

"Yes, but I warn you, I'm not very good. One sleeve might come out a blossomed branch and the other a battered limb."

Rachel laughed and threw herself down in her chair, forgetting that her sewing circular was placed just so on the cushion. Her giddiness swiftly turned to pain. She jumped up with a yowl, clasping her backside with both hands.

"Laws!"

The eye of the offending point glimmered. Everyone in the room stared with alarm.

"What in heaven's name are you shouting about, Rachel?" asked Mrs. White.

Rachel released her skirts and mumbled under her breath, which seemed to vex Mrs. White more than the outburst.

"Speak up, girl! I can't stand muttering."

Quickly, Marilla came to her new friend's aid. "I think she's been stung by something."

It wasn't a lie. A needle was a stinger of sorts.

Mrs. White softened. "Oh dear, how awful!"

The ladies all began to waggle and shake their skirts.

"Was it a wasp? A bee?"

"Wherever did it come from?"

"Mr. and Mrs. Gillis had to tear down their shed because of a hive of carpenter bees wintering in the walls."

"I have chills at the thought—carpenter bees!"

The chatter produced a panic. They all pulled at their collars, shirked away from the walls, and buzzed like a poked hive.

"Ladies, please, please . . ." Mrs. White tried to calm them, while she, too, nervously eyed the cornices, and Ella took up her broom for protection.

In the midst of the chaos, it was only Rachel and Marilla who stood still, not daring to look at each other for fear of bursting into laughter.

"Perhaps we should reconvene after Mr. White has had the place inspected?" Izzy waved a hand over her head, batting away an invisible swarm.

"An excellent idea, Miss Johnson. My poor Rachel has been stung. I'd hate for anyone else to be next. Ella, the ladies' things please!"

Ella returned under a mound of coats and knitted things. The women leapt on her, pulling on whatever item fell into their palms, and rushed toward the door.

"An infestation of carpenter bees in the Whites' house!"

Izzy and Marilla were the last ones to leave.

"We brought this for you." Izzy gave Mrs. White the bottle of red currant wine. "It's got to turn a few more months before it's ready to drink. But if you need it to get you through . . ." She buttoned the top of her coat and studied the walls suspiciously. "Open as you please."

Mrs. White took the bottle. "I may just!"

Izzy waited outside for Marilla. The girls were finally alone in the foyer.

"We can't ever tell them . . ." Rachel began, then looked over her shoulder to her mother, who'd swapped the wine for Ella's broom and was vigorously swatting the ceiling. "It's got to be our secret."

Marilla smiled. She'd never had a secret with a friend.

Rachel covered her mouth to laugh, then held her hand out. "Do you vow to never tell a soul so long as you live and breathe?"

Marilla took it in hers and thought it the loveliest hand she'd ever held besides her mother's. "So long as I live and breathe."

Rachel tightened her grip, then released. "I must help Mother. She's in a terrible state. Will you come over again—so we can work on the amaryllis sleeves?"

Marilla nodded.

"Rachel!" called Mrs. White. "Were you stung near this chair?" She batted the seat with the broom until it fell sideways.

Rachel giggled. "See you."

"See you," said Marilla.

The sun was shining. The snow melted quietly in the unseen

nooks of the eaves and the trees, but the ground remained hard as ice, which Marilla was grateful for as they walked the lane home.

"It looks like you made a friend today," said Izzy.

"I believe so," said Marilla.

Izzy winked and took Marilla's hand. It made her think of the vow she made to Rachel and the vows Izzy would not make to Mr. William Blair. Marilla still found it hard to believe that Izzy had nearly been Mrs. Blair, daughter-in-law of the general store. It seemed there were many things she didn't know about her family and her town.

VI

INTRODUCING JOHN BLYTHE

Marilla and Rachel were halfway done with their two amaryllis sleeves by April. The process had been slower than anticipated because Mrs. White said they could only work on the design after they did at least ten rows each on the Avonlea Ladies' Sewing Circle project: prayer shawls for the Hopetown orphans of Nova Scotia. Seven of the ten ladies also belonged to the Presbyterian Sunday school class, so they had held the majority vote. The circle had reconvened after the county inspector found not one wasp, bee, horsefly, or the like on the Whites' premises. The inspector said it would've perished soon after losing its stinger anyhow, presumably in Rachel's bottom.

"Mrs. White, your home is pristine," the inspector had determined after checking all the boxes on his inspection list.

Prior to his arrival, Mrs. White and Ella had scrubbed from floor to ceiling, making Mrs. White even prouder of the result, which she quoted to all who passed over her threshold: "'Pristine,' said the inspector. Officially."

The snows had melted and the rains had come, making everything and everyone in Avonlea sticky. Water seemed to come from every direction, even up from the ground where the drops splashed in puddles. You couldn't walk a yard without being soaked through.

Marilla had run over to Rachel's while one storm was moving off to Newfoundland and another was approaching from New Brunswick. She had barely made it to the Whites' when the clouds broke open again. From the shelter of their porch, she turned to look out over Avonlea: the gulf in the distance roared; the wind was scented with melted icecaps and blew the trees like stalks of kelp; the rain fell faster and faster until it looked as if a veil had been drawn over the island, tinting everything wet gray. She hardly recognized Avonlea as home. From someone else's front door, it looked so different.

"Come on, before you're drenched!" Rachel pulled her inside. "I've done it! See here—I've perfected the rosette. Every bridal pattern from Paris to London is using it. They say Princess Victoria will have at least ten thousand rosettes on her coronation gown. I can't even imagine!"

Rachel proudly held up her circular for admiration. The rosette chain didn't look terribly different from the standard cable stitch, but Marilla kept silent.

"It's exceedingly difficult. I can teach you," Rachel offered. "But don't be disheartened if you don't pick it up as quickly as I did. It takes some people years if they haven't the God-given knack."

Rachel had determined on their second meeting that Marilla didn't share her "God-given knack," but her work showed potential, Rachel thought, if Marilla diligently applied herself.

"I'd be very glad to learn," said Marilla.

"Let's get our prayer shawl stitching done first. Mother counted my rows before she and father left for Four Winds." Rachel pulled the skein of thick, fleecy yarn from her hamper. "They took my cousins some of Ella's cooking. Poor dears. It's the chicken pox. All five children broke out at the same time." She started to loop her crochet needle around and through, around and through. Marilla joined her, working her crochet hook through her own shawl.

"The pox is the most wicked illness," Rachel continued with a maternal air. "Mother wrapped my fingers in cotton so I couldn't scratch. Her mother did the same to her. You could scar your face for life if you aren't cautious. Afterward, I healed without a single blemish. I once read a magazine serial about a beautiful girl with a pock perfectly placed on her forehead so that it looked like she'd been anointed with a holy wound. That's how it was described in the installment: *anointed with a holy wound*. I thought it the loveliest thing I'd ever heard. I started drawing a little scar on my forehead with a dab of crushed carmine petals. When Mother forced me to confess what on earth I was doing with her rouge, she said it was wicked foolishness. She took me down to see one of the little French boys living on the wharf row—sorrowful child was pockmarked from ear to ear! A face like a corncob. I was so ashamed. I never wished for such a thing again." She shook her head. "Have you had the pox?"

Marilla nodded. "When Matthew was nine and I was one year old. Mother said I was the sickest she's ever seen. I was too young to remember the fever or itching, but Matthew and I have matching scars, so I know it must've been."

"Do you *really* have a scar?" Rachel set down her crocheting.

Marilla thought it strange that Rachel would have such a morbid fascination. It was a chicken pox scar, as common as a freckle and unsightly as a mole. She couldn't understand why Rachel would romanticize it. But then, Rachel was an only child and Marilla understood how an imagination left to its own could make the unknown a grand and beastly thing. So in this way, she knew something Rachel didn't.

"It's right here." She rolled up her left sleeve cuff to reveal the inner crook of her elbow, white and soft from hiding. There, in the bony divot between flesh and bone was a teardrop hollow, no bigger than one of the rosettes on Rachel's circular.

"Yours is the prettiest pock I've ever seen! If it's any consolation," said Rachel.

"Matthew has one on his right elbow," Marilla explained. "Mother says it's often that way with siblings. The pain that one feels, the other does too. When you've shared the same womb, it naturally follows that you share your lives."

Rachel's eyes softened to a glassy stare. "What if you haven't siblings?"

Marilla rolled down her sleeve. She'd hurt Rachel, though she hadn't meant to. "Well, I suppose that's why God gave us friends."

Rachel blinked hard and smiled. "Yes. Reverend Patterson gave a right nice sermon on that very subject last week. It's a proverb: 'A man with many friends comes to ruin, but there is a friend who sticks closer than a brother'—or sister in our case, right?"

Marilla nodded.

"Maybe I don't have a scar on my elbow like you, but I have one right in the middle of my you-know-where after sitting on that stinger last month!" She giggled. "You saved me from eternal humiliation, Marilla Cuthbert. I'm forever grateful."

Marilla didn't see the accident or what she'd said as anything worthy of humiliation or gratitude. But again, she was fast learning that how she saw the world and how another did could be entirely dissimilar.

Ella interrupted their sewing. "Mademoiselle Rachel, Monsieur Blythe has come about a barter?"

Rachel tilted her head and frowned. "Mother and Father didn't mention anything to me."

"Nor to me. It's Monsieur *John* Blythe," Ella clarified. "Says he's come on his father's request regarding a gun."

"A gun?" Rachel wrapped the yarn she was using back around the skein. "Father must've spoken to Mr. Blythe at the town hall meeting on Monday." She put the sewing things back in the hamper. "Tell him that they aren't home and to come back later."

Ella nodded half-heartedly. "I suppose so . . . but he came all the way over in the downpour. Do you think we might offer him a warm drink? A chance to dry some? Seems the charitable thing to do, *oui*?"

Rachel looked to Marilla, who shrugged. She'd never met John Blythe, but she'd felt the force of the rain. It was enough to cut your nose off. Letting the worst of it pass before sending him back seemed sensible.

"All right then." Rachel rose, smoothed her skirts, and pinched her cheeks.

Marilla thought that odd. She'd long ago given up on her appearance. She had Hugh's angular cheekbones that caught the sun too much and so were never the alabaster of fashion but tanned like deerskin. Rouges and pinching only made her look a-splotched. She was just as she was. It didn't bother her to be plain. Besides, it was only the dairy farmer's son.

John Blythe sat two grades up from her at the Avonlea School. There weren't any girls in his grade eight class. Most had left to help raise their younger siblings and do house chores. If anything, they home-studied like she did. So John Blythe had been little more than one of the rumpled dark heads in the crowd of older boys. However, there was a notable difference in Rachel as Ella brought him through the kitchen door. He seemed to have an effect on Ella too. Her tone changed. A jingle under its usual flat inflection.

"*S'il vous plaît*, come in, Monsieur Blythe. You must be chilled to the bone. Here, let me hang your coat to dry by the stove. I'll make a *tasse de thé*. Mademoiselle Rachel and her company are waiting for you in the parlor."

"Very kind of you," he said.

Marilla thought it a pleasant voice.

Rachel moved a ringlet forward onto her forehead at his footsteps down the hall. Marilla scratched her neck.

The toe of his boot came out of the shadows first, followed by the rest of him. He was tall and muscular. The rain had plastered his shirt to his body like a second skin, revealing the outlines of his chest and arms and back. His wet, dark curls hung low on his forehead, making his hazel eyes look nearly golden in the parlor light. When he changed his gaze, from Rachel to Marilla and back, it was like being in the shine and then in shade.

"Hello, Rachel."

"Why hello, John Blythe," said Rachel. "This is my friend, Marilla Cuthbert."

He nodded. "I know your brother Matthew. We schooled together before he went to work for your father. Nice to meet you." He smiled, and his eyes gleamed brighter.

Marilla had to look away. It nearly pained her. Like staring into the sun. "Nice to meet you."

"As Ella informed you," said Rachel with one hand on the curve of her hip, "my parents are not at home. They've gone over to visit my cousins at Four Winds. Was there some pressing business you needed?"

A drip of water fell from his temple to the parlor carpet. John pushed his hair back, and Marilla nearly gasped at the little pockmark nestled in his left temple. So small a thing. It would've gone unnoticed by everyone except . . . they were just speaking of their scars. *Anointed*, Rachel had said. Chills ran the length of Marilla's body.

"My apologies for intruding. We didn't know they were gone today," explained John. "We arranged a barter. One of our Jersey cows for a Ferguson that Mr. White purchased from a London exporter last year. My father sent me over to appraise the condition of the rifle before we bring over the heifer."

Rachel cocked her head. "I remember that gun. Father said it was a waste of money. He's never so much as loaded the thing. Not much to shoot at but bunnies and birds in Avonlea. Father hasn't the time or bloodthirst for such diversions."

John nodded. "He said as much to my father."

"Well, feel free to have a look. He keeps it right over here." She led them to the hall closet and pointed to the top shelf. "Practically new. Still in the box."

"May I?" asked John.

"Have at it. I'd hate to think you came across town in a storm for nothing."

John pulled the box down. His arms flexed beneath the damp cotton. The three found themselves standing too close together in the confinement of the narrow hallway. Marilla could smell the ripeness of wet leather and sea salt on his skin. He opened the box, and they gazed inside at the long, polished wooden barrel.

"I forgot how pretty it looks." Rachel ran her fingers over the shiny metal trigger. "Almost like a royal scepter."

"A dangerous one, perhaps," said John.

Rachel lifted her chin. "Depends on how it's used. If the aimer hits nothing but blue sky, it might as well be a scepter." She laughed, a tinny sound that echoed down the tiled foyer.

Marilla had never seen a gun up close. She wasn't even sure her father owned one. The gunpowder alone was too expensive, never mind the rifle. And as Mr. White had pointed out, there was no use for such a weapon in Avonlea. It was a civilized town on a civilized island. There were no dangers larger than an occasional vermin provoking their livestock, and for that a pitchfork did the job just as well as anything else. Mr. White had obviously bought it on a lark. But now, John had been told to trade a pricey cow for this fancy firearm, and Marilla was curious why.

"What would the Blythes need of a rifle like this?" asked Marilla.

John turned his face to her and her cheeks burned. "For protection."

"Protection?" scoffed Rachel.

"We haven't any enemies here," insisted Marilla. "No wolves or bears. It's an island."

"'No man is an island, entire of itself. Every man is a piece of the continent, a part of the main.'"

Mr. Murdock had read that to them once. The author's name danced on the tip of her tongue . . .

"John Donne," she said, having come to it.

John smiled at her. "You're a smart one."

Marilla felt something pull inside her like sands to the tide.

"Of course it's an island," Rachel huffed. "You think you're so clever because your father lets you study all day. But my mother said there's more to life than books." She closed the lid on the rifle box. "You've seen it. Now you can go home and say so."

John's mouth twitched with a smile. "I'm obliged to you for letting me do the business I was tasked. I am but a lowly farmhand, Mademoiselle White." He bowed like a liege man.

"Don't try to sweet-talk me. I'm immune to highbrow hooey." Rachel flipped her skirt and went back to the parlor.

Marilla turned to follow, but John stood directly in her path.

"There's rumor of an insurrection," he said.

Marilla's heart quickened to a gallop.

"By whom?"

"Canadian farmers, townsfolk, and tradesmen against the corrupt aristocracy—the Châteaux Clique and the Family Compact."

Marilla knew of the Americans' domestic warring, but such conflict had not been Canadian. Canadians were peaceable with their countrymen—or at least, so she'd believed. Seeing her unsettled, John put a hand on her elbow; his fingers wrapped round to the very spot she'd uncovered to Rachel the hour before. She could nearly feel his skin through the muslin sleeve.

"Don't worry, Marilla. You'll be safe."

Marilla dared to meet his stare.

"I will?"

"Of course. I'm sure Matthew and your father are taking precautionary measures. Everyone is. Well"—he looked away to the parlor where Rachel had returned to her sewing—"most everyone. Mr. White told my father that the only reason he'd trade this rifle is because he's already purchased another. A musket, more suited for targets at a close distance."

Marilla's palms went clammy, the danger suddenly close, too.

"Tea?" Ella carried the tray.

John released Marilla's arm. "Thank you, but I better get going."

Ella didn't hide her chagrin. She slumped her way back to the kitchen.

"I'll be sure to tell my father the rifle is in excellent condition," John called to Rachel. "I'm sorry for interrupting your afternoon, Mademoiselle White. I hope you can resume your rousing stitchery upon my departure."

"You are insufferable, Mr. Blythe!" said Rachel, but Marilla heard the giggle in it. So did John.

"Good day, Rachel."

Rachel gave a mouse huff in reply.

"Good day, Marilla."

He winked, and she thought it an awfully bold thing to do on their first meeting. Even bolder than taking her by the elbow. "Tell your brother Matthew that I said hello. It's been too long since I came down to the Cuthbert place. Maybe I should."

All three of the girls watched John trot away, his horse's hooves splashing through fresh puddles. The rains had cleared, and the sky had opened up to a shimmering pink sunset.

Ella sighed. "He's as handsome as the devil."

Rachel twisted a curl around her finger. "I've seen handsomer. Besides, it seems the only one he's interested in being civil toward is Marilla."

Marilla shook her head. "Only because he's friendly with Matthew."

Rachel raised her eyebrows high. "Surely you would've met already if he and your brother were so close."

Matthew had little time for friends. He and Father were too busy on the farm. And after the drunk fire, he hardly went out socially again. She wondered if John had been at the party that night. Probably not, she decided. Matthew was twenty-one to John's sixteen. Too far apart in age to share schoolmates. So why then was John so terribly interested in visiting her brother now?

Rachel finished the crocheted row on her prayer shawl. "He's not my type, but he's mighty nice to look at. Don't you agree, Marilla?"

"Handsome is as handsome does. What a person says and thinks are what count."

It was getting late. Mother and Izzy would have supper waiting, so she packed up her sewing notions. Ella lit the oil lamps while Rachel walked Marilla out to the porch. The air was fresh-scented of earth and mineral with the approach of night.

"So tell me this in truth, Marilla. What would you do if John Blythe showed up at your gable door?"

"I'd welcome him. Just as I would to you or any Avonlea friend."

Rachel nodded. "Be careful walking. The light's going quick, and I'd hate for you to fall into a mud hole."

The whole way home, Marilla thought about the pock scar at John's temple. It was hard to imagine his face born without it. Such a small feature. A flaw, by most opinions, and yet, to her, it was one of the interesting parts of him. It carried a story, and she understood why Rachel found the idea of a holy wound desirable.

VII

AUNT IZZY GIVES A LESSON

The merchants and farmers were gathering in Carmody to discuss the skyrocketing price of spring oilseed. Winter had been harsh across Canada, and the economic crisis had crippled the mainland farms. The meetings would take three days, so Matthew was to stay behind to run the farm while Izzy looked after Clara. Still, Hugh was worried about going. The baby was due in less than a month, and Clara had begun having pains whenever she stood. Dr. Spencer insisted she remain in bed.

"You must go, or we won't have a harvest to feed any of us," Clara argued. "It's only a few days. This child still has a few weeks of growing to do. Plus, I'll have Izzy, Matthew, and Marilla with me. I'm more worried about you on the road by yourself. You could be attacked by rebel thieves!"

"The only rebel thieves on the island are chipmunks stealing our costly seed," Hugh grumbled. "What if the baby comes early?"

"Then you'll miss the hollering," teased Clara. "I won't give one push without you by my side. This baby will see no face but its father's first. I promise you."

He kissed her hand.

Marilla and Matthew stood outside the bedroom. In the wake of John's warning, the idea of anarchy seemed more real than ever.

"He'll be safe on the road, won't he, Matthew?"

Matthew furrowed his brow. "A'course he will. Why do you ask?"

Marilla shrugged. "There's been talk."

"By who?"

She wondered if she ought to say the name. But this was Matthew. She'd never before had a reason to hide anything from him.

"John Blythe. He came over to Rachel's house on an errand for his father—a bartered rifle. John said it was for protection. He said common folk might take up arms in rebellion."

Matthew pursed his lips and looked away to their mother telling their father to pack an extra undershirt. There was a chill to the wind.

"Is it true?" Marilla pressed.

His gaze fell back on her, studying her a moment. "Aye, suppose so."

Anxiety fluttered in Marilla's throat.

Matthew put a hand on her shoulder. "Needn't worry. No danger will come to the Gables. We'll keep you safe."

"That's what John Blythe said too."

Matthew nodded. "He's a good fellow. Ought to listen to him."

"I'd rather listen to you."

Matthew grinned. "I'd best hitch up Jericho for Father now. He needs to be heading out."

He went down, and Hugh followed directly with his overnight case. "Take care of your mother," he said to Marilla and kissed the crown of her head as he passed.

Alone, Marilla entered her parents' bedroom.

"Come lie with me a minute," Clara beckoned.

Marilla climbed into bed, relishing the familiarity of her mother. Clara was doughy and smelled of milk and honey. She wrapped an arm around Marilla, and Marilla wished for time to go on as it pleased while they stayed right as they were.

"When you were little, I used to lie in bed for hours and hours holding you like this, telling you stories about my day." When Clara breathed, her rounded belly rose and fell dramatically. "It's not so bad when you've got company, but when you're alone, it can drag on awful long."

"Then I won't let you be alone," said Marilla.

"My sweet Marilla, as much joy as it would bring me, you can't stay here forever—you've got to grow up and live on your own."

Marilla pressed her face closer to her mother's side and breathed in deeply. Quiet guilt made her ache: as much as she wanted to stay the same, she also wanted to be all grown up. She hated that her heart was divided.

Clara stroked her hair. "Childhood goes by too quickly. You'll see. One minute a babe is a tender young bud, and the next she's bloomed tall and beautiful in the world."

"I'm not so tall or beautiful," whispered Marilla.

Clara tilted Marilla's chin up so that their eyes met. "Oh, but you are! And soon enough you'll find a young man who thinks so too. You'll fall in love and marry and start your own family."

Marilla pulled her chin away and buried it back down in the comfort of Clara's embrace. "How did you know that you were in love with Father?"

Clara inhaled and held it a beat before continuing. "I knew because we'd grown up side by side, but I didn't notice him until just the right time. Then it was like he was the newest shiny thing in all the world. That's when you know it's love . . . when you can't deny destiny."

Marilla felt John Blythe's stare in her mind. It brought on a burning in her chest, not altogether uncomfortable. But it was too early for her to be in love. She was nothing but Matthew's little sister to John. Somehow that gave her solace. She could lie in her mother's arms a while longer. A bud wrapped up tight.

∞

True to Clara's prediction, winter made its last stand that night. An April snow brought Marilla and Matthew together by the parlor fire.

Izzy had just finished taking Clara a bowl of creamy neep soup and was washing up in the kitchen. Matthew read the *Royal Gazette* while Marilla finished the seams of the baby gown that she and Izzy had cut from the yellow cloth with ivy. Marilla was proud of how it'd turned out. She might not have had the knack for artful embroidery like Rachel, but she had a fine hand for tailoring like her aunt. The gown was masterfully constructed with stitches that would last a hundred years. Function over frippery. Sensible was just how she liked it.

She looked up from her work and saw the headline of Matthew's newspaper: "Black Canadians Are Now Voting Canadians."

"I thought everybody already had a vote."

"Not the case," said Matthew. "This is a good thing. You women will have the ballot next too."

"We don't?" That came as a surprise. It wasn't that Marilla thought women had the vote. She just hadn't thought they didn't.

Matthew shook his head. "Same rules apply as in courting. A woman can't walk into a room and pick the fellow she wants to dance with. She's got to wait for him to ask her."

Marilla frowned. "Well, that's the daftest thing I ever heard. Why ever not?"

"'Cause it's the rule." Matthew chuckled to himself. "Not saying I agree with it. That's just how things are done."

Marilla thought a long minute before venturing to ask, "Have you ever been courting?"

"Well, I dunno that I have."

Marilla finished the seam, knotted the thread, and cut it with her teeth. "It seems a person would know if he had or hadn't."

Matthew folded up the newspaper. "I guess I haven't then, but that don't mean I don't know the rules."

Marilla laughed. "You're full of hot air, Matthew Cuthbert. Telling me if'n I'm at a barn dance and want to do the Scotch Reel, I can't just pick a partner and dance?"

"That's what I'm telling you."

Marilla shook her head. "Fiddlesticks."

Hearing their talk, Izzy came from the kitchen with Skunk purring steadily in her arms. He never let a soul handle him that way but Izzy. Marilla reckoned it was because Izzy fed him smoked sardines when nobody was paying him any mind. Clara had bought a bunch from a fancy peddler some time ago, but none of them could stomach the smell, never mind a bite.

"Fiddlesticks to what?" she asked.

"To Matthew. He's trying to tell me the rules of courting when he hasn't even done it himself."

Matthew blushed under his shadow beard.

"You've never had a sweetheart, Matthew? Tell the truth. You'll get extra blisters in hell for lying to a relation." Izzy winked. "No shame. We're blood kin."

Matthew mustered up the gumption while clearing his throat. "I haven't had the time or predilection."

Izzy took a seat in the cane-back chair. "Not having the time, I can believe. But not having the predilection . . ." She stroked Skunk. "Seems to me I saw you watching one of those Andrews girls mighty close during fellowship hour at church last week."

Matthew's cheeks went full rosy. He opened his mouth as if to deny what his aunt said, but then closed it.

"Which one?" Marilla piped in.

"Ask your brother to speak his peace."

They looked to Matthew with knowing smiles until he finally conceded by throwing the paper down and standing. "Fine! Johanna."

Izzy gave a hoot.

"She's the prettiest of them all," Marilla agreed.

There were four Andrews girls: Catherine, Eliza, Franny, and Johanna. All were comely, but Johanna had ebony hair, pink peppercorn lips, and a slight smattering of freckles on her nose, which made her stand out from her fairer sisters.

"She don't even know I'm alive," said Matthew.

"Well, make her know," Izzy insisted.

"But how?"

Izzy set Skunk down on the ground, and he sulked around her heels.

"This is probably something your father and mother should be telling you, but given the present situation . . ." She exhaled. "I suppose coming from family is better than from someone else."

Matthew sat down beside Marilla again, his interest renewed.

"In my limited experience . . ." Izzy cleared her throat. "Well, it's quite simple really . . ." she began and stopped again.

The fire log crackled, and she got up to stoke it with the poker. Once it burned bright, she turned back to them.

"All right, let's start with the basics. Matthew, you fancy Johanna, right?"

Matthew gave a shy grin.

"Right. Marilla, imagine you take a shine to a boy someday."

She thought of John Blythe, for the sake of having a tangible example to learn from.

"Now, stand up, both of you," instructed Izzy.

They obeyed.

"So say you ask this *amour* to walk with you. It doesn't have to be long or far. Anywhere would do. But it must be just you and the other on the stroll. When you do, Matthew, that's your cue to take the young woman's arm and place it in the crook of yours. Like this." She moved his hand to take Marilla's and gently threaded it through his elbow.

"And Marilla, you let the gentleman take your hand and do as such. Then just leave it be. See?"

Marilla nodded.

"Then what?" asked Matthew.

"Well then, you put one foot in front of the other and walk. Go on!" Izzy commanded. "Stroll the parlor."

Marilla giggled. It seemed silly, but Matthew led her forward, and they walked to the hallway and back.

"Perfect!" clapped Izzy. "But you mustn't forget to talk. You can't just walk around mute. That won't do at all. This is your opportunity to partake in intimate conversation."

At that, Matthew dropped Marilla's arm. "Inti—what? Conversation? I dunno . . ."

Matthew was so shy. He could bolster the courage to do the actions, but ask him to add communication and it became an insurmountable feat.

"It's easy," said Marilla, trying to help.

She took his arm back. "Mr. Cuthbert, how are your family's crops this year?"

"Just fine," he grumbled.

"Ask me after my family's," Marilla whispered.

"But you are my family," Matthew whispered back.

Marilla shook her head. "Play the game. Pretend I'm Johanna, and I'll pretend you're . . . well, you're *you* for right now."

She gulped. She'd almost said John's name.

"Ask me things you'd ask Johanna."

"Marilla's right," Izzy coaxed.

Matthew exhaled and cleared his throat. "I heard your father bought a carriage from Charlottetown."

"That's good—that's good!" said Marilla before recovering herself in her part as Johanna. "Why, yes, he did. It's a fine carriage."

Matthew began to stammer, not knowing what to say next.

"Ask me what it looks like."

Matthew threw up his hands. "Aw, I ain't no good at this!"

"That's why we're practicing," Izzy said consolingly. "There aren't any rules to it. Don't think of it as something to be good or bad at. Courting isn't anything more than getting to know a person. So every time you step out with them, you're discovering something new."

"Like a newspaper story—telling what's the news with each edition, right?" offered Marilla.

"Exactly," said Izzy. "Like you're curious to read the happenings, be curious about the person you're courting."

It made sense to Marilla, but Matthew still seemed perplexed.

"I dunno," he said again.

"That's the marvel of it, Matthew. You don't have to know from the start. You can't help falling in love any more than you can help breathing. It'll come naturally enough." Izzy smiled.

Marilla wondered if Izzy had been courted by William Blair and, if so, what had made her change her mind about loving him. Or maybe falling *in* love and falling *out* worked instinctively the same. It didn't seem a thing to ask, however.

"Even old Skunk has a sweetheart," said Izzy. "Found himself a Molly in the barn. She's a wild thing, though. Doubt she'll stay through summer—too many chases to be had out in the world."

Marilla scooped up Skunk and nestled him in the crook of her neck, ignoring his mews of protest. "Maybe if we give your girl some warm milk and sardines, she'll stick around."

"See now, that's courting, Marilla!"

"Dunno if milk and sardines will work on Johanna," said Matthew.

They laughed so hard together that Clara awoke upstairs in her bed and smiled.

That Sunday, after Reverend Patterson finished his sermon and the congregation sang the Psalms, they funneled out to the gravel churchyard, where groups of three and four gathered for the fellowship hour. To Marilla's surprise, Matthew walked straight over to the Andrews family. He shook Mr. Andrews's hand, nodded hello to Mrs. Andrews, then said a few words that made Johanna's eyes blink quick as a spring chick's. She stepped forward from her sisters, and Matthew took her hand into his arm, just as Izzy had shown them. When the pair turned, there was a slight color to Matthew's cheek, but his gait was sure and his mouth twitched on the verge of speaking.

"Well, I'll be," said Izzy beside Marilla.

The two looked at each other with grins that could not be repressed for a thousand tries.

"Go on, Matthew," said Marilla as her brother strolled Johanna toward the church picnic area, where the sugar maples budded chartreuse leaves. She hoped to know the secrets of such a walk—and hoped it would come far sooner than it had for Matthew.

It's been too long since I came down to the Cuthbert place. Maybe I should, John had said. At that moment, Marilla prayed to God that he would.

VIII

MARILLA ENTERTAINS A CALLER

Marilla was just finishing up her prayer shawl for the Ladies' Sewing Circle project. The Sunday school had a total of fifty shawls. Hers and Rachel's made fifty-two. Mrs. White said that any number over fifty was substantial enough that the shawls could now be presented to the Hopetown orphanage. So Marilla had it in mind to take hers over to the Whites' house, where she'd been invited to dinner. But suddenly there came the trot and whinny of a horse outside.

Matthew and Hugh were bailing hay in the stables. Clara was resting, and Izzy was on the back porch holding a gummy paintbrush, flecks of yellow on her cheeks. She'd decided that the wooden chair in which she sat to read to Clara ought to be painted yellow: "Bring a little spring sunshine into your mother's room." So she'd gotten a bucket of paint from Mr. Blair and set up a paint shop off the kitchen.

"Somebody's calling," she hollered through the open window.

"I hear 'em," said Marilla.

"Probably Mrs. Sloane. The woman cornered me in church about bringing over their family copy of *Rules of Good Deportment*—as if we needed the refresher. Those Sloanes never change . . ." Izzy shook her head. "Would you mind being my angel and collecting the book? Tell her I'm presently indisposed. Shouldn't take but a minute."

Marilla agreed. But when she opened the door, it was not Mrs. Sloane but John Blythe.

"Why, hello again, Marilla."

"H-Hello, J-John," she stuttered.

Her hair lay in waves around her shoulders. The ribbon that had once secured it had fallen out earlier, and she hadn't bothered re-tying. What did it matter to Skunk and her skeins of yarn? But now she felt exposed and feverish under his gaze.

"I've come to see your brother Matthew."

John wore a linen day suit, not the farmer's togs of their last meeting. All dressed up like Sunday on an ordinary Tuesday.

"Please, come in," invited Marilla. "Matthew is in the barn with Father. I can fetch him for you."

"Yes, thank you."

Marilla turned to go, but he stopped her. "Could I trouble you for a drink first? Spring's a fickle friend. One day freezing and the next the sun would like to bake a man."

Sweat stippled his forehead.

"Of course, I should've offered from the start."

"I should've sent word that I was coming."

They both exhaled and exchanged smiles.

Marilla fetched him a glass of water from the kitchen. Seeing her through the open window, Izzy leaned in with raised eyebrows.

"It's not Mrs. Sloane," Marilla whispered. "It's John Blythe come to see Matthew."

Izzy cocked her head. "The dairy farmer's son?"

Marilla nodded.

"So why are we whispering?"

Marilla cleared her throat without answering and returned to the parlor.

John took the glass and gulped. "Thank you kindly." His lips glinted wet when he spoke.

"Did you get your rifle from Mr. White?"

Marilla thought of Izzy's lesson regarding being alone with a boy. It was as good a time as any to practice *partaking in intimate conver-*

sation, as her aunt had suggested. Even if this wasn't officially court-ing. Or at least, she didn't think it was, but she'd never done it, so she couldn't be entirely sure.

"I did." He seemed relieved by the drink and the question. "My father was pleased. The Whites got our best heifer in the deal, so all around excellent. And how is your sewing with Miss White going?"

"Very well, thank you. I've finished the shawl I was making for the Hopetown orphans." She pointed to the settee, where the fin-ished garment lay neatly folded.

"In Nova Scotia, yes. I believe my mother made one of those too."

"Wouldn't surprise me. Mrs. White leads up the Sunday school. I think she has all of Avonlea making prayer shawls."

"Lucky orphans."

"Not so lucky." Marilla frowned. "An orphan hasn't any home or kin."

"Of course not. 'Lucky' was the wrong word." John studied his glass. Crystal clear. Marilla had strained the well water through the finest sieve so not a dust fleck remained.

"*Glad*," he said after a long beat. "That's what I meant. *Glad* orphans—to have so many loving people that they don't even know."

Marilla hadn't meant to be contrary, just truthful. She'd always felt uneasy with the niceties of small talk. *How do you do? Well, and you? Lovely weather we're having. Indeed, God giveth the sun and God taketh away. How is your mother? Agreeable in spirit, and yours? Fine, fine, so kind of you to ask.* And so forth. Two people could go back and forth for hours and by the end know absolutely nothing more of consequence than when they started. Others might think that an intimate tête-à-tête, but Marilla found it taxing and boring. She'd much prefer a person to say something of earnest interest or say nothing at all.

"Mrs. White is taking the shawls over to Nova Scotia before the end of the month."

"Yes, my father and Mr. White were discussing purchasing gunpowder while in Hopetown. Mr. Murdock brought in the latest headlines from Lower Canada. Reformer Louis-Joseph Papineau has led a number of protest assemblies across the country. He's gaining support among the people. Mr. Murdock believes royal troops will soon be dispatched to keep us all in line."

Marilla wondered what Hugh would say—if her father already knew of the political grumblings. Matthew was careful not to leave his newspapers lying around.

"May I ask why you left school?" John asked.

She was flattered that he'd noticed and grateful for the change to a pleasanter subject.

"My mother's going to have a baby. She needs my help."

He nodded. "But your aunt from St. Catharines is here now, correct?"

Once again, she wondered how he knew so much about her and her family while she knew so little about him and his.

"I hope to return to school again this fall."

"I hope so too. It's my final year before I take the exit exams. Father insists that I have a full education before I begin working in the trade."

"I didn't realize dairy cows required geometry."

She'd meant it teasingly. She hated geometry. All those smeared diagrams on her chalkboard. He shifted his stance.

"Well, no, not directly." John frowned. "But Father believes it's better to have knowledge than to have not—in most every situation."

"Your father is sensible," said Marilla. "From what I've known, to be a have-not is usually the less admired position."

"Indeed." He gulped the last of his water, then set the glass down on the tea table. "That's why I took the liberty of bringing over the clippings from the schoolhouse. Mr. Murdock gave me his permission, since we'd read them already. I thought you—and Matthew and Mr. Cuthbert—might like to see."

He pulled a parcel of newspaper pages from within his waistcoat.

"Very thoughtful of you."

When Marilla reached out to take the pages, the first finger of her hand accidentally grazed the first finger of his. An unexpected heat shot up her arm, and she pulled away as quickly as she could.

Whether John noticed, she couldn't say. She'd turned her face down to stare at the inky letters of the newspaper: "Rebel farmers battle elite politicos raising property taxes and tariffs. Tories look to the monarchy as Reformers cry for a new republic. Make no mistake, change is nigh!"

Marilla folded the newspapers neatly. "I'm sure Matthew and my father will appreciate reading the headlines from the greater province. Thank you, John Blythe."

"No trouble at all. I don't mind bringing over other readings from class, if you like."

She looked up to his kind gaze and dared to speak for herself. "I'd like that very much."

Out back on the porch Izzy dropped her paintbrush, and the noise caught Marilla's attention. "I'll run and get Matthew."

"No."

John put his hand out as if to touch hers, stopping less than an inch away. The space between them was hardly even the breadth of a seam.

"He's busy. You have what I came to give." He smiled. "Tell Matthew I'll look for him at Avonlea's next farmers' meeting. If you come along, maybe we can talk about the headlines together."

She didn't see why she'd be there. Only Hugh and Matthew attended the farmers' meetings. But maybe she would go to town for more red thread from Mrs. Blair. Now that the prayer shawls were complete, she and Rachel could finish their amaryllis sleeves. If she happened to bump into John Blythe, well, that'd be fine.

After she'd wished John good-day and closed the door, Izzy came in, still wearing her painting smock.

"What did the young Mr. Blythe come about?"

Marilla pointed to the papers on the tea table. "Some of the readings I missed at school. He thought Matthew and Father might like to see them too."

Izzy lifted the top page. "Hmm . . . a shake-up in the colony? Well, this is far more interesting than Mrs. Sloane's *Rules of Good Deportment,* wouldn't you say?"

Marilla smiled and took John's empty glass back to the kitchen, where she hesitated a moment before washing away the smudge left by his lips.

IX.

MARILLA AND RACHEL GO TO NOVA SCOTIA

Oh, Marilla, I'm so glad you're here. I have the most sensational news!" exclaimed Rachel when Marilla came over for dinner.

An invitation had arrived on Mrs. White's good bone-ivory stationery: *Miss Marilla Cuthbert is cordially invited to dinner at the home of the White family this Tuesday at five o'clock in the evening.* Marilla had never received a formal invitation before and found it terribly grown-up. Clara and Hugh had given their blessing, of course. Although Marilla was at the Whites' house often, this would be her first tabled meal with the family. Quite an honor. They only hosted tabled meals for adult company.

Izzy helped her cinch her best gingham dress at the waist with a blue satin ribbon. The one modification transformed the entire ensemble, and Marilla thought she'd never seen herself look better. True, the cuff of one sleeve had a tear on the underside, and the collar had to be pinned to hold it evenly in place, but so long as Marilla kept her hands clasped before her and didn't turn her shoulders, no one would be the wiser.

It proved a harder task than Marilla anticipated with Rachel pouncing on her from hello.

"Mother wants to tell you first, but I can't stand to keep the secret!"

She pulled Marilla into the china pantry leading to the kitchen. Ella paid them no mind, continuing to take serving plates from the shelves above their heads.

"Now promise that when Mother tells you, you will act surprised. Can you act surprised even when you aren't?"

Marilla frowned. She was not versed in theatrics, nor did she wish to be.

"It's easy," said Rachel.

She opened her eyes so wide that Marilla thought they might fall out and roll across the floor like marbles. Then she put a hand to her cheek. "Oh my word!"

When she was convinced that Marilla had assimilated the lesson, Rachel dropped her hand to her lap and her eyes recessed back into a natural countenance. "See how?"

Marilla nodded. "But you haven't told me anything, so I haven't anything to pretend to be surprised by."

Rachel took both Marilla's hands in hers and pulsed them with corresponding squeals. "We are to go to Hopetown together!"

"Hopetown? In Nova Scotia?"

Marilla had never left Prince Edward Island. Though Avonlea people traveled off the island every day, this would be her first time. Instead of feeling excited, she was overcome with a kind of landlocked seasickness, a roiling fret.

"I don't know if I should go . . . with my mother about to have the baby and . . ."

"Oh, don't be silly," said Rachel. "Mother has it all worked out. She's already spoken to your parents, and they've given their approval. After all, it's not like we're going alone. We'll be with Mother and Father, and they plan to formally invite you during dinner— well, dessert. Ella has made the most delicious toffee puddings especially for the occasion!"

Marilla's collar had popped up and the pin was sticking her in the neck. She put her thumb between it and the poke. "Hopetown is so far away. Such a big city."

Rachel nodded. "Yes, we'll be gone three days. Father has business there, and we are to help Mother deliver the Avonlea prayer shawls to the Hopetown orphanage."

Three whole days. It seemed an eternity. She'd never been away from her family a night. Even when her parents were in Charlottetown, Matthew was with her on the farm. She didn't own a carpetbag, or a traveling coat for that matter, though she assumed Izzy might lend hers. She'd have to patch up the soles of her boots first. They'd never do on cobblestone streets. And she'd certainly need a proper hat. No one went into the city without a hat.

"When are we to go?"

"The day after tomorrow!" Rachel clapped.

The collar pin slipped from Marilla's hold and pricked her good. She pulled it out and left the piece to dangle off-kilter as it pleased.

"Rachel! Marilla!" Mrs. White called from the dining room. "Where are you girls? It's suppertime."

"Come on." Rachel took Marilla's hand and led her to the dining room.

Just before entering, Marilla smoothed her collar straight as best she could. Rachel pinched her cheeks. It was habitual, Marilla had come to learn.

"Remember to act surprised," Rachel whispered.

Then, hand in hand, they entered the Whites' candelabra-lit dining room, with roasted guinea hens and spring bean succotash on the table. Marilla wished she could've enjoyed the dinner with Mr. and Mrs. White, but the whole time she was anticipating the toffee pudding and her role as surprised guest. When it finally arrived, she gave her best performance, but by the look of Mr. and Mrs. White, they sooner thought she was choking on her sponge cake.

Mrs. White stared with alarm. Mr. White lifted an eyebrow high. Rachel's head *tick-tocked* around the table.

"Marilla is *very* surprised! Isn't that right, Marilla?"

Marilla gave up the pretense with a quiet nod. "I'm grateful for the invitation—both to your table and to Nova Scotia."

At that Mrs. White exhaled. "Well, good. We could use the extra set of hands with all of these shawls. Plus, of course, Rachel is besotted by your company."

"Father has booked us rooms at the Majesty Inn right in the heart of the city," Rachel continued, while spooning saucy pudding into her mouth. "It's the most splendid place you ever dreamed!"

Marilla had never dreamed of what an inn might look like. The idea of not staying in a home with friends or family had never even crossed her mind before.

"It's the most respectable establishment and equidistant between your father's enterprises and the orphanage," Mrs. White explained. "The Majesty Inn is practical, Rachel. But it just so happens to be splendid too."

Mr. White cleared his throat as if to speak, but Mrs. White interceded.

"We're very happy to have you along on the trip, Marilla. We'll come Thursday morning to fetch you in our carriage. So make sure you've had your breakfast. The journey is not short, and once we get going I prefer not to stop until we've reached our destination."

Two days later, Marilla said good-bye to her family wearing Izzy's blue traveling cape and carrying a borrowed carpetbag.

"I wish I were going too," Izzy cheered.

"Bring me back lots of stories about the city." Clara kissed Marilla's cheeks.

"Be mindful of the street carriages. They never look where they're going," warned Hugh.

"Just try to have some fun, old girl," said Matthew.

Marilla's heart was racing by the time the Whites arrived. Hugh, Matthew, and Izzy stood on the Gables' front porch, waving them off. Marilla had to gulp down the urge to cry. She'd only been on the staying side of good-byes, never on the going side.

"We'll take good care of her!" called Mrs. White. "Back by Saturday eve."

While she'd been in a number of dories and fishing dinghies growing up, this was Marilla's first voyage across Northumberland Strait. The ferryboat was as large as a whale and equally terrifying. Mrs. White heightened the girls' anxiety by telling them of a whole family swept overboard by a rogue wave: "Drowned. All seven. Just like that." She advised that they'd best keep to the passenger cabin and avoid the deck. So Marilla and Rachel remained indoors, anchored safely between Mr. and Mrs. White, as the ship cut through the thick morning fog. The crossing took less time than Marilla anticipated, and soon the purser cried, "Coming to port!" She'd hardly seen a ripple, let alone a perilous wave.

A carriage waited for them harborside, and one-two-three-four, they climbed aboard and began the daylong ride across Nova Scotia. The unending *clip-clop* of horses down muddy roads had Marilla lulled half asleep when suddenly Hopetown rose on the horizon.

Marilla had never seen anything like it: a thicket of buildings breathing tunnels of smoke. At a distance, there was a buzz like the drone of a hive. The closer they came the louder it grew, until it was not a symmetric hum but an erratic symphony of clanking, street vendors and newsboys shouting, whistles and hammers, while people and horses moved in every direction, the smell of leather, soot, and mud both close and far. Only when she brought Izzy's cape to her nose and closed her eyes could Marilla find the peace of Avonlea again.

"Isn't it wonderful!" Rachel shouted. "Father says they're building a new bank over there. And an opera house over there. And oh! Look—there's a man selling wafer candies. I just *love* wafer candies! Mother, can we have some wafer candies?"

"We aren't stopping until we reach the Majesty Inn," Mrs. White grumbled. "I've got a headache."

Marilla had one too, but Rachel seemed energized by the chaos. She leaned halfway out the carriage window as the driver brought the horses to the inn's side drive.

They checked in at the front desk, and the porter took Marilla's carpetbag along with the Whites' luggage up to their rooms. The lobby of the Majesty Inn was just as Rachel had claimed. Dark wooden walls were carved with floral branches and decorative loops like the feathered chain stitches Rachel had perfected. Jasmine incense burned in genie lamps so that as soon as Marilla stepped through the doors, she could almost imagine herself in a peculiar spring garden tamped into a perfume bottle. Bright candles winked at every turn; day or night, everything shimmered. Most notable was the grand ceiling painted like the heavens. Pink and blue cherubs flew through a vast span of celestial sunbursts. The lobby guests, gazing up at the fresco, bumped into each other without pardons.

And so Marilla didn't notice when someone, hovering near, touched her elbow.

"It tricks the eye, doesn't it?" came a familiar voice.

Turning too quickly, Marilla spilled sideways as her boot caught on the hem of her cape.

John caught her. Marilla's chin rested against his chest, the comforting smell of Avonlea all around.

"Falling over yourself to see me again, Miss Cuthbert?" He winked and set her stable on two feet.

She threw the edge of the cape up around her shoulder so as not to be tripped again. "Mr. Blythe, what are you doing here?"

The Whites were busy at the front desk while Rachel asked if the kitchen might have a tin of sugar wafers for guests.

"I'm here with my father," said John. "When I was at your house the other day, I think I mentioned—he and Mr. White are business colleagues."

She nodded, vaguely recalling something about gunpowder.

"And you're staying here too?"

John grinned. "The Majesty Inn is the only place that offers a bed without undesirable roommates—vermin," he whispered close. "But then, some might argue their traveling companions are pests enough."

Mrs. White held her handkerchief to her head and moaned while climbing the stairs. Mr. White followed begrudgingly.

Marilla bit her bottom lip to keep off the laugh. "You're wicked, John Blythe."

"Marilla! Wafers!" came Rachel with a plate of treats. "Oh—hello, John Blythe."

"Glad to see you too, Miss White."

She delicately crunched the end of her cookie. "Well, there aren't enough for three."

John stood tall and spoke loudly. "I would never pillage a beautiful woman's desserts on hello."

Rachel nearly choked, then looked round to make sure none of the other guests had heard. "John Blythe, you are villainously indecorous!" She grabbed Marilla's hand and turned them sharply toward the stairs. "If you see us enjoying our supper in the dining room, be ever so kind as to *leave us alone*. The gall of that one," she seethed to Marilla.

"Oh, but didn't you know," John called after them, "our families are to see quite a lot of each other on this trip. In fact, your father has just asked me to accompany you and your mother to the orphanage tomorrow."

"Lawful heart," Rachel hissed to Marilla, "that John drives me to sinful thought! And now we've got to have him around all day tomorrow?"

Marilla turned her face away from Rachel to hide her smile and caught eyes with John watching them from the bottom landing. He tipped his head at her and the bang of his hair fell above the pockmark at his temple. Marilla crossed her arms and pressed the scar at her elbow. She didn't want to be disloyal to Rachel, but . . . she was glad he was here.

X.

THE HOPETOWN ORPHANAGE

Over a breakfast of soft-boiled eggs, cheese curds, and apple slices the next morning, Mrs. White laid out their day's itinerary. Mr. White had already gone to meet Mr. Blythe at the artillery battery down by the wharf.

"We have an appointment with the Sisters of Charity at half past noon to present the prayer shawls on behalf of the Christian ladies of Avonlea. That leaves us this morning to do as we wish. So I have a surprise for you girls." She cleared her throat and paused until she had their full attention.

Rachel swallowed her apple wedge. Marilla set down the spoon she was using to scoop the egg out of its shell.

"We are stopping in at Madame Stéphanie's Hat Boutique!"

Rachel stuck another fruit in her mouth. "Hats?" she muttered through the tart chew, then turned to Marilla. "Mother has a penchant for hats."

"You should be grateful that you have a mother who keeps au courant with fashion." Mrs. White's eyes darted from Rachel to Marilla, then down to her tea, which she ceremoniously picked up and sipped.

Marilla's cheeks burned, and she returned to swirling the gloppy yolk round the shell.

"I never met a bonnet I liked," said Rachel. "They pinch under my chin and make it impossible to see anything past my nose. Nothing so lonely as being stuck inside a bonnet."

"Rubbish," said Mrs. White. "You just haven't found the right one yet. Marilla, you like hats, don't you?"

The straw hat Marilla had worn was a touch lopsided from overuse. But it had done the job of keeping the whirling dirt out of her face. She never understood why anyone would need a hat of silk and feathers. One carriage ride and it was ruined. That said . . .

"I do like hats, Mrs. White." She couldn't deny it. "I think they provide a person with private space even in the middle of a crowd."

Rachel looked at her as if she were Judas, then pushed her apple seeds to the side of her plate.

"We'll try on hats from London and Paris!" said Mrs. White. "I think I'd like something in emerald—I hear emeralds are à la mode this season."

"Might there be an ice cream peddler by the shop?" asked Rachel.

Mrs. White ignored her daughter. "Yes, an emerald hat to go with my mother's emerald pendant . . ." She was lost in parlay with herself.

"Well, I'll enjoy anything à la mode," said Rachel, feigning a French accent, "especially if it's with my dearest friend. *Oui*, Mademoiselle Cuthbert?"

Marilla had to laugh. "*Oui*, Mademoiselle White."

Half an hour later, they were walking into Madame Stéphanie's Hat Boutique. On a white shelf in the shop window stood a line of bonnets festooned with ivory egret feathers and sparkling sequins beside simpler cottons trimmed with lace, silk flowers, and embroidered smocking. Marilla knew Izzy would approve of the craftsmanship. The seams were immaculate. The stitches of the folds were the tiniest she'd ever seen, even smaller than Izzy's.

Most of the bonnets were opulent creations compared to her straw hats at home, but Marilla wasn't the sort to feel comfortable in flamboyance. Only one stood out to her: a burgundy wine bonnet made of velvet, neatly pleated about the face with satin ties, and lined with silk so as not to offend a lady's styled hair. It was exquisite but not ostentatious.

Mrs. White whisked by with the shopgirl holding two hats already. Seeing the one in Marilla's hand, she stopped.

"How lovely. You must try it on, Marilla!"

Marilla set it back on the stand. "Oh no, Mrs. White. I couldn't afford such a thing."

"Well, I didn't ask if you could afford it." While the shopgirl arranged the mirrors, Mrs. White leaned in close to Marilla. "Do you think I can afford that motmot-feathered cap? Of course not. Mr. White would hang me first. But there's no commandment against appreciating finery. Admiration and indulgence are not to be confused, child."

Mrs. White took the burgundy bonnet off the stand. "Marilla will be trying this on," she announced. "Rachel, have you found one? Preferably something that elongates your short forehead."

Rachel was at the counter helping herself to Madame Stéphanie's jar of sugar comfits. Seeing as she would not be able to leave the shop without something, she acquiesced to her mother's bidding and chose a sumptuous, wide-brimmed hat adorned with so much lace, it looked as if a sofa antimacassar had fallen on top of it.

"Venetian Gros Point!" she chirped.

Mrs. White eyed it dubiously but was not about to argue with Rachel's one choice.

In front of the mirrors, all three put on their hats.

"It's like walking in an Italian dream," sang Rachel. The ends of her braided hair stuck out beneath the lace veil.

Mrs. White swiveled her chin side to side so that the motmot feathers flittered bright aqua through the air. After a few minutes of admiring, she took it off.

"These feathers hang off my face like a pair of stockings drying on the line."

She put on a more affordable one: woven pink flowers against a prudent gray.

The shopgirl helped Marilla with hers. "You tie it to the side, like this," she said and made a bow under Marilla's cheek. "See?"

Marilla almost didn't recognize herself in the reflection. A refined woman stared back, not the farm girl she'd seen in the vanity that morning. In a flash of a hat, she'd grown up. She'd been waiting for it so long and now here it was, blinking back at her from beneath burgundy velvet.

"Beautiful. It suits you," said Mrs. White.

Marilla beamed from within the pleated frame.

"I'll take that hat plus this gray one and . . ." She paused with a frown at Rachel.

"Oh, Mother, please!" begged Rachel.

"I thought you disliked hats."

"You said I simply hadn't found the right one—now I have!"

Mrs. White waved a hand of surrender. "Fine, but Madame, would you be so kind as to lessen the frippery. I assume that would cut the cost too, correct?"

"*Oui*," said Madame Stéphanie. "We will make it perfect for Mademoiselle." And off she went with her shears.

"Please don't take away the frill over the eyes. That's my favorite part," Rachel called after her.

Marilla quietly set her hat back on the stand. "Thank you, Mrs. White, but I couldn't accept such an expensive gift. I'm already on this trip by your generosity."

Mrs. White put a finger under Marilla's chin and lifted it so their eyes met. "Nonsense. That hat is meant for you, Marilla."

And so they left the shop wearing Madame Stéphanie's couture hats. Marilla had never felt so grand. Her satin ribbons shone in the afternoon sun, and everyone who passed the trio paused a moment to look upon them.

John waited in the Majesty Inn's lobby. With the women's faces hidden beneath the bonnet brims, he didn't recognize them immediately but turned like the rest to marvel. Then his eyes caught on Izzy's borrowed bright blue cloak. His jaw dropped, and his eyes met Marilla's with a smile.

Mrs. White broke the spell: "The concierge has been kind enough to hold our shawl parcels in their coatroom. Would you be a good boy and fetch them for us, John?"

"It seems I'm accompanying the fanciest ladies in Nova Scotia." He bowed, then proceeded to the front desk, whispering, "I like that color red on you," as he passed Marilla.

Thank goodness for the pleats around her face or he might've seen her cheeks flaming.

The orphanage was a few blocks away—too short a distance to take a fly carriage through the street traffic. It was faster to walk. So Marilla, Rachel, and Mrs. White each took a parcel of shawls and then stacked the remaining four so high in John's arms that he could only blindly put one foot in front of the other.

"I don't need to see the sidewalk. I'll follow your hats. When I see a nun's habit, I'll know we've arrived."

The Sisters of Charity received poor orphans from across the provinces and even America. The building was a modest redbrick without cornices or columns, and casement windows stared down on the street like pairs of eyes. Violet smoke rose from the chimney, and Marilla smelled cabbage in the air. Someone in the kitchen was making a stew. The gravel front yard was encircled by an iron-post fence and swept clean of little footprints. A vegetable garden had been planted to the right and two saplings to the left. Red maples, Marilla recognized. Good shade trees for the children. They'd bring color in the fall. Marilla was glad for it. The place needed some cheer.

"Welcome, dear ones." The Reverend Mother greeted them at the door. Her bright face peeked through her white wimple like Marilla's breakfast egg yolk.

"We're honored to be here on behalf of Avonlea," said Mrs. White.

"We're honored to receive you, Mrs. White." The Reverend Mother nodded. "Whom have you brought along to us?"

"My daughter Rachel and Miss Marilla Cuthbert," Mrs. White said, presenting the girls. They curtsied.

"Such beauties." The Reverend Mother pointed behind them. "And who might that walking stack of parcels be?"

"Oh! John Blythe," said Mrs. White. "A young Avonlea gentleman who has graciously served as our porter."

"A pleasure!" John called from behind the packages. "I would take off my cap, but that might mean relinquishing these fine goods to the street dogs, and I sincerely doubt they'll have much use for fanciful shawls."

The Reverend Mother got a good chuckle out of that. "Indeed not, lad! Do come in and put down your heavy burden."

The orphanage had been the home of a wealthy widow who befriended the nuns on their arrival in Hopetown. Having no heirs, she'd bequeathed all her possessions to the Sisters of Charity. The sisters had turned the home into a residence of many beds. What had once been the living room now contained rows of cots, neatly made with a single toy at the foot of each: a stuffed rabbit here, a yo-yo there, balls and jacks, enough rag poppets to form an army—all waiting quietly for their someone's return. The dining room had been remade into the classroom, with rows of desks and a slate board propped up at the front. The children were presently outside for lunch. There were so many, they had to take turns at the long picnic tables. Half the children ate their cabbage soup while the other half played hopscotch and jump rope in the courtyard. The nuns were just ringing the bell for the children to swap when the group of Avonlea visitors arrived.

Like schools of fish colliding, the children mixed and separated again, full bellies to play and empty ones to table. Little boys wore knee pants. Little girls wore pinafores. They raced round in all colors of fabric and face: French and British, Métis and black, Canadian and American, orphans all.

"So many," Marilla whispered.

"Yes," said John.

Marilla hadn't realized he was beside her. The brim of her bonnet had blocked her vision.

"Hard to imagine growing up without knowing from where you come."

Marilla agreed. She was born in Avonlea and had no apprehensions about dying there someday. It was where she belonged. She wouldn't be Marilla Cuthbert from anywhere else.

Seeing them watching, a little boy whispered to his tablemates, and all ten turned to look at Marilla and John.

"They think you're a couple come to adopt," said the Reverend Mother.

Marilla's heart beat fast. The word spread across the play yard until nearly all of the children were staring, each one imagining what their life might be tomorrow if they were chosen today. Marilla took a step away from John. It wasn't fair—to the children.

The Reverend Mother ushered them down the hall to her office, where a Lilliputian desk stood in the far corner to make space for the shelves of orphan documents. It was so small a room, only two people could fit comfortably at a time. So Marilla, Rachel, and John waited outside while Mrs. White unveiled their gifts.

A handful of girls, not much younger than themselves, came down the hall. One carried a hymnal, another a weathered guitar, while the remaining two chatted excitedly over which song the Reverend Mother would most like them to perform for the littler ones at bedtime. They quieted as they came closer and stopped outside the office to wait their turn. Silence bore down.

Finally, unable to stand the awkward hush, Rachel pushed back her bonnet's lace netting. "We sing from that same hymnal." She pointed to the book the girl carried. "'Amazing Grace' is my favorite." She cleared her throat and gave an off-key hum. "'Amazing grace, how sweet the sound' . . ."

Marilla held her breath. Rachel's pitch was shrill as Skunk's meows. The orphans stood, unflinching.

". . . 'that saved a wretch like me.'" Rachel paused to inhale. "Well, you know how it goes."

"That was very pretty," said the girl with the guitar. "Maybe you can sing with us if you're staying."

Rachel put a hand to her throat. "Oh, I wish I could, but we're not staying long. We have dinner plans with my father." Catching herself, she smiled and pulled the netting back down.

"I like your hat," another said to Marilla.

The girl's skin was a cinnamon hue. Her hair was the color of mahogany and plaited back thickly. An unnatural scar slashed her freckled cheek.

"We've just got them today," Rachel answered. "Aren't they lovely?"

The girl nodded with a gaze so earnest that before Marilla could think twice, she pulled loose the bow at her throat.

"Would you like to try mine on?"

Rachel turned abruptly, but Marilla kept her eyes on the orphan.

"I'd like it ever so much, if you would." Marilla held out her velvet bonnet.

The girl cautiously accepted and placed it on her head.

"You tie it to the side. Here, let me." Marilla looped the ribbons as the shop assistant had done for her.

The girl looked to the window. A gossamer reflection smiled back, and she turned side to side to see all angles, just as Marilla had done in the shop mirror.

Mrs. White and the Reverend Mother came out then.

"The shawls are beautiful. Our girls will love them. What gracious friends we have on Prince Edward Island."

Believing it to be Marilla in the red bonnet, Mrs. White put one arm around the girl and another around Rachel. "Indeed, the ladies of Avonlea will eternally support the orphaned and widowed, so sayeth the scriptures."

The girl turned and Mrs. White saw her mistake.

"Oh! I thought you were Marilla."

"Please, ma'am, I didn't meant to . . ." She fumbled with the ribbons, tears brimming.

"No, no," said Marilla. She took the girl's hand, soft and pink as a begonia bloom. "Mrs. White, I know you bestowed this gift on me, but I would now like to give it to—"

They hadn't even had an introduction.

"Juniper, but most calls me Junie," she whispered with head hung so low that her voice was nearly lost to the wooden floor.

"To Junie," said Marilla. "With your blessing, of course."

"I—I—" Mrs. White fidgeted with her gloves. "Well, of course. If the Reverend Mother approves."

"A charitable heart is the truest reflection of our Heavenly Father. Our Avonlea friends are a continual blessing." She bowed. "Thank you, Miss Cuthbert."

Junie curtsied. "Thank you, Miss Cuthbert," she echoed. "I's will cherish it for all my life."

Marilla felt something in her chest expand and release. She wasn't sure if it was joy for Junie or sorrow for herself. She liked to think it was the former but worried it was a little of the latter. One couldn't hide a fickle heart from God. Nonetheless, she was glad she'd given the beautiful hat away. She already had so many things: a home, family, people who belonged to her and she to them. There would be new hats for Marilla, but perhaps only this one for Junie.

Rachel pulled her lace creation off. "Here." She handed it to the girl holding the hymnal. "Since I can't sing with you . . ."

"I thank you greatly, miss," said the hymnal girl. She held the hat like a delicate bird that might fly off at any moment. Her friends ogled it.

Mrs. White kept her bonnet firmly on her head. "Well now, such a day of blessing! To the givers and the receivers as our Lord Christ exemplified."

The Reverend Mother crossed herself, as did all four of the orphans. Mrs. White did a kind of half-cross, moving her hand shoulder to shoulder and mumbled amen, which Marilla found strange. It was not Presbyterian.

"Now that our duties here are complete, we won't take up another minute of your time. There are the children to attend to," said Mrs. White.

"Please come again. We welcome you always."

"Indeed we shall. The ladies of Avonlea will promptly start on our next batch of shawls."

Rachel gave a groan that only Marilla heard.

"Come, Rachel." Mrs. White ushered her daughter forward.

While Mrs. White chattered her way to the exit, Marilla and John followed a few steps behind.

"That was a good thing you did back there," said John.

"I didn't mean to cause a fuss. She seemed like she needed something that was all hers."

"I'm sure that's true. Did you see her face?"

Marilla nodded. "A terrible scar."

"It's a slave master's mark," said John.

Marilla stopped in the hallway and looked behind her. The orphans were clumped together, staring after them. John took her arm and led her onward.

"I've seen it before—on the runaways from America. The slave masters disfigure them so if they attempt it again, they can be identified."

Marilla leaned in. "Do you think she was a slave?"

"You mean, *is* a slave. Too young to have paid off her master. Wouldn't have a scar if she was born free."

"Where are her parents?"

John tilted his head close so that his words remained between them. "Adults can't be hidden in an orphanage, Marilla. If she still has parents, they'd do well to leave her with the Sisters of Charity. They can find a safe home for her. There are others. Did you see them at the tables?"

There were many African families in the Maritimes. Prince Edward Island had abolished the practice of slavery when Marilla was but a year old. Then in 1834, Parliament issued the Abolition Act, banishing slavery across the British colonies. Hopetown had an African chapel on one side of town and the Royal Acadian School on the other. So while she had seen the black orphans, she hadn't assumed they were American runaways.

The Presbyterian Church was firm in its opinion that owning another man, by reason of moral turpitude, undermined the laws of God. Being that most everyone in Avonlea was a congregation member, it was widely agreed that slavery was as wicked a sin as there was. But off the island was a different world. There were many Canadians who maintained an attitude of tolerance and, worse, *support* for their slaveholding counterparts. It was because of them that bounty hunters scavenged the provinces, taking whom they pleased back to America. The newspaper ads were full of descriptions of runaways that could fit nearly any African on the street, both the runaway slaves and the truly free. And the courts were governed by the elite, who looked the other way so long as the county coffers were full. They still viewed slavery as a business, not a moral transaction. But here Marilla saw its actuality: these people, orphans of heart and land, belonged to no one. The nuns were providing far more than appearances revealed.

"I can't thank you enough for everything." The Reverend Mother unbolted the front doors. "You'll never know how much your gifts mean to these children."

She smiled at Marilla.

"The outfitting of your little lambs is my new calling," Mrs. White declared. "We will be in touch again soon."

"Blessings on you and safe travels home." The Reverend Mother waved, then closed the door and slid the metal bolt through again with a solid *thunk*.

"Well . . ." Mrs. White exhaled and looked to Marilla curiously. "Perhaps our Ladies' Sewing Circle should take on the knitting of bonnet caps to complement the shawls. A wonderful idea, Marilla." Then off she went, pulling Rachel down the sidewalk beside her. "We mustn't keep Mr. White waiting, and I'm sure Mr. Blythe would like his son returned to him."

Marilla and John walked beside each other. Their arms brushed one another's. When a puddle stretched across their path, Mrs. White and Rachel circumvented it in a wide arc, but John didn't waver in his course. He took Marilla's elbow to help her over. His grip there felt like a buttress for all they'd just seen and all she couldn't put into words. When the Majesty Inn came into view, a new anxiety budded: she didn't want him to leave. Silly, she chastised herself, when they were leaving to arrive at the same place.

XI

THE MAY PICNIC

The annual May Picnic celebrated spring in all its glory. The sun had nearly melted away every drop of cold. Now the marbled blue-green sea on the horizon was banked by emerald green forests and broad fields of pink and purple lupines. Wild lady's slippers yawned their mouths open to drink in the light. The happy ivy and crossvines crawled another few inches up, up, while the apple and cherry trees made every turn a delight of white promise.

Mrs. White was diverted from assigning new tasks to the sewing circle and the Sunday school until after all the women of Avonlea had finished their picnic dresses. It was tradition for everyone to wear something new and as bright as the island.

Marilla woke each morning expecting to welcome her new baby sibling. Clara was due to deliver at any moment, and they were all glad for it. Her belly had grown round and hard as a melon, and she had disappeared beneath it, white as a ghost and weak as a blade of seagrass. Izzy had finished her yellow chair and moved it to Clara's bedside, where she read and sewed at all hours. The only time she left Clara was to help Marilla cook meals, but she ate beside Clara, often sharing a bowl. One spoonful for Clara, one spoonful for herself. Marilla watched and wondered what it would be like to love and care for someone that much. Guilt pricked her conscience. Truth be told, she was glad she wasn't the one sitting in that chair day after day. She worried that made her wicked deep down and prayed for forgiveness if so.

Rachel and Marilla finished their amaryllis sleeves. The stitching was delicate as the petals it depicted. A finer pair Marilla had never seen. To her surprise, Rachel insisted Marilla have them.

"Put them on your May Picnic dress," she urged. "Then we can prove to all the Avonlea School girls that we're official members of the Ladies' Sewing Circle, not just looping on childish circulars like the rest. Besides, Mother is having my picnic dress made from new chintz on special order—these wouldn't match at all."

That said, Rachel admired the sleeves with a sigh, and Marilla knew how hard it was for her to give up things she was keen on. It made the giving more meaningful.

"Exquisite. Did you make these?" Izzy marveled when Marilla brought the embroidery home.

"I did one and Rachel did the other."

Izzy inspected each. "They're both so smart. I can't tell them apart. Look at your daughter's hand."

Clara smiled weakly from beneath the bed quilt and hovered her thin fingers over the stitching, following the amaryllis tendrils, leaf to flower. "Beautiful."

Marilla beamed. "I thought . . . well, I hoped I might put them on my May Picnic dress. That is, with your help, being that I've never made one before."

A request for a dress seemed trivial. Izzy was busy caring for Marilla's mother. But still, she hoped . . .

"Of course!" Izzy agreed. "We just finished reading *Ivanhoe,* and we need another project to keep us occupied until the baby arrives. Isn't that right, Clara?"

Clara nodded and grasped Marilla's hand. "We'll make you the most beguiling dress, my dear."

"I have just the material to match," Izzy said. "A Spitalfields brocade that I've been saving for something special. I brought it with me." She winked. "I had an inkling that something special might be here. It's in my trunk—interlacing cream and red ribbons on a pale blue background." She marched to her room, carrying the amaryllis sleeves.

"Come sit with me a minute," Clara beckoned. "My girl, all grown up. Tell me again about the coast."

It had taken Marilla two full days to tell Clara everything about her trip to Nova Scotia. Her mother had closed her eyes as she listened so she could picture it in her mind. She hadn't been to Hopetown since she was a new bride buying pewter spoons and forks to last a lifetime. Marilla left out the parts about the fancy hats and the slave girl named Juniper. Instead, she described the land and sea and the goings between.

Unlike the departure from the island, on the return Mr. White convinced Mrs. White to let the girls venture out on the ship's bow, given the day was clear with hardly a whitecap. The sailing was Clara's favorite part of Marilla's story. The Cuthberts might've been farmers, but Clara's people, the Johnsons, had been Scottish sailors. Marilla understood now how the sea could lure a spirit. So she told it again: how the wind whistled a note sharper than the clear sky. How the water seemed to crackle as they glided through. How they bought hot cocoas from the ferry vendor, and he dropped a peppermint in their cups for good luck. And how when she breathed in, she could smell the tides. Marilla found that each time she told the story, she knew more and saw more than when she first lived it. The memory became its own rainbow arcing from the past to the present.

"Tell me about the red beaches . . ." Clara's eyelids fluttered on the edge of sleep.

Unlike the oyster shores of Nova Scotia, Prince Edward Island was ringed red like the skin of a cut apple.

"I never knew our island was different from the others."

"*Abegweit*," Clara murmured. "That's the native Micmac name. They say the god Glooscap made our island by mixing all the colors of the earth and stroking the ocean with his paintbrush. *Abegweit* means 'cradle on the waves.'" She put her hand on her belly. "It's a pretty name, isn't it?"

Marilla nodded, though she couldn't say she knew anyone named *Abegweit*. It sounded like a fairy name—something from a make-believe kingdom—so perhaps it was rightful in her story. Clara's breathing turned over to a gentle purr.

"*Abegweit*," Marilla whispered. She kissed her mother's warm forehead and then tiptoed out.

Izzy was in her room with the brocade fabric rolled out across her bed. She'd laid one of her own party dresses on top as the pattern, pinning the amaryllis sleeves neatly in place. "We're nearly the same height, but I can hem the skirt if it's too long. Do you like the brocade?"

Marilla ran her fingers over the meticulous weaving. "It's the finest I've ever seen."

Downstairs came the thud of men's boots followed by the low tenor of Matthew's voice. It was midday. The men were never inside at this hour.

Izzy stuck her sewing pin back into the cushion. "Does Matthew have company? Your father took Jericho down to pick potatoes. Wouldn't be back already."

"One of the sheep herders might've stopped for water," said Marilla. "I can fetch it."

But her assistance proved unnecessary. Matthew and his companion had moved out onto the back porch. Sitting on the kitchen table was a basket of asparagus so piercing green that they hurt her eyes to look at. The smell of tobacco drifted through the air.

"It's true. Tides are turning . . ." Matthew was saying as she came out. "Marilla." He took the pipe out of his mouth. "Look who's here?"

John was in the same day suit he'd worn on his first visit to the

Gables, only this time he'd left off the jacket. His sleeves were cuffed neatly to the elbow revealing muscular forearms, already tanned from hours of spring sowing.

"Good to see you again, Marilla." He smiled. "I brought over some of our asparagus."

"I saw, thank you. Mother will be pleased. She loves asparagus soup. I don't know how you get yours to grow so nicely. Ours looks like seaweed."

"It's the cows. Dung does wonders for the crops."

Matthew cleared his throat and tapped out his pipe's ash. "I best get back to work. Let you do what you come for. Good talking with you. Come again, and we'll have another smoke."

"That's a promise," said John.

Marilla took a step back in confusion. She'd assumed John had come to see Matthew.

"What *have* you come for?" she asked forthright.

Matthew gave a little chuckle under his breath. John waited for Matthew to walk a piece farther toward the barn.

"I've come to ask you a question, Miss Cuthbert."

She crossed her arms at his use of her formal name. She wasn't in the mood for games. There was supper to start on, and she wanted to help Izzy begin cutting her new dress.

"Don't just stand there asking to ask. Speak your mind."

"The Avonlea May Picnic is in a couple of weeks. My father offered to let me use his chaise if I wished to take someone, which I do. *You.* Care to escort me?"

So unexpected was the invitation that Marilla hadn't the time to kindle flattery or fear. Ride alone to the picnic in John Blythe's carriage? But the Cuthberts went together. Who would hold their pie hamper steady in the wagon, which she had done for all the years she could remember?

"I always go with my family."

He nodded. "Well, seeing as Matthew is asking Johanna Andrews to ride with him, and your father and aunt said they wouldn't leave your mother behind at home . . ."

She didn't know what ruffled her more—that he'd already spoken to her kin or that he was telling her things she didn't know. And so, for the first time, she stopped wondering what she ought to do as a daughter-sister-niece and asked herself what *she* wanted to do as Marilla.

"I think that would be nice, John. Very nice."

It wasn't like they were secreting off alone. They were riding openly to a prominent town affair. Everybody would be there, and it wouldn't really matter who came in whose buggy. Nonetheless, her stomach pinwheeled.

John threaded his fingers through his hair and only then did she see the light sweat sheen on his brow.

"I'll come for you then."

XII

THE AMETHYST BROOCH

Two weeks later on the picnic day, Izzy helped Marilla lace up the girdle and slip on the brocaded gown. The sisters had worked ceaselessly on the dress. Izzy did most of the heavy tailoring, with Clara working the button eyelets with such tender determination that when fastened, Marilla swore she could feel her mother's hands across her back. For her part, Marilla had ensured that the seams and hem were stitched to perfection. Her fingers were dotted with needle pricks. She counted every one worth the sting. The dress was the most exquisite that she owned—the most exquisite she had ever seen. After she'd dressed, Izzy plaited Marilla's hair in two loops that joined together at her crown, mimicking the serpentine pattern of the amaryllis embroidery, then applied beeswax to her lips and lashes so that Marilla's face shimmered like honey.

Clara gasped when Marilla entered her bedroom.

"My darling child . . ." She fought against her belly to raise herself upright. "You're a grand lady!" Tears ebbed. "I was just about your age when I started stepping out with your father."

Marilla turned her cheek down. "We're only riding together, Mother."

"Yes, of course, but soon enough you'll fall in love with someone and move on to greener pastures."

A knot formed beneath Marilla's ribs. The girdle was too tight. She didn't want to move on to greener pastures. Theirs were just the shade of green that suited her.

"I'll always be your Marilla."

Clara smiled and beckoned for Izzy to fetch the little velvet satchel on the nightstand. "I have something for you."

Turning her daughter's palm up, she poured out the contents. An oval brooch rimmed in the purplest gems, like the petals of a flower.

"Amethyst. A present from a seafaring uncle. He said he got it from a holy woman who claimed the stones were blessed with protection. It's yours now, Marilla."

Marilla ran her thumb over it. The amethysts sparkled. She had seen her mother wear the brooch on Easter and religious holidays. The rest of the time she kept it safely tucked away in her steamer trunk alongside her wedding dress, locks of ribboned baby hair, and other keepsakes.

"It will be her crowning jewel," said Izzy.

Clara cupped Marilla's cheek. "Now go and have the most marvelous time at the picnic. I'm sorry to miss it and everyone there. Give my love to Avonlea."

"I will." Marilla kissed her mother's hand. "Thank you."

Hugh nodded approvingly when she came down the steps of the Gables.

"Best take a shawl. The wind has a bite, could mean weather coming on."

She did as her father said and pinned the brooch over her heart.

Outside, Matthew sat in his buggy with Johanna Andrews primly beside him. He smiled when he saw her come down the porch steps.

Waiting beside his chaise was John, scrubbed fresh as a Sunday reverend. He reached out to her, but she hesitated, looking back to Hugh and Izzy on the front porch. Accepting his hand felt too significant a thing. Once taken, she could never go back. So instead, she picked up her skirts and helped herself into the chaise. John settled beside her in the seat.

"Hold on," he whispered, then cracked the reins and his horse took off in a bolt.

Marilla had no choice but to lean close and hold on to his arm to keep from tumbling out.

"Apologies," said John once the horse calmed to an even trot and the Gables looked like a portrait miniature behind them. "The horse is young—too much bottled vigor."

Marilla nodded. She hadn't much experience with colts. Jericho was an old gelding that followed them reliably with Matthew and Johanna.

Like waves crashing on the shore, they heard the roar of the picnic crowd before they crested the knoll. The lawn was teeming with Avonlea folk sitting on picnic blankets and dawdling between gingham-covered tables of fruit juice and cordials, cucumber boats, pickled eggs, frosted cakes, and puddings. Reverend Patterson stood beneath the outstretched arms of the sugar maple, giving instructions to the band arranged in a semicircle of chairs beneath. A Maypole had been constructed where the meadow grass had been flattened by treading. It was festooned with colorful ribbons, daffodils, crocuses, lupines, and ivy greens like a garden rainbow.

To the far left was the picnic's showstopper: the carousel, owned by the Clarences, a family of circus workers who had sailed over from Bristol to start anew in Avonlea. Marilla had never seen such a thing. The wooden horses were carved with giddy expressions, their manes painted coral and cobalt, their tails lilac and lemon. Mirrors hung between every pole so that when the crank turned the horses, the colors blurred and multiplied. The force of the spin made the charges fly without touching the ground. Marilla thought it the closest thing to magic. Avonleaers of all ages stood in a long line, waiting their turn on the merry-go-round, and Marilla hoped to get her chance too.

Mrs. White had signed up to run a tent for the Sunday school, selling ornamental shells painted in flashy colors: the Sunday school's spring project. Seeing Marilla and John ride into the gravel yard, her mouth dropped open, and she turned to murmur something to the Reverend's wife. They both smiled at Marilla, which only made her raise her chin higher. There was nothing to hide. Their relationship was one of respectable chastity. But then, once again, John felt compelled to fly in the face of convention.

Instead of helping her down as he would any other woman, he grabbed her by the waist, lifted her over the foot guard, and set her on the ground with his arms around her for all to gape at. She knew she ought to put a hand between them and push him away, but she didn't . . . because the sun was shining bright and the air smelled of roasted kettle corn and crushed grass. Because the band started a cheery tune at just that moment. And because the breeze blew the curls of John's hair free, the curls of hers too. Why change a thing? He was a boy helping a girl out of a carriage on a perfect May day.

"You look lovely," said John.

"My mother and Aunt Izzy helped make the dress. Rachel and I sewed the sleeves—see?" She let the shawl drop to her elbows and turned her shoulders so he could look upon their needlework.

"I've never seen a prettier thing."

Matthew cleared his throat. "I'll tie your buggy beside ours so they can share an oat bucket."

Johanna Andrews's sisters had seen them arrive and surrounded her to ask how the drive alone had been. None of them had been asked to court yet.

Matthew needed something to do to pass the time until they dispersed. Communal groups like this made him nervous. Groups of girls made him doubly so.

"Much obliged, Matthew," said John. "I'm going to take Marilla over to get a drink and then maybe a spin on the carousel. Care to join us when Johanna is ready?"

Relief washed over Matthew. He had a plan for what to do now and what to do next. The Cuthberts were people of planning. Spontaneity was not in their marrow. Marilla was grateful to John for understanding them without explanation.

He took her arm in his, and she rested her hand in the crook of it as they walked onto the picnic grounds.

"Hello there, Marilla! Hello there, John Blythe!" called Mrs. White. "Fine day for a pair of turtledoves, eh?"

"'Let the bird of loudest lay, on the sole Arabian tree, herald sad and trumpet be, to whose sound chaste wings obey,'" recited John, which left Mrs. White standing in a scowl of confusion.

"That's Shakespeare, Mrs. White. 'The Phoenix and the Turtle.'"

"Never heard of it," sniffed Mrs. White. "But I'm selling seashells in support of the Presbyterian Church. If you're in a mood for quoting verses, perhaps you ought to invest in biblical ones."

"You're terrible," Marilla chided him when they were out of earshot. "Mrs. White is sure to tell your mother."

"Aw, my mother is the one who read me the poem in the first place. She values a sound mind."

"I haven't read much Shakespeare. Only the sonnets in our school primer. But I think I'd like to read more after hearing that performance."

"And so you will when you return."

She nodded. "My parents would like me to finish schooling."

Marilla had thought it through. If she pushed herself hard enough in home study, she might even be ahead of her fellow students in the fall. Rachel said she wasn't going to study another minute. She was content having schooled up to grade six, but Marilla wanted to finish grade eight. She was determined to be the first in her family to do so. Matthew had never been one for books. The maths required to do farm business came naturally to him, so he'd stopped going to the schoolhouse as soon as he was old enough to drive a plow.

"It'll be nice to have you back."

"Marilla!" Rachel called from the picnic table. She stood with a handful of flouncy girls from the Sunday school.

Marilla knew them by their mothers: Mrs. Gillis's girl Clemmie, Mrs. Sloane's girl Olivia, Mrs. Gray's girl Nellie, and so forth.

"Hello—hello—hello—hello," they parroted in turn.

"I was just telling them about my chintz." Rachel swished the skirt of her dress. "We had to drive all the way over to Carmody to buy it—it's a toile de Jouy from France." Then she saw Marilla's sleeves. "Oh!" She ran her hands over them. "We made these! And where did you get the skirt material? It matches perfectly!"

"Aunt Izzy brought it from St. Catharines."

The girls circled round to ooh and aah. Marilla thought she might suffocate under their pawing. John came to her rescue holding two cups of cordial.

"Excuse me, ladies, I thought I might have company on the carousel."

All fell silent. Three of the girls looked like they might like to drink John Blythe. But it was Marilla to whom he handed the cup.

Rachel's eyes were wide as goose eggs. She gave a priggish smile. "Be careful, Marilla. Mr. Blythe told my father that John too often lets the reins get away from him."

"Aw," John raised an eyebrow. "To the unknowing eye it may appear, but to the horseman, it's an impassioned dash without restraint."

Mrs. Sloane's girl gave a swoon-sigh, and Mrs. Spencer's girl elbowed her steady.

Rachel harrumphed. "I was speaking to Marilla, not to you, John."

"Thank you," Marilla interceded. "Lucky for us, the carousel has *toy* horses," she reminded her friend. "If I fall off, it'll be my own doing and I'll deserve the trampling."

"I won't let you fall," said John.

"*Humph,*" said Rachel. "I think I'd rather play croquet. Leave the carousel for the children. Come on." The girls followed her like ducklings.

"You really shouldn't irritate her so," Marilla chastised after they'd gone. "Why do you?"

John laughed before seeing her sincerity. "It's just—teasing. I don't mean harm."

"Teasing is like a nettle. You play in a patch of it long enough and somebody's going to get pained."

"If you want me to stop, I will."

Marilla would never ask a man to do anything on her request, but now she did.

"Yes. Please. Rachel's my friend."

He lifted his cup in solemn oath. "I promise." He gulped, then looked into his cup. "What is this anyhow?"

"Ginger cordial. Reverend Patterson's wife read an article about ginger keeping away the spring sneezes. Better for Avonlea's health, so she claims."

"I like the berry better."

Marilla agreed. So they put their cups aside and went to watch the three-legged race, the ring-toss, and a game of John Bull. Then they rode the carousel until Marilla was breathless from laughter and the fervor of the flying spin. Afterward, they picnicked on pickled eggs with creamed mustard and shared a wedge of angel cake that they pulled apart with their fingers. About the time when the first of the fireflies began to wink, Reverend Patterson gave a call:

"To the Maypole! All eligible men and women—to the Maypole!"

Marilla had been dancing round the pole since she was old enough to stand. The children would have their turn, but the first dance always belonged to the unmarried young people of Avonlea. So Marilla and John took their places in the circle. Across from them were Matthew and Johanna.

"Even number now," directed Reverend Patterson. "Everybody got a ribbon? If you don't, then you'll have to wait for the next round. Remember, women go clockwise, men counter. Right-left, right-left, over-under, over-under. Ready? Set? And away we go!"

The band played a melody led by two fiddles.

Marilla took a purple ribbon. She raised her ribbon high, then brought it down low. The circles moved round like the gears of a clock. The colors braided the pole, and when they reached the bottom, everyone released the ties and grabbed the hands closest for the final reel. John was beside her. He threaded his fingers through hers and hers through his. A seamless fit. The fiddles went faster, as did their feet. Marilla was dizzy on the rainbow pinwheel. When it was done, the whole town erupted in whistles and shouts.

No one saw the pair dash hand in hand out of the Maypole circlet, past the mighty maple with the band beneath and the row of poplars guarding the church cemetery, down to the far quiet corner of the meadow where the sea holly and cornflowers were so thick a person could drown in them. They sat together under a canopy of meadow grasses and a sky of spun sugar. Marilla's heart still beat fast from the dance. John's did too. She felt the pulse in his fingertips. From the magazines she'd read, she thought she'd feel embarrassed or ashamed to be holding a boy's hand. The same way she felt holding the pages of the romance quarterlies. But she didn't. She only felt John: simple, solid, and true. That she understood. What she didn't understand was why he had led her to this spot.

"What are we doing here?"

"I wanted you to hear something—a secret."

He let go of her hand. Coolness crept into her palm. He leaned to the side and snatched something from the fuzzy wild rye.

"You've got to come close to hear it."

She leaned her forehead toward him, and he lifted his fist to her ear. *Chirp.*

"A cricket?" She laughed.

"My mother said the first ones of the season aren't crickets but fairies in disguise. They'll listen to your wishes and make them come to pass."

It seemed everyone had a way of wish-making. She doubted any of them were real and at the same time hoped all of them were.

The little bug gave another merry chirp. Marilla smiled. She missed their sound during the long winters.

"So how do I do it?"

He came closer, only the width of his cradled hand between them. "You close your eyes and whisper."

She closed her eyes and felt like she was falling, tumbling into flares of purple behind her eyelids. The rhythm of the dance still pounded in her temples.

"I . . ."

John's breath warmed her lips.

"I wish . . ." *for you to kiss me.*

"Marilla!"

It was Matthew.

"Marilla!"

She opened her eyes to John's confused stare. Something wasn't right. Matthew was calling—yelling for her.

She stood from the tall grass and ran in his direction.

"Matthew, I'm here!"

Reaching him, the sweat at his brow and strain of his eyes told her all she needed to know.

"Mother?"

He nodded.

"The baby?"

He'd hitched up Jericho already. "We've got to go."

"Is Dr. Spencer there?" John panted, out of breath from following her dash.

"Father came for him. They've gone back already. We couldn't find Marilla."

Marilla swallowed hard. The ginger cordial gurgled in her belly. She climbed into the buggy.

"What can I do?" asked John.

Matthew shook his head. "I dunno. I just . . . dunno." Then he gave the reins a flick and Jericho started off.

John and the May Picnic lawn got smaller and smaller. The band's song had tapered to silence by the time they reached the empty road between Avonlea and the Gables.

"Where were you?" asked Matthew. "I've been looking for almost an hour."

Had it been that long?

"Get on, Jericho!" she hollered instead of answering.

The night sky had turned rusty too fast. A storm was approaching.

XIII

TRAGEDY AT THE GABLES

By the time they reached home, the brewing tempest had picked up so that Marilla had to tie her shawl in a clove hitch to keep from losing it to the storm. Her hair had come free from its pins, and the plaits unfurled like reedy branches. The wind howled at her back and pulled the strands straight up to the sky.

"Get inside!" said Matthew. "I'll barn Jericho!"

Marilla jumped out of the carriage, then raced up the porch steps and through the front door. Shutting it behind her, there came an eerie quiet. A pitch rang in her ears.

"Father?" she called.

The parlor was empty. The blackened hearth was burned down to ash.

"Aunt Izzy?"

The kitchen stove had been lit, but the pot of broth was set to the side. Congealed. Bread had been cut and left naked of butter. Skunk circled her ankles, crying for hunger. She tossed a slice to the ground.

"Hush now," she comforted and left him to tooth and claw.

At the bottom of the stairs, she hesitated. Her breath stalled. Her head went light. The climb she'd done all day, every day, now seemed insurmountable. It was too quiet. She forced herself up one foot at a time, until she was at the top.

"Mother?" she whispered.

Hugh, Izzy, and Dr. Spencer encircled the bed.

Izzy faced Marilla first, with swollen eyes and tear-streaked cheeks. "Oh, child . . ."

Hugh and Dr. Spencer turned, but she didn't see their faces. Her vision tunneled.

Red.

Her feet slipped from beneath her. The jolt of the floor was like falling on ice—pain so shockingly raw that she'd pushed herself up and away from it before her father could help her.

"Mother?"

Izzy covered Clara with the muslin bedsheet. Its pallor accentuated the blood beneath. An ivory dress with a crimson hem.

"Marilla?" Clara whispered back.

Her eyes were flat and dark. Her lips a strange shade of violet.

"I'm afraid . . ." Clara's breath was shallow. "The baby is gone."

Marilla looked to Izzy, who didn't hide her tears. She shook her head.

"The child was stillborn," said Dr. Spencer. "Nothing to be done. Even if I had been here. Nothing to be done."

Clara blinked toward Marilla.

"My bold, beguiling girl . . ." Her vision flickered to Izzy. "Take care of her."

Hugh buckled at the foot of the bed, hands around Clara's feet. "Save her. Please."

"If I could . . ." Dr. Spencer's voice gave way. "She's lost too much already."

Clara smiled weakly. "My love, don't be sad. It was all worth it."

Hugh buried his head in the sheets and let out a mournful wail.

Matthew came through the bedroom door, taking them each in silently. His gaze settled on his father. He staggered back.

Clara turned to Marilla. "They need you. Promise me?"

"I promise," said Marilla. "I promise. I love you. I promise . . ."

She couldn't stop saying it, even after the light left Clara's eyes and her hand turned cool.

Time evaporated. At some point, Hugh left. Matthew followed him. Dr. Spencer checked Clara's vitals a last time, then scribbled the date of death in his ledger before moving the baby's body out of the room. Marilla's mind fixated on the empty space where it had been. Babies died. That was a fact of life. People mourned, planted crosses, and then moved on to making anew. But nobody had told her that mothers died too. Nobody had warned her that life and death could be split by a breath.

Only Izzy stayed in the room with her. She sat on the opposite side of the bed. A living mirror of her twin. Deceptively beautiful, death had spared Clara's delicate features. Her silken lashes brushed her alabaster cheek. Her golden-brown hair lay smooth against the pillow.

Izzy ran her fingers through it, softly crying, "You can't leave me alone . . . I need you."

The storm broke overhead. The eaves of the gables groaned against the downpour. Thunder rolled.

I should've been here. That's all Marilla could think. While she was wearing silly flounces, eating cake, and dancing, Clara labored in agony. While she wandered off to trade secrets with a boy, her mother was dying. The smallest elements produced the most significant change. Salt in bread. Water in soil. Light in darkness. If she had been there, she could've saved her mother.

The storm raged for hours and then left nothing but trickles down the windowpanes.

Izzy pulled Marilla into her arms. She'd fallen asleep against Clara's side.

"It's after midnight."

Izzy's bare face was so exactly like Clara's. Her loose hair fell on Marilla's cheek, smelling sweetly of the Gables. Only then did the tears come. Marilla let Izzy rock her like her mother would've when she had a bad dream. She closed her eyes and wished it so—to wake up to Clara shushing her fears and assuring her that all would be well tomorrow.

◆◇◆

But the next day brought only grave silence. And the day after and the day after that. They moved about the house like ghosts. Izzy cleaned the bodies and prepared them for burial. Hugh and Matthew went down to the hollow by the brook and split white birch for a single coffin. Mother and son would be put in the grave as one. Hugh called the baby boy Nathaniel. It meant *as God giveth* . . . and taketh. Mrs. White arranged the funeral with Reverend Patterson's wife.

And Marilla? She did everything she could to keep busy: sweeping, washing, cooking, churning, scrubbing . . . sweeping, washing, cooking, churning, scrubbing . . . over and over. It was never right enough. She saw stains everywhere and was determined to atone. When she stumbled on the yellow-and-ivy baby gown, she shook with raging guilt and packed it in the bottom of her mother's trunk alongside Clara's dresses. She couldn't stand to see them hanging bodiless.

Before they laid Clara and Nathaniel in the velvet casket, Marilla braided delicate strands of her mother's hair, cut it, and looped it behind the oval of her mother's amethyst brooch. It was her most treasured possession. A reminder of the promise she made to watch over Matthew and Hugh. They needed her. Even if they didn't say so. Even if they said nothing at all.

Hugh went so long without speaking that Marilla started to forget the sound of his voice. Her own too. He said nothing at the funeral.

All of Avonlea gathered in the poplar-shaded cemetery. The Keiths, their third cousins on the Cuthbert side, came up from East Grafton with their sons. In addition, there were a number of folks Marilla didn't recognize from Carmody and White Sands.

Mrs. White gave the eulogy. "An honorable woman of an honorable family. Her life was in service to them. She leaves behind the proof of her righteousness in her children and husband."

Marilla winced. If only they knew the truth. Clara had needed her, but she'd chosen selfishness, vanity, desire. She shouldn't have gone to the picnic when her mother was so near to giving birth.

Reverend Patterson said a prayer. "'The wise shall shine brightly like the splendor of the firmament, and those who lead the many to justice shall be like the stars forever.' So may it be with our sister Clara Cuthbert. Amen."

It was the only time the Cuthberts spoke, together in unity: "Amen."

The splendor of the firmament . . . the description struck Marilla like the *holy wound* had struck Rachel. It gave her a headache to imagine something so vast. And while beautiful, it made her mother feel even farther away. The throbbing at her temples increased. So she cataloged the practical: the cow needed milking; the handle on the door between the kitchen and pantry was broken; the cuff on the shirt Hugh wore was one stitch from coming unraveled. These needs were within her control. They comforted her.

When the time came, everyone lined up to pay their respects with flowers. Marilla, Hugh, and Matthew went first, each dropping a Scotch rose into the grave. Clara had brought the bush over from Scotland as a girl. It had blossomed powder-white pompoms just that week. Marilla found it nearly inconceivable that nature could thrive while her mother perished . . . and yet, it did.

After them came the whole of Avonlea.

"A true angel on earth," said Mrs. Blair. Pink columbines.

"A beautiful mother," said Mrs. White. "Cherished by all," followed Mr. White. "Oh, Marilla . . ." cried Rachel. Crimson peonies.

"She is with the Lord and the Lord be with you." Reverend and Mrs. Patterson. Purple Adam and Eves.

Even the widow Pye and her kin. She lifted her black veil, and it was the first time Marilla had seen her face outright. It was soft and full. Widow Pye said nothing, just laid down her bleeding hearts.

They moved Marilla. These loving friends. Some she knew well, others hardly at all. But they were her people: Avonlea. Without them, she was sure she'd crumble into the grave with Clara. To each, she nodded with appreciation so great, it humbled her to trembling.

John and his parents waited until the last.

"Mr. Cuthbert." John took off his hat. "Miss Johnson. Matthew. Marilla."

Marilla dared not meet his gaze. She was sure it would harpoon her through.

"Hugh, if you need anything," said Mr. Blythe.

"Anything at all," repeated Mrs. Blythe.

John carried a nosegay in his hand. The very hand Marilla had held instead of her mother's. Yellow lady's slippers.

She lifted her stare. "They were her favorite." A tear wet her cheek. "Thank you."

John's eyes were steadfast on her even while he addressed her father.

"Mr. Cuthbert, I'd very much like to lend a hand however I may."

"We have a French farm boy coming to us. Part of a trade," explained Mr. Blythe. "One of our Jersey cows for an extra set of hands this summer."

"My family can spare me," said John.

Hugh looked to Matthew and Marilla. He worried about how to proceed alone with his two children. He and Clara had planned for

Marilla to finish her studies, but how with only the three of them to run the Gables and farm? Marilla saw the wheels of his mind churning. John's extra set of hands would help them with the fieldwork so that by fall they'd need only to tally the harvest.

"Mighty good of you. Izzy will be returning to St. Catharines. So we'd be obliged."

Marilla reared back. Izzy was leaving? Marilla hadn't thought past the present. Enough in that to flood an ocean.

❧

The Gables' windows and mirrors were covered in black like coins over the eyes. The men went out to inhale their burnt sorrows through tobacco pipes, leaving Marilla alone with Izzy for the first time since the night of Clara's death.

In her room, she packed her suitcase.

"When?"

It was a question and a demand. Marilla didn't want any more surprises. Only hard truth.

Izzy put down the fabric she folded. "The end of the week." Her eyes brimmed. "I can't stay in Avonlea. It belongs to my sister, not me. I have a home and business in St. Catharines. My life is there."

Marilla shook her head. Clara and Izzy were born of the same womb. They shared each other's makeup. A lifetime of secrets, dreams, and wishes. Why then could she not stay with them? For Marilla, if no one else. Had Izzy already forgotten her mother's last words—to take care of her?

"Please."

Izzy went to her room's east-facing window and moved aside the black drape to open it. The breeze brought with it the sweetness of the cherry tree sapling outside. She inhaled as deep as she could and stood a long minute gazing out. Her back to Marilla.

"No one will be able to move on if I stay," she whispered. "Everyone still sees Clara, except for me."

Outside, Matthew's and Hugh's figures, small as ants, were making their way up the hill.

"I don't want you to go."

Izzy turned. The wind batted the curtain.

"Come with me to St. Catharines. I know the headmistress of a wonderful girls' school. I live above my shop with the entire attic empty. It would make a cozy bedroom. Dormer window and pitched ceiling. Hugh and Matthew could take on a live-in hire. You wouldn't be leaving the island forever. Just until—until . . ." She faltered.

The future was nebulous. Neither one knew how to answer the unsaid question: until when? It was futile anyhow. Marilla had already given her answer to her mother: *I promise*. She wouldn't leave Hugh, Matthew, or the Gables. Not ever.

"My place is here."

Izzy nodded. "I know it is. Just as I know mine isn't."

While it wounded her, Marilla respected Izzy's decision. Her aunt could never step into her mother's role, nor did Marilla wish her to. Staying would be a constant reminder of their loss and an eternal comparison to what once was. The only way for Marilla to move forward was to cleave her life in two: Marilla the mothered and Marilla the motherless. The distinction fortified her.

At the end of the week, Matthew loaded Izzy's luggage into the wagon with Jericho at the lead.

"Write me how you're doing or I'll worry," she told Hugh. His silence was agreement.

Marilla balled her hands under her apron, determined to be strong.

Izzy embraced her. "I'll miss you most of all, my pretty flower. Will you promise to write me too?"

Marilla gulped against the tears.

"That's all right." Izzy kissed her cheek. "I'll write to you, and you can reply or not, but I'll keep writing." She turned for the buggy and Marilla's resolve broke.

"Aunt Izzy!" She threw herself into Izzy's arms and buried her face against her aunt's lilac-powdered neck.

"I love you, dear girl. So very much."

And then Izzy let go and took Matthew's hand into the seat. He gave a whistle and Jericho began to trot down the long lane. Izzy didn't wave good-bye or turn back, but they could see the shudder of her shoulders from afar. Hugh and Marilla stood silent on the porch until Jericho vanished over the dewy June horizon. Then he put on his cap and went on to the barn, while Marilla walked down to the garden with a bucket. Sheep's sorrel had grown neglectfully between their green peas, and she had a mind to weed it out clean.

XIV.

GREEN GABLES IS NAMED

A fortnight later, Marilla was coming up the maple lane from gathering forest herbs as John brought their cows down to pasture.

"Oh—" She jumped when she saw him and dropped her summer savory.

He picked it up and returned it. "Good morning, Marilla."

"Good morning, John." She waved the bouquet garni. "I'm making an herb bannock. Are you staying for supper later?"

He adjusted his kerchief. The sun blazed down despite the mottled shade of the bear-clawed leaves. Beads of sweat dampened both their faces.

"Thank you, but I promised my parents I'd be home."

She nodded. "Maybe I'll send you back with a portion."

She'd picked enough for four. She didn't know how to cook for any fewer.

"Now that you've got the French farm boy to feed, and we have one fewer." Her eyes welled. She bit her lip.

John reached out to take her hand.

"No." She pulled away. "Thank you but . . ."

"I only meant to . . ." He sighed. "We haven't really had a chance to be alone since . . . you know."

"Since the day my mother died? Yes, I know." She lifted her chin hard. "I need to get back. Chores are waiting." She started that way.

John stopped her by the elbow, his hand gently grasping her secret scar. She went slack.

"My father says grief can make a heart hard for a time. I understand, Marilla. I'm not going anywhere."

A breeze caught the maples and rippled through. She leaned into him, ever so slightly, then straightened.

"I'll leave the bannock in the kitchen for you."

She didn't look back over her shoulder as she walked to the Gables. It wasn't until she was at the kitchen door that she heard the cowbells moving along.

Marilla wrapped the extra bannock wedge in wax paper and left it on the chopping table. It was there one minute and gone the next. John must've come in while she was sweeping the yard, and Matthew and Hugh were washing up for supper. She was glad she missed him—and sorry too.

Marilla fed the silent men at the table. She ate bites between washing dishes and wiping crumbs. Too hot from the day to sit indoors, they all went out on the back porch afterward. Hugh and Matthew lit their tobacco pipes, and Marilla took to her wicker chair. A flight of tree sparrows descended on the gravel, hopping back and forth and twittering some tune known only between their flock.

Hugh cleared his throat. "This place needs a name."

It surprised Marilla.

"A name? But we have a name."

Hugh shook his head. "Your mother wanted it to be called something particular. I've been thinking on it a time, but can't seem to find the right thing."

As they thought, the sun slowly sank into the horizon, throwing a golden shimmer across the Cuthbert pastureland. The last reach of day. Fireflies blinked and disappeared, blinked and disappeared.

Here and gone, here and gone. The fields rolled green blade to green leaves to green gulf beyond . . .

"Green Gables," said Marilla.

The men took a beat to consider.

"I like it," said Matthew.

"Simple and good," said Hugh. "Your mother would've agreed."

The three of them stayed sitting there as the purple haze of night fell over all and the crickets began their bittersweet song. Marilla was exactly where she wanted to be—where she was meant to be. Home at Green Gables.

part two

Marilla of

Avonlea

XV.

REBELLION

February 1838

Matthew's not taking supper again?" Marilla asked when Hugh alone came to the table. "That's the third time this week." She spooned out beef pie from the cast-iron. "Not sure how he's going to keep up strength for the farm when he's out every night fooling about."

"It's a political gathering. Boys his age feel the need for activism."

Marilla placed a clean fork by her father's plate. The metal gleamed in the lamplight. She'd taken to scouring things with vinegar.

"Enough activities in a day to stay busy."

Hugh gently speared his beef pie, crumbling the crust into the sauce. "National activism, I mean. Young men get an itch to make their marks in the greater history. It's hard for women to understand."

"Why so?" she countered. "Don't we get the same itch?"

Truthfully, she didn't understand. Since her mother's passing, all she could focus on were the particulars of the here and now: get out of bed in the morning, wash her face, plait her hair, put on her apron, grind the grist, beat the eggs, flip, fry, stew, serve, wash, and repeat. Day after day, month after month. Every minute felt on the cusp of overwhelming. She'd known that if she stopped for a beat, the grief would overtake her. Sometimes she had to close her eyes and tell herself to breathe: in and out; and again, in and out. Otherwise, the heaviness in her chest would hold her steady until her head throbbed and her whole body became a weather vane for pain. It took every ounce of will to get out of bed then. The only comfort she gleaned was in Green Gables. Clara was there. In the wooden slats of the floor she'd walked, the hearth she'd kindled, the prayers she'd said, and the poems they'd read aloud while turning water into red currant wine. Marilla wondered if the world outside had always been so cumbersome but she hadn't known it because Clara had been her shelter. With her mother gone, there wasn't a crevice that didn't seem ashen.

While Hugh ate, Marilla scrubbed the silver candlesticks. The flame and wax had left them smudged.

He pushed back from his empty plate. "Very good."

"That's the last of the butcher's beef until spring." She dipped the cloth into her vinegar-water bowl and rubbed hard until the silver flashed.

"One of the Blythes' bulls. I can taste the strawberry apples. Only ones in Avonlea."

She nodded. "Yes, John said they give them to the livestock. Sweetens the heifers' milk too."

John had worked through the autumn with them. Far longer than the initial offer. He'd come over straight after school to bring in the cows while Matthew and Hugh gathered the crops. He'd started to feel as much a part of Green Gables as any of them. When the harvest ended and the first snow arrived, he went back to his studies after school.

Then in November, a rebellion sparked. The Reformers were calling it the Patriote Movement. At the Battle of Saint-Denis, Canadian Reformers had surprised them all by defeating the British army. The uprising quickly spread across the provinces. Martial law was declared in Montreal. Handbills circulated.

Half of them cried out: "Independence for Canada! Down with the Monarchy!"

And the other half proclaimed: "United we stand! Long live the Queen!"

Each week the newspapers reported more outbreaks of violence between the two parties, Reformer against Tory. Soon the dissension had reached the Maritimes. Just as Mr. Murdock had foretold, British troops arrived to patrol the town. Everyone in Avonlea assumed anarchy was soon to follow. So they bolted their doors and kept arms close at hand. John had been right all those many months back. Rachel said her father had two new muskets: one by the front door and one by the back. It seemed that Hugh owned a rifle too. He brought it in from the barn one day and kept it behind his parlor chair. Marilla thought she'd feel more distress at its presence but was surprised to find it comforting instead. They were ready to defend Green Gables if necessary.

By the New Year, most of the rebel leaders had been shot, hanged, or arrested. But the Patriote Movement was not finished. Like an epidemic, it swelled in the hearts of the people. Even in Avonlea, the political factions had become all anybody talked about. From the mail runners to the sheepherders, everyone was at verbal war: the conservative Tories against the liberal Reformers. The young men of Avonlea were assembling to debate in an old barn missing half its roof, just off the road between the woods and the schoolhouse. They'd named it the Agora.

"It's a cold night. Bet your brother'd be mighty grateful if his sister brought a warm pie to fill his stomach." Hugh eyed the pan. "Enough there to feed two men, I reckon."

Marilla put down her cleaning cloth. A lock of hair had come loose from her braid and hung down to tickle her nose. She pushed it back and caught a whiff of the vinegar on her hand.

"Women aren't welcome at the Agora."

"You're not just a woman," countered Hugh. "You're Marilla

Cuthbert. Matthew's kin." He took out his pipe and headed to the parlor, leaving Marilla alone over her uneaten pie.

"Serve him right if I ate the rest myself," she muttered to Skunk.

The cat sat at her heels, looking up with a gaze of utter obedience.

"If it were a mackerel pie, I'd give it to you in a snap, but it's the last of the beef."

So she wrapped the remaining pie in paper, washed her hands with lye soap, and rubbed a vanilla bean on her wrists to hide any leftover tang. Then she bundled up in her good winter coat, mittens, and quilted bonnet.

"If I'm not back in an hour, the wolves may have taken me."

"There are no wolves on the island." Hugh yawned.

"A guilty conscience can gnaw on a person is my point."

"Near to fifteen years living in Avonlea, I trust you not to fall into the sea or be devoured by wild beasts." He kissed her cheek and she set off.

It was a cold but windless night. The moon hung crescent as the pie she carried. The trees on the lane were naked and sheathed in ice, leaving her eyes to wander up to the starry sky that domed over in a giant, twinkling gable. The snow gave a gratifying crunch under boot, and the smell of burning pine grew bolder the closer she came to the Agora. In the warmer months, the meadow she crossed was a sea of bright violets. Now it was merely bruised shadows. On the opposite side of it, a bonfire smoldered through the Agora's open barn loft. The hot smoke plumed up to the sky, then fell back down cold to crawl across the land. It made her eyes burn and turned everything hazy. She was glad when she finally reached the light of the door.

Pushing the latch aside, she opened it without invitation and was met by a dozen phantoms. The fire cast odd shadows under their eyes and across their jaws. While she knew them to be farmers' sons, neighbors, and the boys who'd sat behind her in Avonlea School, they wore the masks of warring men. Matthew stood up from a bench at the far end. In the center was John, in midsentence, with his back to her.

"—cannot remain compliant with the way things are. Aristocracy by peerage does not predetermine leadership and cannot rule the modern people." He turned in the direction of the men's attention and smiled when he saw Marilla.

"I've brought beef pie," she said. "For my brother Matthew and anyone else who might be missing supper."

Matthew, familiar and true, was quickly by her side, taking the parcel and ushering her back out.

"Thank you," he whispered. "I'll be home soon."

"Maybe we should hear from a feminine mind," John announced to the circle.

A low grumble ensued.

"No women in the Agora," said someone who sounded a lot like Clifford Sloane.

"You're breaking the rules," protested Sam Coates beside him.

"We're here because of daring men who challenged the law!" John raised his fist. "Put it to a vote then. Who says nay?"

The room quieted. A log in the fire split and spit a mist of embers.

"Yea?" asked John.

He and Matthew locked eyes.

"Yea," said Matthew.

"That's two to none, so let the question be asked."

Matthew led Marilla forward, although she dragged her feet. No one had asked *her* yea or nay to speak! Standing beside John, she seethed inwardly at being put on the spot like this. The heat of the bonfire was suddenly too much. She took off her mittens and hat and crossed her arms over her chest to keep her nerves at bay.

"As a young woman in our community, I ask you: whom do you side with on the matter of the rebellions—the Tories or the Reformers?"

Rachel had come over frequently since Clara's death, feeling it her duty to fill Marilla's emptiness with talk of the world. She'd told Marilla how the Whites had come down on the side of the liberal Reformers, proponents of progressive change for an egalitarian society and a more responsible government representing its citizens. She even went so far as to say her family favored *no* royal family at all, but an autonomous republic like the United States. Seditious talk! Marilla was flustered from the listening, but Rachel insisted that everyone was openly discussing these things, including the Blythes. The Whites and the Blythes being friends and business partners, they were in agreement that the old rules of class and wealth could not unite a nation.

Marilla had said nothing during Rachel's harangues. Politics seemed inconsequential compared to the loss she felt and the regrets she carried.

Still, Marilla had brought it up with Hugh one evening.

"Where do you stand, Father?"

"We're conservative Presbyterians—Tories—and loyal to the Crown. It's the holy order of things. We must trust in God's sovereignty and the sovereign hand that he anoints. Otherwise, what's to stop every man from crowning himself a king?" Then he'd read a long, cautionary passage from Deuteronomy.

First and foremost, Marilla was a Cuthbert, loyal to her kin and their ways. So now, in the audience of the Agora, she deferred to her brother.

"Matthew speaks for the Cuthberts. Whatever he says, I agree."

"Tories!" someone shouted proudly.

John raised a hand for quiet.

"We know what Matthew says. What do *you* say, Marilla?"

Frustrated by his insistence, she met his gaze straight on and frowned. Neither blinked for a long minute.

"I have nothing to say, John."

"I don't believe that. You're too smart."

The calls of "Tories!" and "Reformers!" returned and crescendoed.

Matthew pulled her out of the ring, through the Agora door, and into the moonlit barnyard. There in the quiet, his long exhalation colored the air gray between them.

"Come on," he said. "Let's go home."

Silently, they retraced the footprints she'd made coming. But Marilla's mind was back at the Agora, replaying the scene over and over, imagining what she could've said: That progress didn't have to come with sacrificial bloodshed. That she had faith in her family and faith in the land. That they were farmers—they should know the ways of nature! A cow didn't have to die to make way for a new calf, nor a monarchy for a new nation. But then she thought of her mother and Nathaniel buried together in the Presbyterian church cemetery. Her eyes welled. She closed them against a blast of cold air and trudged ahead.

By the time they got home, Hugh had gone to bed. The pie had congealed into a mass of mush from the to-and-fro. Matthew ate only the beef chunks from the pap. She gave the rest to Skunk, who'd vigilantly stayed awake as if knowing his time would come.

XVI

TWO TO STUDY

March

A last light snow blew over the island, lacing the tree buds in silver frost while the sky opened clear as a bluebell. After the night at the Agora, Marilla found herself reading every newspaper clipping Matthew brought home, every political bulletin on the post office wall, every book lying around the Gables. Her mind was hungry for words. They kept her thoughts from wandering and her heart from feeling the dark sorrow.

"I think I'd like to take the school exit exam early," she told Hugh over breakfast. "I'll have to study," she explained. "Which may take time away from my chores."

Hugh lifted a shiny tin cup. Marilla had soaked it long enough to pickle the metal, then scrubbed until it looked better than new.

"I think that'd be all right. You'll have to get Mr. Murdock's permission."

"Mr. Blythe asked to borrow our hoof nippers. I'm going over there tomorrow," said Matthew.

"Schoolhouse is on the way," Hugh replied.

Marilla looked from father to brother. Matthew winked and slurped his coffee. It warmed her to a grin.

It'd been so long since she'd gone to school that she'd outgrown her day dresses. All she had were her house frocks and Sunday best. So she ventured into her mother's things. Izzy had pressed all of Clara's white cotton shirts with her own lilac water. Marilla was grateful that they smelled of her aunt and not her mother. It took all her will to open the trunk at all. She retrieved a cream blouse and a patterned skirt that she'd never seen Clara wear. A black spray of flowers against a forest green background. It fit her to a T.

The family was still in mourning. The black curtains remained over the windows all winter—to keep out the drafts, she'd told herself. It'd been nearly a full year, and the warmer months were approaching. She'd have to take them down soon. But she was determined to wear her mourning black no matter the season. She slipped the black crepe armband over her blouse. She hadn't the energy to plait her hair, so she pulled it neatly into a bun. She wanted to prove to Mr. Murdock that she was more mature than her years and thus capable of passing the exam early.

Matthew waited with the sleigh. When she came out, he gave a shy whistle, which she ignored but appreciated. She needed all the confidence she could get.

The new snow was melting into the old as they slid across the fields to the east, through the woods, and over the road that led to the village of Newbridge. Outside the Avonlea School door, the students' lunches were stacked in a row. A handful of pull sleighs were parked beside. The windows winked as bright and warm as she remembered. How simple life within had been: the hours broken into segments of learning. Each day filled up like a jar of beans to be taken home, digested, and filled up again tomorrow. If only they could've stayed that way.

Marilla timed it so that she wouldn't interrupt Mr. Murdock's lesson. He was a stickler for keeping schedule, and she wanted to stay in his good graces. He'd break for lunch recess soon.

Matthew brought Jericho to a stop on the east side of the schoolhouse beside the apple tree that bore forth unlimited after-school treats in the autumn. Now, however, it was barren as a bundle of brushwood.

"I'll wait for you here," said Matthew. He leaned back and tilted his hat to block the sunshine from his eyes.

Marilla hopped down from the sleigh and peeked through the schoolhouse window to see if Mr. Murdock was still at the board. He was, but before she could lean out of sight, one of the younger students caught a glimpse of her and began pointing frantically. Marilla put her finger in front of her lips to shush him, but that only made him cry out.

"Mr. Murdock! There's a lady at the window!"

Mr. Murdock's bearded face popped up, an inch of glass between their noses. He narrowed his gaze like a stingy elf.

"Miss Cuthbert, may I help you?" His voice muffled through the glass and left a puff of frost on the pane.

"I—I've come about my studies," she replied.

"Then I would presume you'd properly arrive through the door, not the window."

Marilla's cheeks went hot. "Yes, sir," she said and made her way round to the front, where she paused, unsure if she was supposed to knock before entering. She decided to err on the side of etiquette given that Mr. Murdock was already piqued.

It took three raps before he answered, "Please come in."

He stood at the front holding his cane pointer. Little Spurgeon MacPherson was in the dunce's corner with the cone cap forcing his flappy ears to stick out.

"Miss Cuthbert, come to the front so you may tell us the purpose of your visit?"

Her knees buckled momentarily, but she obeyed, walking down the long aisle while the entire schoolhouse looked on.

"I'm sorry to interrupt, Mr. Murdock. I thought you'd be at recess by now."

"Did you not know the time?" He pulled his watch from his

pocket. "We have five entire minutes before recess. Five entire minutes in which my diligent students should have been learning the topography of Upper Canada, but instead you have distracted them. They will just have to make up these five minutes by concluding their recess early."

The class moaned. A little girl in the front row put her head down on her desk pitifully and cried, "Toad warts!"

Marilla's hands shook so badly that she had to ball them into fists at her side.

"Mr. Murdock, I pray you do not punish the class on my account." She prayed he would not punish her either. "You see, I've come to ask if I might sit for the exit exams early—this spring."

"The exit exams? Well, Miss Cuthbert, those are only for our most advanced students who have faithfully and successfully mastered a Christian education through grade eight, as specified by the Lancastrian System of our Queen and country." He cleared his throat. "As you can see, my back-row pupils are small in number, and only they are prepared for the exits."

She turned to the back row; she vaguely recalled the five seated there from the Agora, only now they wore suspenders and innocent expressions. John was the last in the row. He spun his short chalk stick between his fingers, watching her. She was determined not to falter in her mission.

"I understand, Mr. Murdock, but I've spoken with Rachel White, who has been on home study for a number of years. She says you are allowing her to take the exit exam when she pleases."

Mr. Murdock gave a huff. "Miss White's mother has assured me that she is under direct tutelage. That is why I consented for her to sit despite not having completed her work at Avonlea School."

"As you know, I haven't a mother anymore to make assurances for me." Her voice bent to crack, but she wrenched it steady. "But you have my word that I will study as hard as I can so that I do you credit and exit properly."

Mr. Murdock softened at the mention of Clara and set down the pointer. "As true as that may be, I must adhere to the rules. The uneducated can't educate themselves based on what they do not know. You need a tutor."

Marilla didn't know any tutors, nor did her family have the finances to afford one like the Whites. It was an impasse for which she had no solution.

"I'm sorry, Miss Cuthbert," said Mr. Murdock. "For this and your loss." The gentleness of it cut her to the quick.

She'd rather him be curmudgeonly. She knew how to hold herself up against that, but his empathy loosened her fortitude.

"I'll do it, Mr. Murdock!" John stood from his desk chair.

Some of the younger children began to giggle. Mr. Murdock gave a menacing warning point to Spurgeon in the corner, and they all shushed.

"Students, you may orderly and *silently* file out for lunch. Remember not to take your sleds too far into the woods. Be back five minutes early. Tardy pupils will earn extra homework. Mr. MacPherson, you are relieved from your punishment, but you must bring in the firewood for the afternoon. Mr. Blythe, come here."

John made his way to the front against the current of departing students. Marilla and John waited, side by side, in front of Mr. Murdock until the last student closed the door behind him.

"Mr. Blythe, I do not condone outbursts from my pupils."

"I apologize for my lack of restraint but not for what I said, Mr. Murdock."

Mr. Murdock screwed up his nose.

John continued. "I would be willing to tutor Marilla in all subjects. You recently told my father that I was ahead of the rest of my grade and could probably sit for the exam tomorrow and pass with flying colors."

Mr. Murdock smacked his gums. "That was a conversation between your father and me."

"If you be a man of knowledge and truth, then your assessment would stand as good authority on my ability to successfully tutor Marilla."

Mr. Murdock pushed around a handful of papers on his desk, then let out a loud exhale that sent the chalk dust swirling.

"Fine. You may tutor Marilla with the stipulation that it be daily and after you complete your full studies in my classroom. This will significantly impact your work for your father's farm, you know?"

John nodded. "Yes, sir."

Marilla's heart leapt around like a jackrabbit.

"Miss Cuthbert, you will report to me before the exit exam date so that I may evaluate whether or not you are ready to sit with the others."

"Yes, sir, thank you, sir. I promise I won't fail you!"

"Don't worry that you'll fail me—worry that you'll have wasted all of young Mr. Blythe's time and talents." He turned to John and held out his hand in a handshake of agreement. "Mr. Blythe, her failure is your failure."

John shook his hand without batting an eyelash.

Outside, the younger students raced around Jericho, who hoofed the ground, perturbed.

"Thank you, John."

"Like I said, you're smart. Smarter than any other girl I know."

It flattered her more than other compliments she'd received. Her mother had been virtuous. Izzy was beautiful. She, Marilla, would be smart.

"When do we start?" she asked.

"Now. Today!"

"Today?" She laughed. "John, you are positively the most impulsive person I know."

"*Carpe diem!* Do you know what that means?"

"It's Latin." Marilla raised her chin to the sunshine. "'To seize the day.'"

"Very good, pupil." He cleared his throat and affected Mr. Murdock's tone. "And where does this Latin phrase originate?"

"The Roman poet Horace."

He clapped. "Well done. Let's show that old Mr. Murdock."

XVII.

JOHN BLYTHE SUGGESTS A WALK

Every day John took the back way from Avonlea School, over the meadow that bloomed a purple sea, through the spruce woods made sappy by the sunshine, and down the lane leading to Green Gables. The arch of maples had put forth their spring pomp. Furry pink blossoms adorned the boughs, and winnowed by the breeze, they dusted all who walked beneath in pollen. John would arrive at the back door sneezing and haloed in gold.

They studied at the kitchen table so Marilla could keep an eye on the supper pot. Though she offered him a meal, John never took it. He said his mother wouldn't rest until after she'd fed him and his father had smoked a pipe. It was the Blythes' routine, and he honored it. Marilla understood. Family came first.

John brought over Mr. Murdock's lessons and shared them with Marilla. Math came easiest, but it took nearly two weeks to study through history, geography, and civics. Then they began on grammar and composition.

"Mr. Murdock's composition homework is to write about our travels."

"But I've never been anywhere except Nova Scotia."

"That counts," said John. "Write about that."

He pulled out the bronze pocket watch his father had given him on his last birthday. It was inscribed: To my one and only son. He habitually rubbed the face shiny.

"The exam's written portion is timed. So I suggest we practice."

He eyed the second hand of his watch. "On the count of three, two, one—begin!"

The kitchen filled with the quick *click* of chalk sticks against slate.

"Time!" called John.

Marilla smiled. She'd finished with a minute left to double-check her spelling.

"Let's read them aloud," said John.

"That's not part of the exam." Rhetoric was her least favorite of the school curriculum.

"How else are we to review each other's compositions?"

Marilla saw his point. Reluctantly, she cleared her throat and held up her slate to shield her face from John's stare.

The world goes unsteady when you're standing aboard a steamship crossing the Northumberland Strait. To the south, the beaches of Nova Scotia are rocky gray and rimmed with boats. Their sails flutter like ruffles on a dress. To the north, our island glows at sunset. The sand shines like red fires. My mother said that far before our British prince namesake, the Micmac natives called it Abegweit. It means "cradle on the waves." A land of new birth where all colors of men and beast are free to live their brightest. A more fitting name, I believe. An island born from the sea should be red at its bedrock. So very red . . .

Marilla's throat tightened as the memory of Clara's last hour came to her, sharp as a hatpin.

"My mother liked to hear that story, but I never told her all of it. I never told her about Madame Stéphanie's hat shop or about Junie, the slave orphan. Reverend Patterson says secrets can be as sinful as blatant acts of deception. If I had known my mother would . . ." She gulped to steady her voice. "I wish I would've told her everything."

John put his hand on hers.

"You might not have told her, but she knew your aim was for good—then and now. This is a composition to be proud of, Marilla."

He pressed his thumb into the back of her hand, and she didn't pull away.

"It's your turn."

"Mine is not nearly as well done."

"Then you'll just have to be satisfied placing second."

He gave a lopsided grin and dropped her hand to pick up his slate. "'I spent a year in Rupert's Land visiting my mother's kin . . .'"

Marilla hadn't known he'd gone to Rupert's Land as a boy. John read of his Uncle Nick, his mother's boisterous younger brother; of gallivanting through the woods with his seven cousins; of fishing in glacial lakes, climbing mountains, and air so clean it made him feel twice as alive. Marilla relished the descriptions. It seemed a fantastical land made ever more daring by John's retelling.

"I couldn't say who won. That was very good," she conceded. "You made me see a place I've never been."

"You made me see the place I've always been like I never knew it. That takes greater skill."

"Then it's a tie." She smiled.

Outside, Matthew stomped his boots clean on the porch.

"I better get food on the table," said Marilla.

"Maybe one day you'll go to Rupert's Land and see it for yourself."

She laughed. "Fancy that. A woman traveling by herself like a buccaneer." But even as she said it, she thought of Izzy and wondered, *Perhaps so—and why not?*

"Maybe I'll take you."

Her heart lit up. The pea soup on the stove bubbled. Matthew came in.

"Hello, John. How's studying?"

"Learn a new thing every day." He winked at Marilla, collected his books, and pulled on his cap. "Please give Mr. Cuthbert my best. Tomorrow I'll bring back the hoof nippers we borrowed."

"No rush," said Matthew. "What's ours is yours, neighbor."

John left with a nod.

"He's a good friend," Matthew said. "You're lucky to have him."

"Me?" Marilla served out a bowl with a side biscuit for sopping. "He's just as much your friend."

Matthew chuckled. "Fine, fine. A good friend to us all. Darn near family for as much time as he's here."

Hugh came in soon after, and she made up a bowl for him too but forgot the biscuit. Her mind was busy mulling over John's story of Rupert's Land and what Matthew had said about him. It felt nice . . . to think of him as family.

∞

The warmer season finally arrived in full form. Gone were the night frosts and blustering winds. The mornings glistened with dewy blades of grass. The lupines plumed bold fingers to the sky. The afternoon fields fluttered with life stirred by the promise of longer days.

Izzy had faithfully written them. At first, the letters brought on such an aching that Marilla could hardly stand to look at the handwritten address on the envelope, but it dulled with time and routine. Izzy wrote about the shop, the ladies she dressed, the political rallies in St. Catharines's streets, and the new influx of Americans to the city. Her last line to every letter was *Give my love to my Marilla girl. I'm eager to hear from her when she's ready.* It made Marilla prickle oddly.

She'd once gone so far as to take up paper and pen to reply, but in pausing to think, her mind was quick to fasten on the latest newspaper sheet John had delivered. He had been unrelenting in his tutelage.

It was the *Prince Edward Island Times*, a liberal Reformer publication that Hugh didn't purchase. The article read: "Mr. Mingo Bass, African footman to Miss Elizabeth Smallwood of Charlottetown, has gone missing. Miss Smallwood believes her servant was taken unlawfully by slave hunters from America. He originated from Virginia."

John had penciled to the side: "Can you locate Virginia?" But she knew that he'd singled out the article for more than her geography studies. John was the only one who knew of Junie and the Sisters of Charity's work with escaping slaves, a secret she'd kept even from her mother and shared only with him. And so she'd been distracted from writing Izzy—what did she have to say anyhow?—and had taken up her maps instead. Geography was her weakest subject. She simply hadn't the empirical evidence to draw from. The atlas mountains, rivers, and borders seemed little more than chicken scratch in dirt. But she would not let that be her undoing.

Marilla was on the back porch in her wicker chair so she could feel the fresh breeze while she studied. The exam was a week away, and John had just come from the schoolhouse.

"Mr. Murdock gave me this for you," he said.

She opened the folded note:

Miss Cuthbert, please come to Avonlea School prepared to be evaluated this coming Wednesday before the Saturday exit exam.
—Mr. Murdock

Marilla turned the note so John could see. "Here it is. Judgment Day."

"You're ready. More than ready."

She smoothed her hand over the open atlas. "I still can't remember all the Danish colonies—they're scattered everywhere!"

"I'm willing to bet 'What are the Danish colonies?' will not be a question on the exam."

"It could."

He cleared his throat authoritatively. "You've studied hard, Marilla. You're more ready than anyone in Mr. Murdock's class."

"Including you?" She raised her eyebrow.

"Well now, the reflection of a great teacher is a student who equals his knowledge." He smirked then continued in earnest. "Besides, schools can't expect that they've taught us everything there is to know. Nobody knows *everything*, Marilla. Not even you. They just expect us to know enough to pass." He snatched the book from under her and closed it with a gratifying *thwack*. "You want to study your geography? Come on, let's go."

She crossed her arms. "Go?"

"No better way to learn the land than to explore it."

"The most exasperating individual—this is because you want to beat me in the scores, isn't it?"

"Aw, you've figured out my villainous scheme. Villainous: V-I-double-L-A-I-N-O-U-S. We can practice our spelling along the way."

He could charm the devil.

"Biology too, I suppose. Exercising the body does improve the mind," she relented.

And off they went, through the apple-cherry orchard blooming pink and white; down to the perimeter of the Cuthbert farm where their green field gave over to the tangle of forest ferns, tree bark, and wet moss. Under the wooded canopy, the air changed, thick with honeysuckle and pine tree sap. The winds of the island combed only the treetops so that the sky seemed to dance overhead while their feet remained planted. The brook had thawed and gurgled merrily through the creek bed. Marilla hadn't been there for over a year, a lifetime ago, when she was a child who read frivolous magazine stories and had a mother.

Still, she instinctively knew the way.

"Follow me."

Past the fern grove and around the tree with the hollow so large that she'd once been convinced a family of fairies lived within. The brook widened there and picked up current as it angled downhill. They had to remove their shoes to keep from slipping. She took John's hand to steady herself.

"It's just over here."

"What is?"

She didn't answer. Gravity pulled them forward, faster and faster. The brook cascaded over rocks and bare feet until reaching level ground, where it pooled around her island . . . so much smaller than she remembered. The slender maple clung to its islet, roots dripping off the sides like living lace. Sunshine fell through the open canopy, making the water twinkle blue-gold.

Marilla fought to catch her breath. Her heart thumped in her earlobes. Her toes tingled from the cold and her fingers from the heat of John's hand. She was nearly delirious. How very long had it been since she'd felt so free? Not since her mother was still alive. Not since that May day when John put a cricket to her ear and told her to make a wish.

She lifted her skirts and waded out until her face came under the fullness of the sun.

"This was my secret place. When I was a girl."

"It's beautiful." He took a step toward her and the water rippled against her calves.

Then—suddenly—he slipped and fell. Only two feet deep, but it was enough to soak him through. Marilla threw her head back with a laugh and nearly tumbled in too.

"I'm glad I amuse you," said John. "Care to help me up?" He extended his dripping hand.

She took it and pulled with all her might. The water gave a soft *whoosh*. Rivulets ran down. The gossamer shirt clung to his skin. Her heart did a queer double-beat. Before she had time to turn away, he pulled the shirt off over his head. Grumbling, he wrung it out. The muscles of his back flexed like newly churned butter, soft and yielding. His stomach bent narrow at the waist where his suspenders hung loose. He turned, their eyes met, and in that moment there came a silent roar inside her, as if all the love and heartache she'd ever known had been uncorked.

John moved forward or she moved forward—she couldn't say. The water swayed. The trees whirled. And then his hands were around her. His lips on hers. She closed her eyes, kissed him back, and let her skirt slip from her grasp. As the cloth took on water, it pulled her deeper. His mouth was hard and sweet like a plum. His naked body smelled of melted snow, glacial and alive, just as he wrote, just as he was. She ran her hands along the ladder of his ribs, under the swell of his arms, over the stretch of his belly, and up the channel of his chest. While she'd seen her brother and father shirtless, she'd never known the feel of a man. Flesh under her fingertips.

He cupped her face; his thumbs traced their mouths as one. Behind her eyelids, she saw him in red bursts and wondered if a person could die of loving.

A downy woodpecker started after some tree bug. Its loud staccato jolted them apart. The sun was setting, its light slanted from the west, casting new shadows across their faces. More time had passed than they'd realized. Coolness settled over them. It would be dark in an hour.

Marilla remembered: Matthew and Hugh would be coming in from the fields soon with no supper to fill their hunger. Her decisions affected others, not just herself. She caught a chill and goose bumps rose up on her arms.

"You're cold," said John. "We'd better get back."

His shirt had floated off to the shallows. He fished it out and put it on, wet as it was.

"I hope we dry up before home."

Marilla hated to think what Hugh and Matthew might assume.

"Tell them the truth. I was an oaf and fell into the stream. You saved me."

John pulled her close again and kissed her. Red warmth. She let it consume her. She needed to believe it was worth dying for. She desperately wanted to understand her mother's last words to her father.

XVIII

AN EXAM, A LETTER,
AND MAYFLOWER REGRETS

M r. Murdock might've been harsher in his examination had he not suffered from a chest cold that had him sputtering like a kettle with too little water. He'd deemed Marilla literate enough to sit for the exams, and then went home to apply a mustard plaster. His phlegm had abated enough by that Saturday morning, though he smelled awfully rank. Marilla was grateful to be seated a few rows back.

John and the other grade-eight boys had been moved up to the front row. When he saw her enter, he smiled. Sam Coates threw an elbow into his ribs. Marilla and John hadn't spoken of their walk in the woods. How could they?

Once, she had accidentally turned the corner into the kitchen and seen her mother and father in an embrace. They'd jumped apart as if a horse's whip had been lashed, and her modest father's cheeks had colored so shamefully that Marilla knew it had to have been an egregious disgrace. That night before bed, she'd prayed for God to forgive her parents. Though she'd grown up and understood the natural way between men and women, it remained a thing of unmentionable unmentioning. Especially now when her mother was dead.

So she smiled back primly at John and hung her hat on one of the hooks.

"Pupils on home study, please take a seat in the third row," instructed Mr. Murdock.

Marilla slid into her seat and relished the feel of the timeworn desk. The wood was rubbed smooth at just the right places so her knees and hands felt welcome.

"*Psst—*" Rachel hissed. She'd just come in and taken a desk beside Marilla wearing a new school dress of white-and-indigo stripes. She pointed to the cuffs. "I crocheted the lace myself."

"Very pretty," said Marilla.

"This is an examination, not a sewing circle!" Mr. Murdock glared at them.

"I'd rather the latter," Rachel mumbled under her breath.

Marilla didn't dare move a muscle, even when Mr. Murdock turned away to hack into his handkerchief.

"I'll walk with you home after," Rachel whispered. "Mother wants me to ask Mr. Cuthbert if he'd lend us a few cucumber seeds for the garden . . . don't you just love summer cucumbers? I do—"

"Miss White, would you kindly move from your seat with Miss Cuthbert over to the empty desk by the window."

Rachel picked up her box of chalk and sponges. "Yes, sir."

John dared turn around again. He winked. Thankfully, Rachel didn't see—too busy grumbling over being reseated alone.

On the stroke of nine o'clock, they began.

By noon, it was over. Marilla had used every minute to scrutinize her answers until Mr. Murdock called the time. John had done the same, while Rachel had finished early and waited outside under the apple tree, now pink and petal-fluffed.

"Marilla!" she called to her.

But John had followed Marilla out and caught her by the hand to the side of the schoolhouse.

"How'd it go?"

"I think well."

He smiled. "No questions about the Danish colonies to ruin us."

She had to laugh at herself.

He leaned in close, and she smelled the sunshine on his skin. The memory of the brook's current swirled around them.

"John." She put a hand on his chest.

"Ma—rilla?" Rachel came round the schoolhouse.

Marilla dropped both hands to her sides.

Rachel's head swiveled like a sparrow eyeing two worms. "Like I told you, I'm going by Green Gables on my way home." She took Marilla's arm. "The Ladies' Sewing Circle is meeting this afternoon, if you care to join."

Marilla had nearly forgotten the Ladies' Sewing Circle. It seemed so long ago that she was worried over perfect knots and even stitches. It shamed her to remember how concerned she'd once been with the women's appraisal of her needlework. She couldn't even say where her circular was now.

"I've got to get supper on," Marilla declined and gave an apologetic glance to John. "We best be going."

"I'll come see you when Mr. Murdock posts the scores," he called after them.

"Oh, fiddle-dee-dee, who cares about scores. If we don't pass, we'll take it again next year. Come on." Rachel marched swiftly, pulling Marilla along with her.

When they reached the violet meadow, Rachel's steam petered out. Her gait slowed to a normal amble. The monarchs, swallowtails, and ladybugs alighted from their hiding spots, sending the field into a rainbow of winged motion.

"What is between you and John Blythe?"

Marilla shrugged. A ladybug landed on her wrist and followed a blue vein up the soft, pale underside of her arm. "We've been studying every day for this exam. He wants me to do well . . . to prove Mr. Murdock wrong."

"Is that all?" Rachel's voice edged on caution. "Because there are those who think John is rather handsome. The kind of boy that a girl could find herself in love with."

"In love?" Marilla balked. "With John Blythe?" And then she saw the strawberry blush crawling up Rachel's neck. "Oh!" Her stomach dipped. "I didn't think *you* . . . I assumed you and John disliked each other. Rachel, I promise I didn't know."

Rachel gave a sad, thin smile. "He's yours now, Marilla."

Marilla shook her head in protest.

"Yes, whether you like it or not, it's as plain as the nose on his face. He's in love with you."

She thought of their kiss—was it one or many? The memory of his arms around her made her tense her own. The ladybug took its leave.

"Love," she whispered. "What do any of us know of it, really?"

Rachel leaned into Marilla's side. "We know we want it. I'm envious is all. I wish it had been me, but then, I'm glad it wasn't. Handsome as he may be, John Blythe thinks himself some kind of know-it-all." She stuck out her tongue. "He would drive me mad!"

Marilla had to laugh. "Yes, humility is not his most notable characteristic."

They crossed into the spruce woods, where the needles carpeted the ground and crackled lightly underfoot and the air smelled clean and warm.

Rachel patted Marilla's hand. "Don't worry about me. I'll find my husband soon enough."

Husband. The word choked Marilla. Who said anything about husbands? Suddenly, she felt ten times her age, heavy with the burden of what was to come and wishing they could turn back the clock to a year ago: when they were girls sewing pretty sleeves and planning May Picnic costumes; when her mother was full of new life and Green Gables was their Promised Land. It'd all turned out so differently than expected.

They'd just come over the log bridge when they spotted Matthew on the crossroad. He was not alone. Johanna Andrews was with him.

"Speaking of love . . ." whispered Rachel.

But the closer they came, the more certain Marilla was that this was not a meeting of lovers.

Johanna held her basket stiffly in front of her, back straight as a chair, face hidden beneath her straw bonnet. Every time Matthew stepped forward, she stepped back so that there remained a wide gap between them. His head hung low. His shoulders were more slumped than usual. Hearing their approach, Johanna turned. Her face was red as a raspberry.

"I'm sorry, Matthew," she said. "This isn't what I want. Please, just let me go!" And then she ran down the lane toward Avonlea.

Matthew's eyes were coals burnt to cinder. He blinked open and shut without seeming to see them.

"Nothing but meetings and partings in this world. Dear me," Rachel whispered. "I best come back another time for the cucumber seeds. Or you can come over whenever you wish. We're doing prayer shawls and caps for the orphanage, plus I've just started on my first cotton warp quilt. I have extra yarn."

She quickly kissed Marilla's cheek good-bye, then dashed ahead to catch up with Johanna and inquire what the disagreement had been about—for surely there had been one.

Marilla went to Matthew. They said nothing, just started down the opposite path to Green Gables. Matthew pulled a long blade of bluestem from one of the tufts bordering the road and peeled it into strips with a gentle *zip*. He tossed the strands off to the dirt; his fingernails were stained green from the task.

"Care to tell me what happened?" Marilla asked when he reached for another blade.

He exhaled. "Can't say I could, even if I tried."

She nodded. "Quarrel?"

"I dunno."

"Was there some offense done?"

He shrugged. "I just dunno what happened. One minute I was walking her home and showing her where Father and I hope to plant turnips next year, and the next minute she's gone off."

That did seem strange. "Maybe she doesn't like neeps. Did she say?"

"Not to my recollection. She just said she hated the stink of pasture on everything, and she wasn't going to spend her days churning buttermilk and peeling potatoes."

"I don't like potatoes either, but you never mentioned potatoes."

Matthew shook his head. Marilla shook hers too.

"Maybe it doesn't have anything to do with you, Matthew. Maybe something happened at the Andrewses', or maybe it's just an upset inside Johanna."

Marilla had her blue days. She couldn't explain the expansive melancholy that often overtook her in the form of a headache. She'd learned that it was simply best to lie down with a cold compress and wait for it to pass, so as not to impart suffering by way of her tongue.

"Just a storm," she comforted. "By tomorrow it'll have blown over."

But at church the next day, Johanna seemed ever more set in her coldness. She said nothing, but gave off such an unfriendly disposition that even her sisters looked afraid to intervene. Matthew steered clear of all the Andrewses, following Hugh once more in departing the fellowship hour as quickly as Jericho could take them. Rachel waved to Marilla with a pitiful look, and Marilla longed again for her mother. The church ladies would've talked to Clara about Matthew and Johanna. Then they'd all know how to help. But Marilla was still a shy child in their eyes, even if she felt older.

Matthew didn't speak of Johanna after church, and Marilla didn't bring her up. They simply went on: bringing in the cows from pasture, bedding down Jericho, feeding the chickens, sweeping the yard, putting supper on the table, reading the Bible before bed, praying in the darkness, sleeping and dreaming of things forgotten by sunrise.

Mr. Murdock promised to post the exit exam scores the following Monday after school let out. That morning she'd gone to the Whites' with the cucumber seed and picked up an apple-leaf pattern with corresponding yarn for a cotton warp quilt. Marilla didn't think Rachel would let her leave without agreeing to rejoin the Ladies' Sewing Circle project. It was for the "dear little orphans, after all," said Rachel, and how could Marilla argue with that? Rachel didn't mention Johanna Andrews, and Marilla didn't ask.

Despite her reservations, Marilla was glad to do something for the orphanage again. She thought of Junie often and hoped the red bonnet had kept her cool through summer and warm in winter. A wine red shawl would look good with it, she thought, and had it in mind to pop by Mrs. Blair's for the extra skein after the post office. She never made it. A letter arrived from Izzy. Unlike all the others, it was addressed specifically to her. She hurried home with it in her hamper, her mind churning on what Izzy could want to say to her alone.

She cracked the seal as soon as she came in the door.

Beloved Marilla,

Has it already been a year since your sweet mother, my sister, took her leave? It's hard to believe. The pain of it remains raw as

*a new wound. With the anniversary of her death near, I find my-
self unable to think of anything but you, dear flower girl. It's been
so long since I heard from you. Your father and brother write me
that you are well and running Green Gables with the fortitude of
a queen. You have your mother's gift in that regard. I was never
so good at maintaining a home. I haven't even a pet, knowing too
well that I'd let it run wild as it pleased. The discipline of a family
was never my forte.*

Skunk slinked to Marilla's feet. She picked him up and gently
scratched her fingers beneath his soft neck until he purred.

*I understand why you declined to come live with me in St. Catha-
rines. I worry that your lack of correspondence may be for fear that
I'll try to force you from your home. Never! I respect your decision,
as I trust that you respect mine to return to my own.*

*That being said, I do believe my sister would've liked us to be
close—closer in her death than we had been in her life. I hear her
voice in my own sometimes and see her reflection at every turn.
She reminds me that she is not gone from this world. While her
body may vanish to dust, her spirit lives on in you. I don't think I
could stand to miss you both. Please write to me. It would mean
ever so much.*

With all my love,
Aunt Izzy

Marilla could barely read the closing through her trembling.
Was the calendar right—was it May already? She hadn't lingered
in the Avonlea social circles long enough to hear the talk of picnic

planning or anything else. Of course Rachel hadn't brought it up, knowing the painful memories of last year. So Marilla had been left to tunnel into her daily regimen without the mindfulness of time and life beyond. Izzy's letter pulled her from her blindness like a groundhog blinking at the sun.

Her chest heaved. Skunk squirmed under her hold, so she put him down. Her empty hands yearned to grasp something solid. Her mother. She wanted her mother's hand. She curled her fingernails into her palm until crescent moons formed. The aching shot to her head. She closed her eyes and saw flashes of purple: the amethyst brooch with her mother's hair. It was in her box of sewing notions and precious things. She hurried upstairs to her bedroom. Her temples throbbed. The purple flashes spotted her vision. Opening the box, she thrust her hand in and felt the bite of metal.

"What the devil!"

Her finger returned: red. The droplet grew round and rounder until it could hold its form no more and ran down the side of her hand. She put it to her mouth. Mineral on her tongue. With her other hand, she carefully found the brooch and then lay down on the bed, running her thumb around the oval of braided hair.

"I'm sorry, Mother," she whispered. "I promise. I'm sorry." She closed her eyes to let the bursts of pain be absorbed into the darkness.

A knocking below woke her. She didn't know how long she'd lain there—minutes or hours. Her finger had clotted and scabbed with crimson. She set the brooch on her vanity and smoothed back her hair with a little water before going down to answer.

"Marilla!" John stood on the front porch with a bouquet of mayflowers.

There was no denying—it was May. Her heart sunk at the certainty. She'd lived a whole year—twelve months, three hundred sixty-five days—that her mother never saw.

"Congratulations!" John beamed.

Marilla turned her face away to hide her welling tears. "It shouldn't have been this way."

"What do you mean?" He laughed. "Of course it should!"

He reached out to her and she bristled.

"Don't."

His arm fell and the flowers dangled upside down. "Marilla, I don't understand."

Her finger smarted. She cupped her hands together to keep the pain from traveling to her head again. "Well, I'm sorry. I haven't the time or energy to make you understand at the moment."

"But I—"

"Please go," she told him.

He took a step forward, and she pulled back sharply. *"Please."*

His face changed from soft concern to a frown. He set the bouquet on the porch banister.

"I only came to say how proud I am of you. You beat out Sam Coates and Clifford Sloane and all the naysayers. Mr. Murdock himself told me to congratulate you—and me. We did it together, Marilla."

She'd passed the exit exam? A swell of emotions spilled over. She wished her mother were there to hear the news. She wished she hadn't treated John so harshly. She wished she had the words to tell him all that she felt. But it was like trying to fill a teaspoon from a waterfall. So her tongue stayed tied as he walked off the porch and down the lane, the dark curls of his head diminishing to a decimal point. When he finally vanished into the dip of the log bridge over the spring, Marilla took in the mayflowers, put them in a pitcher of water, and watched as their little star heads slowly lifted.

Never mind today, she thought. There was no undoing the mistakes in it. But tomorrow was new with time aplenty to make things right.

XIX

AVONLEA MAKES A PROCLAMATION

There's to be a town hall meeting tomorrow night," Matthew said from behind the *Royal Gazette*.

They were in the parlor. Hugh was having his nightly whiskey, while Marilla worked on her cotton warp quilt.

"Aye, so I hear," said Hugh.

The front-page headline of Matthew's paper read: "Lord Durham in Charlottetown on Royal Investigation of Rebellions." Every village across Upper and Lower Canada had been issued an ordinance to prepare a representative statement regarding the political upheaval of the past year.

"Councilor Cromie has promised to stay as long as it takes to hear every opinion. With the likes of the Whites in attendance, it's going to be a long night." Matthew chuckled.

"Well, it'll just have to get on without me." Hugh stood and rubbed at some invisible ache in his arm.

Marilla worried about her father. He pushed himself too hard on the farm and didn't eat near as much as he used to. At first she'd taken it to heart—her cooking wasn't right. But she'd been cooking the same for her family since before Clara died, so that reasoning didn't hold water. As well, his hair had turned entirely gray in the last year, and his skin had dried crepey over his knuckles. He looked twice his age. She reckoned that, like herself, death had changed him. Talking about it wouldn't change him back. So she let him be and simply put an extra pat of butter in his breakfast oats.

Matthew lowered his paper. "You aren't going to the meeting?"

Hugh nodded. "I don't believe in debating with the opposition. At the end, they'll still stand on their side and we'll stand on ours. Like two bulls pulling on opposite ends of a square knot. Just makes things tighter. Politics is a young man's fancy. I'm set in my ways."

Marilla frowned. His words rang of fatalism, and despite her no-nonsense nature, she was covertly a hopeful spirit.

"But your opinion would be calculated into the whole of Councilor Cromie's proclamation. He's sworn to report back to Queen Victoria the convictions of *all* of her royal subjects, not just those in attendance at the meetings," she argued.

Her outspokenness startled them.

Since passing the exit exam, she'd felt a burgeoning confidence in using her abilities for more than just domestic duty. She'd been appraised beside her schoolmates—future men of Avonlea—and found equal, even smarter. There was power in knowledge. Like the gears of a steam engine, the more active knowledge was, the more force it produced.

"If you be of a mind to go, Marilla, then you and Matthew can carry the Cuthberts of Prince Edward Island's opinions to the councilor," said Hugh. "I'm to bed now. G'night to ya both."

They wished him good-night.

Matthew raised an eyebrow to her.

"Either say what's on your mind or go back to reading, but don't sit there ogling me," she said, not unkindly.

He folded the newspaper. "I was over at the Blythes' today helping Mr. Bell take ownership of a couple new cows."

The Bells' farm was adjacent to Green Gables on the west side.

"Spent some time talking with John while I was there."

"And?" She quickened the *click* of her needle loops.

He cleared his throat but seemed to swallow the words before they came out. "He'll be at the meeting tomorrow too."

Matthew rose and went out on the back porch to loudly suck his pipe.

She hadn't seen John for three weeks, not since the day the exit exam scores were posted. On the way back from town, she'd often thought about stopping by his house and had come up with half a dozen excuses to do so—from borrowing dough starter from his mother to returning one of their study books. Then she'd chastise herself: if John wanted to see her, he knew good and well where to find her. For her to seek him out wasn't something proper young ladies did, and she was determined that although her mother wasn't there to show her the ways of womanhood, she would grow up proper.

She was glad to know that John would be at the town hall meeting. She cared for him more than any other boy in Avonlea. Besides Matthew, of course. Blood being thicker than water. If she couldn't make John understand why she had acted the way she had, she hoped to at least show him that she wasn't upset anymore. She stayed up later than usual that night, knitting her apple-leaf patches and stitching them together with the others. She might not have been as skilled as Rachel, but she gleaned great gratification from seeing a work come together nicely.

Before the meeting the next day, she finally replied to Izzy. She wrote of her sewing project. It was a topic they could both take pleasure in while staying away from the ones that caused pain. Marilla decided it was the best way to begin their one-on-one correspondence. She also wrote about passing the exam, Lord Durham's coming visit, and their cow Darling's new calf, Starling. Mother and daughter were virtually indistinguishable: Darling and Starling. She ended the letter, quickly added a concise "Love, Marilla," and then mailed it on the way to the meeting.

Avonlea's town hall was built in an odd place, too far off the beaten path from the rest of the municipal buildings, and on mired ground that had the consistency of sponge cake. Wagon wheels were perpetually getting stuck, and everyone knew where you'd been by the mud on your boots. Mrs. White said she had been "catastrophically against" the location. Marilla thought it odd for anyone to be so indignant over a plot of land.

The Whites sat in the front row, with the Blythes directly behind them. Rachel turned to wave at Marilla when she and Matthew took their seats at the back of the crowded chamber. John's head didn't flinch.

"We're here to represent the family," said Matthew, and by that he meant silent conservatism.

Councilor Cromie took his chair at the front table, and the meeting came to order. The gathering swiftly grew from civil debate to grumblings to heads of families raising fists.

"We should be faithful to God and country," argued Mr. Murdock.

"Silk-stockinged administrators holding power over the common man!" said Mr. Phillips. "With all due respect, it's not as simple as 'God and country.' The people need a responsible government."

"What are you suggesting—a republic like America? Treasonous!" scoffed Mr. Sloane.

"If it came to that, yes. The Tories fight for the old ways of sovereign rule, but the Reformers understand the complications of our modern politics," Mr. Phillips continued.

"I don't see anything complicated in following the precepts of the Christian community," said Mr. Murdock, sending Mrs. White into a tizzy in the front row.

"As a *Christian* woman in this community, I'm tired of the Tories taking full ownership of our Lord Christ. Sacrilege!"

"Reformer guilt," someone jeered.

Mrs. White stood straight up then and gave the gimlet eye to the whole of the crowd. "Care to say that to my face?"

Mr. White pulled her down to sit.

"God save the Tories, the Queen, and England!" shouted Mr. Blair.

"God save the Reformers and the people of Canada!" Mr. Andrews retorted.

Hostility lit the crowd like gunpowder.

"I'd rather die than have the Tories tax my lands as they please, raise tariffs on our crops, and rule over us simply because they have titles and wealth. They see us as little more than peasants come to work the farms and send money back to their coffers!" said Mr. Phillips.

"If discourse does not bring change, then *liberal* action is required," added Mrs. White.

"All four of my sons would fight to the death to uphold the government of the God-ordained royal family," said Mrs. King, who played the organ at church. "The old ways are old for a reason: like the biblical commandments, they work!"

"Now, now—order!" Councilor Cromie called. "Everyone!"

Marilla sat beside Matthew with her chin tucked into her chest. How flippantly they spoke of death. Her mother was dead. Tory or Reformer didn't matter when it came to the heart beating. These were her neighbors, the very people who'd come together beside her at her mother's grave and held her upright. Now they threw hateful barbs at one another based on credos constructed by men who didn't even live on Prince Edward Island and had no notion of their ways—old or new. Life as she knew it was unraveling beyond her control: her mother, Green Gables, John, Avonlea . . . the sum loss was too much for Marilla.

She stood, heart clanging in her temples like cymbals.

"I have something to say."

The Cuthberts hardly spoke in private, never mind in public. The crowd hushed. Every head turned toward her, including John's.

She gulped hard, but it was too late for silence. The words perched on the tip of her tongue.

"I—we—the Cuthberts—have lost a great deal in the past year. I'm a God-fearing Presbyterian and a loyal subject of the Crown." She sipped air and willed her thoughts steady. "Changes in Avonlea are going to come. Some for the better. Some for the worse. Some we won't know, good or bad, until long after. Some we won't ever know. I can't say I understand why God saw fit to take my mother away. It's changed my life. I look at the world differently now. Not as a child anymore. I see the morning sun, and I'm grateful for the people alive under it. *You*, neighbors, friends, and family, remain. I reckon we can disagree about a great many things, but we must find a way to be peaceable. Tory or Reformer, we are Avonleaers first. We must choose to compromise for the sake of our town and those in it. After God, loving thy neighbor is the greatest commandment, is it not? That's what my father reads from the Gospel and what my mother believed."

Then she sat with her hand over her mouth. Shocked at the echo of her voice in the room.

It was John who stood first and clapped. Marilla's lips trembled.

The applause gathered mass, reverberating through the town hall. People stomped their feet and cheered, "Hear, hear!"

Matthew looked at her dumbfounded.

She wished Councilor Cromie would hurry on with the official business.

"I've said my piece," she said to Matthew.

"And more," he replied.

The hall was overly warm. Her vision began to blotch. She thought she might keel over. "I need fresh air."

Quietly, she exited out the back door while the town hall recorder took down the official statement dictation from Councilor Cromie.

The lupines and June bells were in full bloom, lacing everything with the sweetness of honey even at night. The spring peepers in the pond chirped their song under the sky, cavernous and pulsating with stars. The distant forest was a blind spot in the nightscape, with Green Gables hidden somewhere in the folds between. She closed her eyes and breathed in the scent of sleeping clover fields and balsam firs.

"'To slowly trace the forest's shady scene, where things that own not man's dominion dwell, and mortal foot hath ne'er or rarely been,'" she whispered. She enjoyed Lord Byron, despite the many who called him a heathen.

"'But midst the crowd, the hurry, the shock of men, to hear, to see, to feel and to possess,'" quoted John.

He'd followed her out and leaned against the side of the building.

"From Shakespeare to Byron. You do impress." Marilla smiled to see him.

He came a step forward so that the starlight lit the grooves of his cheeks, the little pockmark at his temple, each whorl of his hair.

"I can't say 'Solitude' is my favorite poem. I prefer 'She Walks in Beauty.'"

Marilla blushed and was grateful for the darkness. "That's an easy choice. I like the lesser-known verses. Their shine hasn't been rubbed off from overuse."

She heard him laugh, though she couldn't see it. He stood closer than the night let on.

He took her hand, and she let him.

"I liked what you said in there."

"When you asked me in the Agora, you didn't give me time to think it over. I need time to think things over before I know my mind."

"That's wise. But we don't always have the time. Sometimes you just have to act. On a feeling."

She could smell the tobacco on his vest, peppermint on his lips.

"We never spoke about—"

"I know." She cut him off. The past was done. There was no un-doing. There was only now, with tomorrow fast approaching. "I'm sorry about the other week, John. I didn't mean to be . . ." *cold, cruel, angry, hurt, scared* . . . "the way I was."

Sometimes, even after thinking over a thing, she still didn't know the right words.

He touched her cheek, drew her face up to his.

"Marilla?" The doors of the town hall opened, light and voices spilling out.

They separated.

"Marilla?" It was Mrs. Blair. "There you are." Seeing John, she cleared her throat. "I see young Mr. Blythe has found you first. Well, I hope you don't mind if I borrow her for a moment. I have a proposition."

John tipped his cap. "Be seeing you," he said to Marilla.

She nodded and watched his figure evaporate into the night.

Mrs. Blair took her arm with a good-naturedness that Marilla was unaccustomed to from the stern merchant. "The womenfolk of Avonlea have been discussing the formation of an official Ladies' Aid Society, unassociated with any religious institution or political party. Currently, we have a diaspora of groups, from the Presbyterian Sunday school to the mission's aid run by the nuns to a wide net of sewing circles and everything in between. So many branches collecting funds in support of worthy charities. How much stronger could we be in helping the poor and unfortunate if we united? The Avonlea Ladies' Aid Society would bring us together for the greater Avonlea—as you so astutely said in the meeting. We could use a powerful voice like yours to lead."

Marilla shook her head. Mrs. White was the leader of the Sunday school and sewing circle. She couldn't usurp the older woman's position. While Marilla didn't agree with the Whites' politics, she was loyal to Rachel and her family, who had always been so kind.

"I thank you, Mrs. Blair, but Mrs. White would be a better candidate."

"Eugenia White can retain supervision of her individual flocks, but we need someone young and spirited."

"Well said in there, Marilla." Mr. Blair came to his wife's side.

The rest of the town exited the hall. Couples clumped together in discussion while ambling slowly toward their homesteads. Their chatter drifted on the night breeze.

"We best be going," said Mrs. Blair. "But I hope your answer is yes."

Matthew was the last one standing in the soft circle glow of the building's lanterns. Hands in pockets and cap pulled down over his eyes, she couldn't read his countenance.

She came closer until he saw her and gave a shy smile. He offered the crook of his arm and she threaded hers through.

"Proud of you," he said.

"I guess I've broken the curse of the Cuthbert tongue."

He nodded. "If somebody was going to, you'd be the one."

She squeezed his arm. It felt wholly good—this moment—like awakening in the dark to the comfort of moonlight.

"Let's get home to Green Gables," she said, and they walked home arm and arm, without a word passing between.

XX.

FIRST VOTE OF THE LADIES' AID SOCIETY

June arrived in a torrential downpour of sunshine. Everyone in Avonlea was outside, drinking in the light like parched castaways on a deserted island.

The first meeting of the Ladies' Aid Society was held at Green Gables. Marilla had never been the hostess of such a large gathering. She had to borrow chairs from Mrs. White, who loaned Marilla her best from her own dining room set. No one could dare say she was begrudging about not being asked to lead the new collaboration. However, Rachel confessed that when Mrs. Blair told her the news of Marilla's appointment, Mrs. White had screwed up her nose and nearly set to fulminating. But Mrs. Patterson had been in agreement, and Mrs. White would not speak a word in opposition to the Reverend's wife. So Mrs. White had swallowed her steam and said she would gladly mentor Marilla in the ways of charity administration. And so, having taken Marilla under her wing, she made good on her word. Marilla was grateful.

Matthew brought over the extra chairs in the wagon and helped Marilla arrange them in a circle, per Mrs. White's recommendation.

"So no one squabbles over who's in front or behind. All the ladies are equal—like King Arthur's Round Table," she'd explained.

Marilla did her best, but the Green Gables parlor was more oblong than round. Allowing for the furniture, the circle looked like a lopsided fried egg. She put out their best rosebud tea set and brewed four pots of Darjeeling, feeling glad it was summer so the ladies wouldn't mind it at room temperature. She baked a vanilla cake the day ahead and slathered it an inch thick with butter frosting. Everything was ready.

In her room, she buttoned on the amaryllis dress. It'd been over a year since she'd dared to take it out of the wardrobe. She'd contemplated packing it away in her mother's trunk, but she hadn't another summer frock as nice. Buying material and making a new one seemed a waste of time and money when she'd only worn the dress once. Izzy had used such a fine brocade on the skirt, and Clara's hand was in the stitching. To not wear it seemed a greater travesty.

It was still scented with the meadow lilies and clover she'd raced through with John. She was relieved that it held those memories and not the ones of later—iodine, vinegar, and blood. She turned her hair back into a soft chignon and wore her mother's amethyst brooch over her heart. It twinkled like captive moonlight and gave her courage.

The ladies of Avonlea began arriving on the stroke of the tea hour. Mrs. White was first, of course, bringing with her a majority of the sewing circle. Mrs. Patterson and Mrs. Blair came next with many of the Sunday school women. Mrs. Sloane, Mrs. Gray, and Mrs. Barry also came, each with her girl in tow—mothers and daughters, two by two, as if Green Gables were Noah's Ark. Marilla welcomed them as decorously as she imagined the ladies-in-waiting around the soon-to-be coronated Queen Victoria, only five years older than she. The newspapers were top to bottom with articles related to Lord Durham and the royal court. They claimed that spies were everywhere, taking notes and sending information back to England so Lord Durham could put together his final report on how best to resolve the fractured Canadian populace. The English law was clear: taking up arms against countrymen was rebellion.

All those inciting or participating in such were to be hanged. But what was to be done when everyone in the colony was guilty? The answer had Avonlea folks polishing their teaspoons and attending church with uncustomary vigor. Even brazen Reformers, like the Whites, were keeping their carriage wheels shined to a sparkle, smiling and waving to their Tory neighbors as they passed by.

Best behavior was the masquerade of the moment, while rumors stirred that the Agora had doubled in members, minus one Matthew Cuthbert. He'd stopped attending the political meetings. There was too much to do on the farm. Besides, Marilla had said enough for all the Cuthberts at the town hall meeting.

For her part, Marilla was pleased to bring the women of Avonlea together while the men gathered in dissension. "'The whole is greater than the sum of its parts'"—she quoted Aristotle to start off the inaugural meeting and made sure everyone had tea and cake in their mouths, leaving them little choice but to nod in agreement. Mrs. Blair had given her the bylaws of the Aid Society and the rules of decorum. In her first act of governance, Marilla assigned a provisional vice president, secretary, and treasurer. If any of the volunteering women could not perform their duties, they were free to abdicate their role to another—with the permission of the group, naturally. Everyone seemed in favor of that, and they took a break to refill their glasses.

"I'd like to be vice president next," said Rachel. "After Mrs. Barry gets tired of it. She's the most cantankerous woman. I don't know how you'll manage, Marilla."

No one else had volunteered for the position after Mrs. Barry put her hat in the ring. Her prickly demeanor was certainly a contributing factor. But then, Marilla secretly appreciated a churlish nature. You never had to wonder what Mrs. Barry *really* thought—no idle chatter or disingenuous smiles. She was the woman she was and solid in her opinions. Marilla admired that.

"I'll serve our red currant wine next meeting. That'll soften her around the edges," she teased.

Rachel giggled and ate the butter frosting rosette off her second piece of cake.

The first vote was next: choosing the Aid Society's first philanthropic recipient. Since so many of the women were involved with the Sunday school already, she thought it a good time to call to attention the issue of the orphanage prayer shawls. They'd crocheted these for as long as she could remember, but having visited the Hopetown orphans, Marilla understood there was far more at stake than keeping off a spring chill. Prayer shawls were little help to a hungry belly, a fever, or an ex-slave's freedom. The Sisters of Charity needed funding for food, medicine, and, yes, paperwork and passenger tickets should they be required. She'd thought it over for a long time and had decided that the good Lord had given her the Aid Society scepter so she could use it. But she had to be as wise as King Solomon in acquiring the endowment.

"Now, to vote on the Ladies' Aid Society's first order of business." Marilla cleared her throat. "We are all familiar with the Sisters of Charity in Hopetown and their work with orphans. Since the Sunday school and the sewing circle so generously provide them with garments, I thought the Aid Society might collect a donation purse."

A couple of the women harrumphed—such open talk of money displeased them. Unless, of course, they were boasting of how much their porcelain cups and saucers cost.

Marilla pressed on. "While I know all here would generously and freely give, I thought we might procure the monies through a fund-raiser booth at the weekly farmers' market. All items would be made and sold by the Ladies' Aid Society to benefit charities locally and abroad."

"What did you have in mind for us to sell?" asked Mrs. Barry, already emboldened by her vice presidential title.

Marilla had thought that through too.

"Raspberry cordial," she announced and sent the women into a carousel of chatter.

In passing, John had mentioned to Matthew that their raspberry bushes were becoming a menace to the Blythe farm. They couldn't harvest the berries fast enough, and the thicket had become a safe haven for every crow on the island. Marilla was sure the Blythes would be happy to have the women pick the bushes clean at no charge. She'd hoped Mrs. Blythe would be at the meeting so they could ask her permission, but she was sixty years old and the Sunday school was as much socializing as she could take. John had been born late in his parents' marriage. There'd been another child, a daughter who died of typhoid at age eleven. John's birth had been the unexpected cure to their sorrow, and he was devoted to them.

"The Blythes have raspberry barrens, and we all have a recipe. It's an easy and financially responsible commodity that many a thirsty shopper would enjoy. All proceeds would go to the orphanage, minus the cost of the sugar and bottles. Each member will be given a berry allotment to make her cordial. I can speak to the Blythes about their bushes. Shall we put it to the vote?"

And vote they did. A unanimous agreement.

"Well done," Mrs. White said on her way out. "Your mother would be proud, Marilla."

Rachel kissed her cheek. "The cake was scrumptious."

"I knew you were the one to lead us," Mrs. Blair crowed.

Marilla was glad the meeting had gone to form. The wink of the amethyst at her breast reminded her that she wasn't alone. Her guardian angel had been there.

After the last member left, Marilla changed back into her everyday housedress. She washed the tea dishes, swept the living room of cake crumbs, and made a smelt stew for supper. Then she hung her apron on the hook and set off down the maple lane, through the evergreen woods, and over the violet meadow to the pond where she knew John led his herd for a drink before nightfall. Dusk-drowsy ducks and dragonflies took flight from the cattails on her approach. John's lone figure stood tall and solid beside the shimmering waters.

"Well, hello there," he said.

"Hello, John."

"Passing through?"

He knew she wasn't. Town was north and the Blythes' place was west.

"I came to see a man about raspberries."

"Raspberries?" He raised an eyebrow. "I know a fellow who's got a few."

She nodded. "I think we know the same fellow."

The cows started back toward the barn on their own. Thirst quenched, they were ready for the soft silage of the barn.

John leaned his elbow out to her. "Care to walk a spell?"

She didn't hesitate. After all, she was there on the business of the Ladies' Aid Society. So if the Barrys, the Whites, the Blairs, or any of Avonlea happened to come down the road and see them ambling arm in arm through the field of frenzied buttercups, Marilla would have an explanation. They couldn't see how his hand wrapped around hers or feel his thumb drawing slow circles against the inside of her wrist.

XXI

RASPBERRY CORDIAL SECRETS

So it was agreed upon, and the following week the Ladies' Aid Society gathered at the Blythes' farm. After two hours, their baskets were full, and they'd made great gains in trimming back the bushes, much to the chagrin of the crows that cawed from the birch trees.

After church that Sunday, Rachel came to Green Gables with her share of berries and bottles. Mrs. White was convinced that she had yellow fever, though Dr. Spencer said it was merely a cold. She'd put herself to bed with a cloth over her head and a mirror so she could check her color. The house was on quarantine, with every spoon scalded in soap and boiling water.

"I'll never forgive myself if my only child contracts this peril!" she told Mr. White, who consented to Rachel going over to Green Gables for the day, if only to appease Mrs. White's histrionics.

"Never can be too careful," said Rachel. "You catch a sneeze to-day and—*poof!*—tomorrow you're in the grave."

Remembering herself in the Cuthbert kitchen, she quieted.

"Lawful heart, I'm sorry, Marilla. I always speak without thinking first. Mother says it's my Achilles' heel."

A year ago, the mention might've cut her, but like the cherry sapling beside the Gables, Marilla had grown a new ring of bark. She felt sturdier.

"You're only saying what's true, Rachel. No need to apologize for it." Marilla was at the stove, mashing raspberries with sugar.

Rachel picked up a lemon and rolled it between her palms so that the juices ran loose within.

"Let's play Twenty Questions while we cook. I'll start. I have a secret."

Marilla usually wasn't in the mood for Rachel's games, but summer was seductive: the breeze played with the curtains, the sunny fields sparkled like the gulf, and the smell of raspberries filled the kitchen with sweetness. Why not indulge Rachel while they boiled and stirred? Especially if it was not Marilla's secret being ferreted out.

"Is it a place?" asked Marilla.

"No."

"A thing?"

"No."

"A person?"

"Yes!" Rachel tossed the lemon from hand to hand.

"Hmm . . ." Marilla thought and put a kettle of water on the stovetop. "Someone in Avonlea?"

"No."

"Someone in Carmody?"

"No."

"White Sands?"

"No."

"Well, how do I know this person?"

"Only yes or no questions!"

Marilla exhaled. "Okay, *do* I know this person?"

"No."

"How on earth am I supposed to guess someone I don't even know, Rachel?"

Rachel frowned and tapped her chin. "I hadn't thought of that."

Marilla shook her head. While skilled in many a thing, Rachel wasn't the quickest of wit.

"We won't make it to twenty questions, so you can go on and tell me."

Rachel seemed fine with that. "I have a beau."

Marilla spun round from the stove. "Rachel White!"

"It's a secret. Mother would have a conniption if she knew." She giggled. "I can hardly believe it's finally happened to me. And he's not even from Avonlea. He lives down in Spencervale."

"How positively Romeo and Juliet of you."

"I met him when we were driving back from visiting our old neighbors in East Grafton a couple months back—when that big storm came through and flooded all the roads, remember? Well, we had to stop the night in Spencervale. Friends of my father's, Mr. Lynde and his wife, graciously offered us their spare room. Over dinner, I met their two daughters and elder son, Thomas."

At the mention, she blushed. The kitchen kettle gurgled to a boil, and Marilla took it off the heat.

"We've been meeting off and on ever since. He drives up to see me. He's four years older. Mother and Father have said I can't marry anybody until I'm eighteen. Thomas being the honorable sort, he's obliged to wait it out. He says by that time he'll have earned enough to buy a farm in Avonlea. He wants to be financially set when he makes his proposal. His family doesn't have heaps of money . . . but I don't mind so much. He's kind and pious and pleasant-looking. That's more than most brides get. Rachel Lynde," she said dreamily. "It has rather a nice ring to it, don't you think?"

Marilla was shocked speechless. Firstly, that Rachel had kept this hidden for as long as she had, and secondly, that it had progressed from beau to husband in less time than it took to make cordial!

"Marriage?"

Rachel nodded enthusiastically. "Of course. Girls our age." She shrugged. "It's the natural thing. Wait too long and you'll be past your bloom. Then nobody will want you. You could end up a spinster."

Marilla frowned. "I guess I just never thought about marriage much."

Then it was Rachel who looked shocked. "Never thought about it? Why Marilla Cuthbert, you know good and well that John Blythe is head over heels in love with you!"

A sweat flashed up and down Marilla.

Rachel didn't notice. She was busy taking a paring knife to the lemon and squeezing out the juice. "Mother was engaged to Father at sixteen. We're only a year from that age, give or take a few months. John's bound to ask you to marry him, and then you'll move over to the Blythes' farm, and we'll be neighbors. It's ever so much closer to Avonlea than Green Gables."

The tart citrus scent was the only thing keeping Marilla's head from reeling. Leave Green Gables?

"No," she said in such a tone that Rachel flinched. "I won't leave Green Gables. Not now. Not ever. I promised my mother."

She took the little bowl of lemon juice from Rachel and poured it into the pot with the raspberries. Then she stirred and strained until there wasn't so much as a fleck of seed in the liquid. Rachel silently helped Marilla turn the puree into the boiling water and funnel the batch into bottles. She was so uncharacteristically quiet that Marilla knew she'd hurt her friend's feelings.

"I'm sorry," Marilla said while tucking corked cordial bottles into Rachel's hamper. "I shouldn't have been so selfish. This isn't about me and—anybody. It's about you and Thomas. I'm truly happy for you, Rachel."

Rachel leaned into her side. "I think you'll get on with my Thomas. He's a listener, like you." Then she picked up her basket. "Tell Matthew and Mr. Cuthbert I said hello. See you!"

"See you."

Rachel ambled down Green Gables lane. With her hair pinned up under her straw hat, she could've been mistaken, Marilla thought, for one of the ladies of the Aid Society. It made something inside Marilla pinch with terror. When had they stopped wearing their hair in plaits? Age had come on quick and quiet like a leaf bud on a branch. She took in the bleary outline of herself in the window's reflection. No matter how she searched the face, she couldn't see a married woman staring back. She only saw herself: Marilla.

The Ladies' Aid Society stand opened to grand success. They put out a pink striped awning to match the raspberry cordial. With ninety-eight of one hundred bottles sold at five pence each, bringing in a total of just over two pounds, they declared the fund-raiser an enormous success. Many of the women had left by way of the Blythes' so they could pick what was left on the bushes for the following week. Marilla took the last two bottles home to keep for John. It was the least she could do. The Aid Society would have had nothing without his generosity, and she'd promised him a thank-you picnic.

The next day they went down behind the Green Gables barns where the grass was matted with starflowers and the wood line was edged with ruby red pokeweed lending a spice to the air. There they sat on a fallen maple trunk and sipped the cordials through rye straws that cut the sweetness with a reedy tang. Marilla told him of the Ladies' Aid Society's raspberry success, and he passed along his parents' gratitude for their dispatching of the crows.

"A mutually beneficial proposal," said John. "You were smart to suggest it."

Proposal? The word stuck her like a pin. Marilla sipped hard. The heat of the day and the juice of the berries had quickly turned her straw to mush, leaving her fingers sticky.

"All the ladies are so very thankful to you and your parents."

She wiped her hands together trying to remove the residue. A soapwort grew nearby. John rubbed the sappy leaves over her fingers to clean them. The tickle of his touch rose up her arm into her chest and made her think of him pressed against her in the brook. She pushed away those thoughts by talking about others.

"I was thinking that if we sell different homemades at the booth through autumn, we should have a presentable amount for the Reverend Mother in Hopetown. Mrs. White has everyone knitting wool caps too. Of course, we won't have enough for all the orphans until next winter, but I don't think they'll mind a donation check instead."

"Do you still think about Junie? With the red hat?" John asked, turning her smooth hand into his so that their fingers fell between one another's.

Her pulse beat fast. She'd mentioned to him that when she was crossing the street from the post office, a young African woman in a red bonnet had ridden by. Her stomach had leapt into her throat. She knew it wasn't Junie, but the bonnet concealed the face, leaving her mind to wonder.

"The Reverend Mother told her that we are from Avonlea, so she knows she has friends here if she needs us."

"Friends?" John smiled. "You've got a liberal heart, Marilla."

Marilla frowned. "Conservatives are just as much against slavery as liberals. On that issue we are in complete agreement. Why must everything come down to politics with you, John? There's a whole world out there that doesn't give a grasshopper hair about the Tories or the Reformers. We're all God's creatures." She tried to pull her hand free, but he held it firmly.

"That's a liberal opinion too. And exactly what we must remind our government. Noble titles alone shouldn't control the populace."

Marilla sighed. She agreed, but she couldn't agree. Didn't he understand? A person couldn't always act on feelings. They had to consider all the factors of influence and consequence. The monarchy represented God. If sovereign rule was removed, what would keep the people from an apocalyptic end? Without a predominant government, they'd be left to the whims of individual desire and greed. All they need do was look south to America for warning—their people were running to Canada for sanctuary.

"What I'm saying is that if Junie, or anyone like her, came here, I would help. It's the Christian thing to do."

"You advocate for equality in that regard. Again, very liberal of you."

"John Blythe!"

Her temper flared but hadn't time to reach a flame before John's lips were on hers in a kiss. She forgot . . . everything. For the moment. She couldn't pull away. The magnetism between them was too strong. His hands slipped round her neck and hers went to his arms. Then she heard the ring of a cowbell from the barn, and she reared back. They weren't at a picnic or in the woods. This was her home, Green Gables. Her father or Matthew could walk up at any moment—or worse, someone from town paying a call. What would they think?

She looked straight at John but suddenly couldn't see him. The barn and gables rimmed his face and the midday sun cast a dark shadow.

John's bound to ask you to marry him, and then you'll move over to the Blythes' farm, Rachel had said.

She wanted to kiss John, but she knew if she kissed him again, she'd want to kiss him for the rest of her life. How could she without agreeing to marry him and leave Green Gables? John was the only son of the Blythe household. His parents were old and expected him and his future wife to take over the farm. They couldn't live in two places. Only if Matthew married could she be free to do as she wished. Until then, she'd made a vow to her mother.

Marilla stood.

"I can't sit here lollygagging. I've got to start on supper."

"I'm sorry about the political talk. I was only joking." John stood too and tried to take her hand back.

She balled her fists. "I've got to go."

"Marilla . . ."

She didn't stay to hear the rest. "Thank your mother and father for the berries!" she called over her shoulder and raced back to the house, leaving him with two half-drunk bottles in hand.

From the kitchen she watched him kick the grass, then start down the lane toward the log bridge. She ached to think he was angry, but better that than the alternative. If he loved her, as Rachel claimed, then he'd be back. She wanted him to come back as desperately as she wanted to stay at Green Gables.

"That John Blythe?"

Hugh startled her.

"Yes."

He sucked the stem of his pipe in response, then went out on the porch. Marilla took the leftover chicken from the cold closet and warmed it in a pan. To make a sauce, she added a glug of the red currant wine that she, Clara, and Izzy had bottled together. It seemed a lifetime ago. The bittersweet vapors reminded her of all that was at stake.

XXII

AN AUCTION OF
UNFORESEEN CONSEQUENCES

The summer flew by, but August stuck like honey.

"Laws, this heat is wretched," Rachel complained. "Anything we cook will spoil in less time than it takes to eat it."

She'd come to get Marilla's biscuit recipe.

The Ladies' Aid Society had gone one further. On the suggestion of Mrs. White, they were hosting a supper hamper auction. Every woman old enough to hold a skillet was invited to participate. The proceeds went toward the collective check for the Hopetown orphans. The rules were simple: each hamper entered had to include a main, a side, and a sweet. The members could team up in pairs or households.

Mrs. White and Rachel were preparing stewed oysters and biscuits with lemon pudding for dessert. Ella was helping Mrs. White with the oysters and pudding, which left Rachel in charge of the biscuits.

"Father broke a molar on Mother's biscuits once," Rachel confessed. "He didn't tell her, of course. Just spit the broken bit into his napkin when she wasn't looking. The problem with that was she kept on making them the same. Ella offered to mix the dough, but she insists on doing it according to her own measurements." Rachel shook her head. "Whoever puts down good coin for our supper hamper will want his money back—if it doesn't kill him first!"

Marilla saw the peril. It could very well be Matthew or Hugh with a wicked toothache on account of a bad White biscuit. For once, both men were coming to the event and planned to bid. The summer orchard and field crops had been good. The farmers' meetings in Carmody had raised the price of seed to market, putting extra coin in every family's pocket. Having Matthew and Hugh at the auction galvanized Marilla to make it successful. She wanted each bidder to feel that the hamper he or she won was the best of all. And no broken teeth.

"Here's our recipe." Marilla handed over the card with her mother's handwriting scribbled across. "Softest biscuits you ever did see. Just be sure not to overbake them."

Rachel took it gratefully. "Mother can *never* know!"

Rachel rushed out with the weight of the afternoon sun throwing a heavy slant to her shadow. Her Thomas Lynde from Spencervale was coming to the auction. Rachel was keen on introducing Marilla and impressing Avonlea folks with her suitor.

"Rachel gone?" Matthew peeked his head around the corner from his bedroom.

Marilla nodded. "She'd not be happy knowing you were eavesdropping a wall away."

He came into the kitchen. Skunk followed. "Hard not to. That girl's louder than a gull after bait."

She laughed. "Well, you should bid on her hamper no matter. It would mean a lot to her."

"I'll bid," he said and rubbed his jaw. "But I won't aim to win."

"That'll do."

He went to Marilla's basket on the wooden table. She'd already packed it full and just needed to dress up the outside with ribbon. He lifted the lid.

"Mmm, jelly chicken, pickled cucumbers, cherry tarts—is that a jar of your plum preserves too?"

"It is," said Marilla proudly. "That reminds me. I'm putting a bottle of red currant wine in. I'm not sure if the other hampers will have a beverage, but in hot times like these, a sip can be more nourishing than a sup."

She pulled a bottle from the pantry and gave the remaining five a half-turn clockwise while she was there.

"John will be sorry he missed this," said Matthew.

Marilla pursed her lips. "I don't know why it would matter more to him than any other hungry belly."

The Blythes had gone to visit John's uncle, Dr. David Blythe, in Glen St. Mary. Marilla was glad that he wouldn't be at the auction. She didn't have to worry about the whispers and askance looks of the Sunday school ladies. Town talk about the two had escalated. In whispers, people were discussing everything from secret engagements to bridal veils, making her avoid the social circles even more than usual.

"It's a mighty good meal is all. The man who takes it home will be a lucky fellow."

"Or woman," she added. "Women are encouraged to bid too. I have my eye on Mrs. Blair's hamper. It's rumored that she ordered a box of chocolates from London, just to up the auction price. I wouldn't mind a taste of those. I can't say I've ever eaten chocolates from London. Have you?"

Matthew shook his head. "You know me. I'm not fond of anything too sweet, too salty, or too sour."

"A man of moderation. That's a virtue."

He shrugged. "A man can't change his tastes any more than he can change his name."

But a woman could? Rachel *Lynde*. Nice ring or not, it brought on an aching to think that her best friend would become a new person simply by saying "I do." Marilla liked who Rachel was just fine.

"Hand me that magenta ribbon," she told Matthew. With it, she tied the hamper lid down with a solid bow.

The next day Matthew, Hugh, and Marilla rode together to the Presbyterian churchyard, where the auction was taking place. Reverend and Mrs. Patterson had given them the use of the same booths, tables, and chairs as for the annual May Picnic. The wicker hampers were arranged in a line across the longest table. An even dozen. Marilla took the count as an auspicious sign: twelve months in a year, twelve hours in a day, twelve disciples, twelve days of Christmas, twelve Avonlea suppers to be got.

She was helping Mrs. Blair situate the cash drawer when Rachel arrived, dragging a bashful young man by the arm.

"Marilla! This is my Mr. Lynde."

Thomas turned with his chin down and didn't meet Marilla's eyes. "Nice to meet you, Miss Cuthbert."

He wasn't terribly handsome or homely. Not too thin or stout, not tall or short, fair or dark. In fact, he was so perfectly undistinguishable that he nearly blended into the background. Like a tree branch or a blade of grass. In that way, Marilla found him pleasant.

"Rachel has spoken highly of you, Mr. Lynde."

He grinned without showing his teeth.

"Do you see this exquisite tortoiseshell comb?" Rachel turned her head aside. "It belongs to Thomas's mother. An heirloom piece. I'm only borrowing it today, but . . ." She leaned into his side with a giggle.

"It's beautiful," said Marilla.

"Thomas, go save two chairs for us. I'd hate to have to stand the entire auction," Rachel directed, and he did her bidding. "Isn't he a dream?" she said in his wake.

Marilla cleared her throat. "How did the biscuits turn out?"

Rachel pulled her in close to whisper. "Perfectly light! Of course Mother noticed . . . I told her we bought fresh baking powder and that made the difference. A small lie, but I'd rather ask the Lord for forgiveness than a disgruntled neighbor!"

"Probably easier to gain absolution too."

Rachel bugged out her eyes with a nod. "That's the Gospel truth."

Marilla was a stickler for timeliness, so the auction began on the stroke of the hour. Mr. Blair took the role of auctioneer, and they led off with Mrs. Patterson's "Divine Dinner" hamper: a ham and mushroom pasty with sweet almond gingerbread. It fetched a good price from one of the Pyes who they all knew had many a reason to earn his way back into the church's good graces. Then came Mrs. Lewis and her daughter Lavender: their basket was festooned with ribbons and bows and lavender buds stuck between every cane of the basket's weave. Marilla wondered how anyone could eat the food within without thinking he'd swallowed a soap bar. It was the prettiest on the table, she had to give it that. One of the Irving boys won it and turned Lavender's head too. The Whites', the Blairs', and the Phillipses' suppers all sold for nice prices. Marilla's basket was up next. She'd purposely placed it in the middle so as not to claim a noteworthy first or last position as Aid Society president. Matthew and Hugh bid first in a show of support, followed by Mrs. Bell, but Mr. Murdock ultimately won the hamper in a surprise turnabout.

"Every Christmas the Cuthberts' Plum Preserves were a favorite. I was sorry to see them go when you left Avonlea School," he said when she handed him his prize.

It warmed her to him. Suddenly, he wasn't the stern, wrinkled headmaster thwacking his pointer against the board, but an elderly gentleman with a kind spirit deep down. She wondered when he had changed . . . or when she had.

"There's a bottle of my mother's red currant wine too," she whispered.

"Another favorite," he confessed. "Thank you."

Next came the Andrewses' hamper: beef olives, potato balls, cottage loaf, figs, and a jar of sweetmeats. A solid feast, but not surprising given that there were so many cooks in their household.

The bidding began with Mr. White, who despite raising his hand on every basket had yet to win. Mr. Bell outbid him and was then outbid by none other than Matthew.

Marilla's gaze, and all of Avonlea's, went directly to Johanna. She turned away to her sister with a frown. Mr. White countered good-naturedly. The baskets were dwindling, and if he left without any, Mrs. White would be fit to be tied. Matthew upped the price by five pence. Johanna fumed in her seat. Whatever squabble had befallen them was obviously not repaired.

Mr. Barry bid five over. Matthew bid again. Marilla knew it was their total funds.

"Going once, going twice," said Mr. Blair.

At the count, Johanna rose from her seat piqued to inflammation and stormed off. Seeing the upset, the banker, Mr. Abbey, lifted a hand.

"Two shillings."

It was twice as much as Matthew had in hand. Mr. Abbey had meant to help alleviate Johanna Andrews's obvious discomfort, but the result was Matthew's mortification. He hadn't a penny more to spend, never mind a whole shilling, and everybody in Avonlea knew it. So he stood and followed in the same direction as Johanna while the rest held their breaths with suffocating determination not to let their neighbor see.

Marilla went after Matthew. No one else could without causing a scene. Mr. Blair continued in the auction.

"Now, now . . . Mr. Abbey has won the Andrewses' supper. Let's move along. Mrs. MacPherson's is next, and I'm willing to bet she's got some of her raisin Bath buns in there."

Marilla went round the church to the cemetery, where she heard Johanna before she saw her.

"Why must you make me say it?"

"B-But . . ." Matthew stuttered.

"But nothing! I'm not your sweetheart or anything else, Matthew Cuthbert. I'd rather die than be a farmer's wife. I tried to tell you kindly at Green Gables, but you didn't seem to hear me. So now I've told you forthright, and I feel wretched for saying it." She began to cry, then ran off.

Marilla had never heard anything so callous in all her life, and from the look on Matthew's face, neither had he. He took a step to follow, then stopped and stood wringing his cap in his hand. His humiliated silence pained her even more deeply. She knew she ought to turn and leave him be, but she couldn't tear herself away. His wound was her wound. That was family.

His shoulders shook, and she went to him. Saying nothing, she put a hand on his back. He didn't turn, and she didn't force him. She stood there, pressing her palm into the growing heat beneath her touch. She didn't see him cry, but she felt it, trembling through his bones and into hers like a tuning fork until her own cheeks were wet with tears.

She went home with him that minute, leaving Hugh to ride back with Mr. Bell while Mrs. Blair counted the monies in the till, the Ladies' Aid Society members picked up the picnic grounds, and the families of Avonlea commented on everything under the sun except for what they were all thinking: Johanna Andrews had broken Matthew Cuthbert's heart. And for such a man as Matthew, there was no undoing the damage.

XXIII

A RETURN TO HOPETOWN

1839

Winter came early. The first snow blustered in from the Arctic that October, completely depriving the island of its usual pageantry. The red maples and yellow birches had just begun to turn when their leaves frosted over and dropped off the boughs. The island was prematurely darkened with a sky as gray as a bucket of laundry water. By Christmas and the New Year, everyone in Avonlea was stir-crazy with no thaw to come for another four months. Suddenly, the Ladies' Aid Society visit to Hopetown became as meaningful as a pilgrimage to Zion. But it wasn't until February that the Northumberland Strait had thawed enough for the ferryboats to run.

Mrs. Spencer had a distant cousin in Hopetown who offered up her spare room to the Ladies' Aid Society delegate. Although Mrs. White had been the spokeswoman since the society's inauguration, her health recently had not been the best. She feared catching pneumonia by traveling and recommended that Mrs. Blair go in her place. But Mrs. Blair couldn't leave Mr. Blair to run the shop alone, so Mrs. Barry was nominated. Then, not a week before the scheduled departure, Mrs. Barry's husband got the gout. And so Marilla and Rachel volunteered.

"My cousin will be there to receive them," Mrs. Spencer assured Hugh. "I was two years younger than they when I first traveled to Nova Scotia alone. It's quite safe so long as they're sensible enough not to fall overboard."

Crossing the Northumberland Strait in winter was a dreary business. No fear of rogue waves. It was too cold for that. The water was just a degree above turning back to ice. They crammed inside the heated passenger cabin, where they couldn't see a thing through the salt-frosted windows. Reaching land, they rode to Hopetown in an enclosed stagecoach with the flaps pulled down to keep the winds from chilling them through. Marilla would occasionally peel back the corner of a flap to see where they might be on the journey, but all she saw was barren road to barren field to barren sky. The minutes ticked by slowly in the dark. Even Rachel ran out of things to say, which didn't bother Marilla. Silence had always been a Cuthbert comfort.

Finally, the driver gave a "Ho!" to the horses, and they slowed to a stop before a brick townhouse; though similar to the orphanage, it was narrow where the orphanage was wide.

"This be the place," said the driver.

On the front stoop, Mrs. Spencer's cousin Lydia Jane greeted them from beneath her woolen shawl.

"Come, come! It's freezing out. Butler Cline will fetch your bags."

Marilla and Rachel made a dash for the door, with the wind snatching their skirts helter-skelter as they went.

"These winter storms are wretched!" Lydia Jane said in welcome. "Hang your coats on the hooks. Go in by the fire. Tea is waiting."

Mrs. Lydia Jane was twice widowed with nine children: three died young, four were married off, one was a missionary in India, and another was a shipping clerk in America. She'd lived in a country house with rooms aplenty but moved to the city when the last of her children were grown.

"She's as thorny as a bramble," Mrs. Barry had warned. "Raised her children by the righteous Word and the rod. Do as she says and you'll stay on her good side."

Mrs. White preferred a strict chaperone to an indulgent one. But

Rachel had never been one to appreciate any disciplinarian outside of herself. Marilla suspected that was partly why Rachel never returned to Mr. Murdock's tutelage at Avonlea School. Bending to someone else was not a gift of the White spirit.

"Drink your teacup empty. I don't want my porcelain stained with a ring," Lydia Jane instructed.

Marilla obediently gulped back every drop while Rachel drank slowly, swirling the contents every so often with a casual "Mmm."

When Lydia Jane determined that teatime was complete, she called for Cookie the cook to collect the tray, with Rachel's ringed cup and all.

"You'll be sharing my spare room."

She marched them up the stairs to a room smelling of dead roses and musty carpets.

"The bed is plenty big enough for two. My cousin says your meeting with the Sisters of Charity is tomorrow, so Cookie will have breakfast on the table at nine o'clock. I apologize in advance for my absence. My daughter-in-law had her fourth child last week. She's come down with milk fever. I promised to watch over the older children while the doctor pays a call. But I trust that you will go straight out to your business and come straight home. The only single young women who dillydally in the streets are those of ill repute. I know you will uphold my respectability by not appearing as such."

With that, she nodded good-night and closed the door with a resolute *click*.

"Lawful heart, if she isn't the most *cantankerous!*" Rachel threw herself down on the bed. A fine dust rose up like slate chalk. She waved a hand through the air to clear it. "Even more so than Mrs. Barry, which I didn't think possible." She rolled onto her elbow. "She's determined not to let us have any fun, but I'm more determined to out-determine her."

Marilla opened her vanity case to brush out her hair before bed. "We were warned! Let's do as she says, Rachel."

Despite Marilla's newfound confidence, she harbored apprehension that she couldn't rationally explain. She knew every nook and cranny of Avonlea. It belonged to her as much as she belonged to it. Here she was an outsider, unfamiliar with the people and the city. All she wanted to do was complete the task and get back home.

"We can have a *little* fun. If we take the long or short way to the orphanage, it doesn't change anything as it pertains to Mrs. Lydia Jane. Our destination points remain the same."

Marilla was exhausted and simply wanted to sleep. No more talking or moving or thinking toward tomorrow. It would come in due time. After ensuring that the Ladies' Aid Society check issued from the Abbey Bank was tucked securely in her purse, and her purse tucked under the winter petticoats in her traveling case, she climbed into bed beside Rachel.

It was the first time she'd slept with anyone besides her mother. Rachel smelled differently in the night. Her gown was scented with chamomile and dried sweetgrass. Warmth emanated from the opposite side of the bed where Marilla was used to cool sheets. It reminded her of when she was young and the Gables had yet to be built. All four Cuthberts slept together on a pallet pulled out before the hearth at night and pushed back against the wall during the day. Clara and Hugh slept side by side in the middle with Marilla fitting into Clara's side and Matthew into Hugh's like soupspoons. Marilla had been afraid of the shadows in the windowsills then. The only way to keep the monsters from nibbling her toes had been to wrap her feet between her mother's. She'd nearly forgotten— both her fear and the magic to chase it away.

"Do you think we'll see the orphans from the last time?" Rachel yawned. Her buttermilk breath puffed warm.

"Hopefully not," said Marilla. "It would mean they've gone on to join families."

Marilla's and Rachel's feet met in the middle.

"Your toes are like ice!" Rachel rubbed her feet against Marilla's under the covers. "You would think Lydia Jane would give us bed warmers if there's no fireplace in the room. I checked under the bed, in the wardrobe, everywhere—not even a hot brick to be found!"

True, it was odd. Even at Green Gables, every bed had a warming pan underneath.

"Maybe she hasn't any to spare."

Rachel harrumphed. "Well, we'll catch the grippe for sure if we sleep another night without."

They were staying two nights with Lydia Jane.

Rachel twitched in the darkness. "It's settled then," she said at last. "After breakfast, we'll *have* to go by the general store. It's on the way to the orphanage. Father has an account. We can pick up a bed warmer there."

Marilla sighed. Trust Rachel to find a justification to do as she wished. "Rachel . . ."

"What?" she replied guilelessly. "If Mother were here, she'd do the same." Then she flopped onto her stomach and brought the pillow over her head. "Good night, Marilla," she mumbled.

Fried potatoes and sausages were on the table the next morning. Marilla was glad for the hot meal. Their night had been far from restful. Every time she came close to sleep, a draft would sweep up from her toes and make her nose run. She'd tried to put the pillow over her head like Rachel, but she couldn't breathe through the down.

She nearly drank her weight in hot tea before she'd rid herself of the shivers.

"Has Mrs. Lydia Jane gone to her daughter-in-law already?" Rachel asked Cookie, slicing her sausage and dipping it in mustard.

"She has, miss, and she asked me to put her collection of *Quebec City Gazettes*—English and French—in the parlor for you two young ladies to enjoy before your meeting."

From their breakfast table, they could see the yellow and molding stack of periodicals from weeks, months, even years gone by. Marilla found the extreme accumulation of any one item to be gluttonous and indicative of a small mind. She'd never understood the popular compulsion to hoard a hundred silver spoons, a hundred porcelain trinket boxes, a hundred stamps, and certainly not a hundred copies of back news. What good did it do a person? When they were dead and gone, it was all fodder for the trash fires.

"How generous of Mrs. Lydia Jane to share, but we must run an errand on our way to the orphanage." Rachel bit the end of her sausage and chewed.

Cookie was of the old French servant ways and didn't say a word in opposition. She merely raised her eyebrows high and gave a low hum under her breath while cleaning away their empty dishes.

The windstorm had passed and the sun was out, making the day warmer than the one before. They were halfway down the front stoop before Cookie shouted out, "Be wary of Spring Garden Road! Trouble there today—a hanging!"

Marilla looked to Rachel.

Rachel grinned.

Marilla frowned.

Together they pushed down the city sidewalk. The bells and whinnies of the fly carriages whirled left and right. Kitchen maids rushed by with baskets full of root vegetables, new bread, and fish in paper wrappings. Newsboys shouted, "Half price!" on the morning edition. The Majesty Inn, where they'd stayed on their last visit, was busy as an anthill. Madame Stéphanie's Hat Boutique was equally so. Patrons hurried from shop door to shop door, keeping out of the cold. Marilla and Rachel were the only ones to pause at the window, ogling the winter bonnets of fur and wool.

"I wish Father had an account with Madame," said Rachel. "Then I could buy another lace hat. I barely got to wear mine for an hour."

"Pining for a thing won't grant you it. Come on."

Rachel might've concocted this bed-warmer mission, but Marilla was determined not to be caught in a lie of circumstance. They would go to the general store and on to the orphanage, then directly back to Mrs. Lydia Jane's. Not knowing the layout of Hopetown, Marilla feared they'd come upon the gallows at any minute. She'd looked into the face of death already. There was nothing about it that she wished to revisit. Unlike Marilla, however, Rachel had never seen so much as a dead hog, and her macabre curiosity was getting the better of her. She dragged her heels and paused at every intersection to look east and west. She even stopped a chimney sweep to ask, "This isn't Spring Garden Road, is it?"

"No, miss, it's—"

Marilla yanked Rachel forward without hearing the rest. The general store was two blocks up, but the closer they got to the city center the thicker the crowds became. A maelstrom of motion swept them up so that they had to link arms to keep from being separated. So many people in the current. They couldn't see one yard ahead. By the anxious tone of the mob, Marilla knew this was not the usual traffic. She didn't dare ask a stranger. So she clung to Rachel and Rachel to her. Then, all at once, they came to a standstill and the murmurs quieted. Her fears were realized.

On a high platform behind the courthouse was the gallows. Marilla pushed to find a way out of the throng, but all eyes were up to the scaffold and all feet planted in the frozen dirt.

"We're walled in."

Rachel nodded. "Look!"

The soldiers escorted a handful of disheveled men from a wagon. The crowd burst into commotion. Jeers and cries mingled to a roar that made Marilla's knees buckle. The vibration sent tremors through her. She covered her ears. When the prisoners reached the top platform, nooses were placed round their necks.

"Silence!" called the magistrate. He wore a grand regent hat and elysian beaver coat.

The crowd obeyed. The light breeze carried the sound of a distant harbor gull and the rumble of icy waves, making Marilla wish she were back on her island, far from this place.

"These are the criminal leaders. They have been tried by the God-ordained court of Her Royal Majesty and found guilty of rebellion and treason. Look well, citizens. This is what befalls insurrection."

The mass erupted.

"Death to treasoners!"

"Tories for the Crown!"

"Hang the rebels!"

"The prisoners will have their last words," said the magistrate.

All hushed. The gull bleated *cah-ha-ha-ha* out of sight.

"Please speak, Chevalier de Lorimier!" A sympathizer dared to shout.

Marilla remembered the name from the newspapers. Lorimier and his comrades were part of the Patriote Movement's paramilitary. They had participated in the uprising for an independent Canada. A seditious act. The sentence was death.

Lorimier lifted his face. The flaxen rope was tight at his neck, but he spoke boldly, as if it weren't there at all.

"I leave behind my children, whose only heritage is the memory of my misfortune. Poor orphans, it is you who are to be pitied, you whom the bloody and arbitrary hand of the law strikes through my death . . . I am not afraid. *Vive la liberté!*"

And then the trapdoors were unbolted and the men fell like weighted jigs.

Rachel cried into Marilla's shoulder, but Marilla stared on, unable to blink.

"May God be with their souls," she whispered, then saw a child, still in pantalets and swathed in a knitted cap and scarf, atop its father's shoulders. Watching. Laughing. Cheering on death. And Marilla was suddenly aware of children everywhere. Some with their parents and many alone in scruffy groups of threes and fours. All laughed and mocked the dead. Justice was a game and had nothing to do with right versus wrong. They were too young to understand that life is ephemeral while death is permanent. These weren't her children or children of Avonlea, and yet they pained her. Like a tendon tethered to splintered bone.

A hole in the crowd gave them pass and Marilla took Rachel's hand.

"Come on!"

Together they ran, the steel toes of their boots clicking on the cobblestones, until Marilla saw the doors of the orphanage. There she pulled the bell and banged the knocker over and over for what felt like an eternity before the bolt slid open and they spilled inside, shaking and sweating despite the frost on their coats.

XXIV

SAFE HAVENS AND LETTERS

I would've insisted you come another day had I known of the executions," apologized the Reverend Mother.

She had hot tea brought into her office, but neither Marilla nor Rachel could drink a drop.

"We bolted the doors for fear of rioters, but the Royal Guard seems to have everything under control." She cleared her throat and stared out the window to the inner courtyard, empty of children in the winter months.

Rachel cried off and on. Marilla sat stony, wishing they'd never gone down that street, never set out on such a folly. They should've obeyed Mrs. Lydia Jane and gone straight to the orphanage.

"Is it over?" asked Marilla.

The Reverend Mother continued her gaze outside. "I fear it's only beginning. The unrest is more expansive than Hopetown. The United States is also in conflict. Our Sisters of Charity there speak of the great divide between North and South. Just as we here are Tory against Reformer. Human hearts are full of strife. It's a fallen world, my dears. We can only do our best to establish safe havens where we can."

It seemed a battle already lost.

The Reverend Mother turned then and picked up the donation check that Marilla had brought. "Thank you for this. Mighty good will come from it."

"But how can we help more?"

"Justice is mine, sayeth the Lord. Let the men of politics rage against each other, spill blood, and live in enmity. It's our duty to love the poor, the orphaned, the weary and burdened. Matthew 11:28. Love can be its own kind of war."

Rachel broke into sobs. "I want my mother . . ."

The Reverend Mother rang a bell on her desk, and the door opened. "Sister Catherine, would you please take Miss White to the kitchen. The poor lamb has had quite a shock. Perhaps a sugar biscuit would help settle her nerves."

Sister Catherine put an arm around Rachel and led her out. The Reverend Mother closed the door to her office before facing Marilla.

"The moment I met you, I saw strength. May I share something in confidence?"

Marilla couldn't imagine what the Reverend Mother might need to share in confidence with a Presbyterian farm girl from Prince Edward Island.

"Of course." She gulped and quickly prayed:

Forgive me for not obeying Mrs. Lydia Jane. Forgive me for being toler-ant of Rachel's deceptive schemes. Forgive me for not being with my mother in the hour of her need. Forgive me for the woods and the brook . . . and John. She wanted to be as absolved as possible to receive whatever the Reverend Mother wished to bestow.

"Do you remember the young orphan you met last year—Juniper?"

Marilla could never forget. "Is she still here?"

"No." The Reverend Mother adjusted the sleeve of her tunic. "Thankfully not. She was adopted by a family in Newfoundland."

The image conjured by that news was soothing: the girl in her red bonnet ambling down some pastoral road with her new parents.

"I'm glad," said Marilla. "I can't imagine it's easy . . ." She strug-gled for the right words. "For a person of her description . . . an older orphan and—"

"An African slave?"

Marilla looked down at her fingers. "Mrs. White is having her sewing circle and Sunday school knit caps. She's determined to have enough for every orphan by next winter."

"That's very kind of her. We have too many cases of head cold in the winters."

Yes, but Marilla hoped the Reverend Mother had heard what she was really saying.

"And I should think," Marilla continued, "that a quality hat might be a simple but vastly important thing to an orphan in need of concealment."

The Reverend Mother smiled and took a seat beside Marilla.

"So you *do* understand."

Marilla nodded. "I believe so."

"To speak candidly, we are receiving more and more children born into slavery and orphaned by their parents' deaths or life's circumstances. It makes no difference to God. They are alone and in need of grace. There are very few safe houses between the southern states of America and our door. They arrive half starved, wounded, sick, and terrified from the journey. We do what we can—*everything* we can. But with so few sanctuaries, it's impossible for the many to take refuge in those few. Our dormitories are overwhelmed. It's increasingly difficult to protect them from slave-catchers who wish to return them to bondage. Despite Canadian law, there are many in power who sympathize with the wealthy slaveholders. To them, these orphans are property, not people. The courts have their hands full with the rebellions. They turn a blind eye to the runaway slaves and the slave owners who come to collect them. It's a broken system for which neither Tory nor Reformer has a solution. So we look to the Word: 'for you are not under the law but under grace.' Romans 6. We obey that and pray it protects. His grace be sufficient." She crossed herself. "Amen."

One land's law outlawed slavery. Another's enshrined it. Both thought they were just. Marilla saw the need for action and the great peril the slaves faced if discovered.

The Reverend Mother lifted the bank check. "I tell you the truth because I must be forthright about where this money goes. It allows us to expeditiously move the orphans, even the ones with no family waiting, to other provinces. God's doves outwitting the serpents' guile, so to say. The Ladies' Aid Society of Avonlea is providing more than silver here. Because of this gift, we are able to help the poor, weary, and burdened. 'The stranger who resides among you, shall be to you as native-born. You shall love them.' So says the Lord our God. Love spinning life spinning love."

"Is there no more to be done, though?"

She gripped Marilla's hand warmly. "If we could multiply our safe houses, we would. But as it stands, we each can only work within our limits."

Marilla respected the Reverend Mother's caution. She understood what Marilla appeared to be from the outside: a young woman from a small town on a small island. And yet she burned with a desire to be more—to do more—within her life's parameters. An idea came to her, but before she could discuss it with the Reverend Mother, Sister Catherine cracked open the door.

"The roads are clear now, and Miss White is much improved. I've called for a fly carriage."

"Good. You girls should be going before it's dark. The daylight hours are few in the cold months."

Marilla stood. "Reverend Mother, I wish you to know that your words will remain in my strictest confidence. Though I wonder if you might allow me to share this matter with my aunt, Miss Elizabeth Johnson, in St. Catharines. I trust her implicitly, and she may have thoughts on how we could be of greater service . . . in addition to Mrs. White's shawls and caps."

The Reverend Mother turned to Sister Catherine. "It seems the goodly women of Avonlea are making every orphan a knitted cap for next winter."

Sister Catherine clapped her hands. "The children will be so pleased. Many of the sisters are near to blind from the amount of darning alone! We are eternally grateful."

"Indeed, we are thankful to all who aid our cause." The Reverend Mother bowed.

Marilla took that as a permissive yes. They led her back down the orphanage hall to Rachel. A sprinkling of shortbread crumbs dotted her coat, but she still looked green around the gills.

"Take them straight to Mrs. Lydia Jane's home," the Reverend Mother instructed the driver, then kissed both of their cheeks. "I pray your next visit will be in more peaceable times."

"I'll write to you," Marilla promised.

"I'll keep my eye on the carrier sparrow." She winked.

Inside the cab, Rachel nestled close. "Thank goodness we don't have to walk back. I don't think I could bear seeing any of Hopetown again."

"Mind the copper warmer under the seat," said the driver. "Be careful not to kick it over and set the coals loose."

Rachel gasped dramatically. "We didn't get the bed warmer for tonight! All for naught!"

Marilla pulled the carriage blanket over their laps. Her mind was too preoccupied to coddle despair over cold feet.

"I wish we were home," said Rachel.

"Tomorrow. It's already on its way."

∽∾

Back at Lydia Jane's, they said nothing of rebel hangings, street crowds, orphans, or the Sisters of Charity. Lydia Jane explained herself to be a resolute Protestant and suspicious of everything about the Catholic Church. She argued that she couldn't believe in a religion with so much obscured behind cloistered walls, confessionals, and nuns' habits . . . even if the concealment was for a good cause. She didn't abide by talk of religion, politics, money, or destitution at supper. It gave her indigestion. So instead, they complimented Cookie's mutton mawmenny and sweet butter pound cake and listened to Lydia Jane talk of her grandchildren's every tumble and cough that day.

They excused themselves early to bed, where Rachel didn't bother taking off her underskirts before getting in.

"I'll be ready to go faster in the morning, and they'll keep me warm."

With flannel petticoats on, Rachel left scant space for Marilla. She didn't argue. Wide awake anyhow, she took her candle to the chaise longue, along with paper and pen.

"Dear Aunt Izzy," she wrote, then explained as prudently as possible the truth of the orphanage's calling. "The Reverend Mother says they need more safe houses in the border cities. I understand it is asking you to shoulder a great responsibility with much personal hazard, but you've always been one to live beyond limitations. Might there be anything you can do in St. Catharines?"

Before the coach came in the morning, she gave Cookie the letter to mail. She didn't want to risk losing it on the journey home.

A week later, Izzy sent her reply to Green Gables:

Dearest Marilla,

I'm glad to hear your visit to Hopetown was successful. I assume you are home to your father and brother by now. Please give them my love and a good head scratch to Skunk too. I miss you all most earnestly.

As to the pertinent subject of your letter. I have heard much about the absconding slaves. The newspapers in St. Catharines report of Africans coming north and narrowly escaping their American captors. I've just recently read an article by Mr. Jermain Loguen, an African abolitionist who has given a number of rousing speeches at Bethel Chapel here. He is quite respected in the community. Mr. Loguen has spoken mostly of the enslaved men and women. I'm ashamed to admit that I hadn't stopped to take into account the many children!

You are right. We cannot sit idly by in comfort while others suffer unjustly. I have thought of little else since your letter arrived.

It is a controversial mission to enter given the conflicting laws of our nations, but as you wrote, I have never been one to conform for fear of the unknown. If anyone arrived at my doorstep seeking refuge, I would not turn them out. The same offer I made you, I give to all: welcome and shelter. I'm sure I could make a safe place in the attic of my dress shop. I am at the Reverend Mother's disposal and yours, foremost, darling girl.

Lovingly,
Aunt Izzy

Marilla kissed the letter and immediately sent word to the Reverend Mother.

Ask and ye shall receive. A miracle of multiplicity.

XXV

APOLOGETIC UNFORGIVENESS

Marilla was thankful that she'd written the Reverend Mother when she had. At the beginning of March, word of Lord Durham's published *Report on the Affairs of British North America* reached Canada, and it seemed a wrench had been thrown in the nation's gears. The post office closed for three weeks following. The Blairs took no customers. The town hall remained dark. It was rumored that Councilor Cromie bolted the front doors of his house with Mrs. Cromie and the entire staff locked within. Even old Mr. Fletcher and his chestnut grate were absent from the heart of Avonlea. It felt like a national apocalypse.

The only wheel that continued to turn faster and faster was the almighty printing press. Newspapers bubbled like boiling stewpots, reporting from Charlottetown, Hopetown, Montreal, Quebec City, and even London. Instead of morning bread, men and women lined the main street ravenous for the breaking news.

Lord Durham had collected all of the township proclamations from across the Canadian provinces and compiled them into his royal report, wherein he declared that the only way to quell future rebellions was to unify the British colonies in Upper and Lower Canada, Prince Edward Island being a British colony of the Lower. Lord Durham argued that this integration would produce a more harmonious union. Peace was contingent on the removal of racial divides. The people needed to feel they were one, no matter their language, religion, creed, or color. Proclaiming one Canadian nation, blessed by the Crown, would allow equal representation in Parliament, consolidation of debt, and uniform application of the law across the land.

"The United Province of Canada Sanctioned by the Queen," the headlines declared. Avonlea took time to digest the news. People were tired of peeping out their windows waiting for bedlam to arrive. "The end times are upon us!" Reverend Patterson had been preaching for years anyhow. So the post office reopened; Councilor Cromie unlocked his doors; and Mr. Fletcher returned to roasting nuts.

In Marilla's mind, it was a draw. The liberals had lobbied for reform. So here it was, conservatively applied. But it seemed that not everyone shared her perspective. The Agora had grown even more popular among the younger set. Matthew did not attend, but that didn't stop John from bringing him daily news of the deliberations.

The only good part of the early winter was the begetting of an early spring. It was the first warm March day. Marilla went round the house opening all the windows to let in the sweet breeze. The boughs of the lilac trees were freckled green, their tips whispering the lightest shade of purple. A couple of house sparrows had made a nest in one of the branch forks. Marilla watched them for signs of life spinning, as the Reverend Mother had said.

Now that the post was running again, a letter came from Hopetown. The Reverend Mother had been in touch with Izzy, who was already entertaining "houseguests." It made Marilla's heart quicken. For the first time, she considered taking Izzy up on her offer to visit. She could help care for the visitors and be part of the greater mission. But with only the one spare attic room, her presence would be at the cost of another. So Marilla put the letter away in her bureau drawer, gleaning private joy in simply knowing the work was under way.

Hugh had left for Carmody at dawn. After the long blackout of

commerce, livestock and seed were being traded again, and most
of the farmers had gone off to fill their empty storehouses for the
sowing. Before supper, Matthew came up the yard from the barn in
earnest conversation with John.

"That's the problem, Matthew," he said. "Too many like you are
afraid to speak for fear of unsettling tradition. But it's plain as day
that we are in modern times and the old conservative ways can't
uphold a new nation."

They reached the back porch, and through the open kitchen
window Marilla heard the scrape of Matthew's matches, the puff of
his pipe. A disagreeable habit he'd taken to more and more after the
supper hamper auction. They hadn't spoken of Johanna Andrews in
months, and Matthew made a point of leaving directly after each
Sunday service.

"God don't require me to rattle off at the mouth to be Christian,"
he'd said.

Marilla agreed.

She thought about closing the window to keep out the smoke,
but then they'd know she was there, and she hadn't time to visit
today. She still had to finish dipping her beeswax candles, fill up
the kitchen water cistern from the well, and turn the pan of skim
milk into the pig's bucket before getting supper on the table. So
she quietly went about her business while conversation and tobacco
wafted through the window.

"I don't disagree with you, John," said Matthew. "I see that we
need reform."

"Then you are a Reformer!"

"It's not as black and white as that." Matthew sucked the stem of
his pipe. "I have ties. Going all the way back to Scotland. Everyone
in my family has been Presbyterian. You can't turn your back on
where you come from. So while I may agree with the Reformers'

convictions, I must side with the Tories by religion. They are God's ordained governance, and as Reverend Patterson preaches, we must be faithful to the Crown."

"I must've missed that sermon. Where does the scripture say that the British Crown is God's holy appointed? Couldn't our French neighbors argue the same for King Louis Philippe? And the Americans for their President Van Buren? And the Dutch and Belgians and . . . tell me, who has God's paramount favor? The world is too large and too diverse for us to stay rooted in social convention when it no longer strengthens the people for whom it was created."

"Again, I can't deny your claims."

"Then why continue to back a political agenda that would see its citizens blind and dumb to the necessary changes for the greater good? The only solution is democracy, but we must have every man's vote to make it happen."

Matthew sighed, and it bothered Marilla to hear his frustration. "Change is happening. The Tories are for unification, and Lord Durham supports the responsible government."

"After we nearly beat him over the head with it—and that's the point, Matthew. Had we not rallied together with grit and clarity, we would have no foothold in demanding equality across the social classes. It's men like you who are holding us back. Men like you who we need to pick a side—hot or cold, but not lukewarm!"

Marilla had heard enough. It infuriated her how John backed Matthew into a proverbial corner. Her brother was far too meek and good-natured to fight back. She wouldn't listen to him being boxed about, especially not at Green Gables. Matthew had endured enough humiliation at the cold shoulder of Johanna Andrews. Marilla could do nothing to defend him then, but now she could.

"You're so full of yourself, John Blythe!" she seethed through the window before coming out to the porch. "Why won't you just let a thing be? I've seen exactly what this kind of talk does—makes men barbaric and bloodthirsty! I saw it in Hopetown. Innocent people—children—are being hunted and strung up while you're busy doing what—talking? Debating war as a sport in your Agora. Making trouble for those who might be taking action, even if it isn't the liberal action you deem adequate. Who are you to judge? Anarchy is never the solution. All I see from the liberal Reformers is rebellion and death."

John's eyes were wide with surprise and concern. "Marilla—"

She held up a stern finger for him to remain silent.

"What is most vexing to me is why it matters so very much to *you* if we are conservative. We don't impose our political beliefs on you, so why must you change us?"

Fuming and perspiring, she heard the pot of tomato stew gurgling over. "And now you're ruining my supper too!" She went back in, slamming the kitchen door behind her.

John followed her, with Matthew behind.

"Marilla, please calm down. No need to be in such a temper," said John.

She pulled the pot off the stove and nearly threw it at him. How dare he come in here and tell her how to behave!

"You think you can enter a person's home and take over? Matthew is a conservative, just like my father and mother, just like *me*. We don't want to change. And if you don't like it, you can go on and never come back."

"Marilla . . ." Now it was Matthew who looked ill. "You don't mean that."

She raised her chin high. "On mother's soul, I do."

She scarcely believed she'd said it until the words hit their target.

John's face went scarlet. The pockmark at his temple purpled. Silently, he nodded to Matthew, turned, and left.

Marilla's head began to pound. Her vision tunneled. Red.

She spent the next day in bed, the headache amplifying every color too bright, every sound too loud, every movement a stab. When it abated on the second morning, she got up and found that Rachel had come by to bring the Sunday school quarterly. Since their Hopetown visit, she'd rededicated her life to the righteous cause of salvation and liberal reform. She claimed the church was the first step in that liberation. She'd seen doomsday with her own eyes and was determined not to be led to the gallows in the Last Judgment. They'd never spoken of the hangings. Marilla hadn't forgotten, but the more time passed the fainter the memory grew, the less it pained her. Some things were best that way.

Matthew was in the kitchen helping himself to a breakfast plate of cold ham and cheese.

"Father back from Carmody?" she asked, tying on her apron.

Matthew nodded. "Already went out to the fields with the new seed."

"You headed that way too?"

"Hoped I'd talk to you alone first." He pushed his plate back and wiped his lips hidden beneath the beard he'd begun wearing.

"Talk—whatever about?" Her headaches acted much like a wet sponge across a school slate, erasing even the faintest reminder of the equations of yesterday.

He cleared his throat. "About the other day with John Blythe."

"I don't see what there is to talk about."

"Then I suppose it's up to me to do the talking."

Matthew talk? It made her nervous to think about, let alone to listen to.

"You've grown up fast since we lost Mother. You've got strong opinions and a newfound tongue to voice them. I'm real proud of you, Marilla. But I wouldn't be able to hold my head up as a man and your older brother if I didn't tell you how I'm feeling. It's time for me to speak *my* mind. You were wrong to say what you did to John Blythe. I was ashamed of you."

It stung her afresh, and the quiet twitching at her temples commenced. She steadied herself against the sink.

"I was standing up for you and our family."

"I don't need anyone to speak for me. I have a voice just as much as you do. It's a choice we make every minute. What truths are important enough to say aloud and what ones are important just to know. That's the power. You've got to be discerning. You can change your mind anytime you want, but you can't take words back. Not ever."

Marilla bit her bottom lip and turned away so he wouldn't see her eyes brimming. She believed what she'd said to John, but hadn't stopped to ponder *if* she should say it, and how. Her pride had been the thing to lash out and yet, somehow, it was wounded now.

Matthew stood and put on his hat. "You should be telling John Blythe that you love him. That's what ought to be said."

She turned quickly to repudiate that, but he was out the back door without a good-bye, leaving her regretful. She'd meant to speak boldly not cruelly. Up until that moment, she hadn't realized how similar the two could be.

A week went by, then two, and three. The cherry blossoms and narcissus burst into pomps of pink, yellow, and white, but Marilla hardly noticed. She hadn't heard from John in all that time, and so he consumed her every thought. This was more than a cold shoulder. She'd argued with him in front of her brother. She'd sworn on her mother's soul. She'd spoken immutable words.

"The Blythes are just back from visiting cousins in Charlottetown," Matthew said from behind his newspaper sheaf one evening.

"I wondered where they'd gone to," replied Hugh from behind his. "I've been meaning to have John come take a look at Starling. Reckon she'd make a good match with one of their bull calves."

Marilla flushed, sitting between the two, her fingers clumsy with the darning. She was relieved that John's absence had a reason and a coming solution.

A day later, she was practically tripping over herself when she spotted him trotting down Green Gables lane. She rushed upstairs to put her hair in a horn comb and crushed dried geranium petals against her wrists.

He arrived by the front door, and she opened at his knock.

"Hello, John, nice to see you."

He took off his cap with a solemn nod. "Miss Cuthbert." His tone was cold. Dark shadows spooned his eyes.

She frowned to see him so formal.

"I've come on behalf of my father—on your father's request—on the business of your heifer Starling."

Heat rose to her cheeks, and she felt foolish for thinking he'd come for other reasons.

"I believe Father is in the barn."

He cleared his throat. "While I'm here, I wanted to have a word with you, if I may."

Here it was: he'd apologize, she'd apologize, and they'd move on without this unsociableness between them. Maybe they could even go for a walk later. The maple lane was dripping with spring crimson florets, and she wanted to tell him about her new idea for the Ladies' Aid Society's market booth.

"I'm sorry if I offended you and your family with my liberal opinions, Miss Cuthbert. I wrongfully assumed I could speak with familiarity. But I assure you, I won't make that mistake again."

It was the cynicism in his tone and the way his eyes darted to the side when he alluded to their affinity. A provocation trumped up as an apology. She squared her shoulders hard.

"You must learn that impudence has consequence, Mr. Blythe."

He made a sound between a sniff and a grunt.

"Good day to you then."

Marilla inhaled sharply, ire in her lungs. "Good day, Mr. Blythe."

She shut the door and stood with her back against it for so long that John walked to the barn to speak with her father and returned before she moved. When she heard him out front again, she took the doorknob. If she opened it, he'd see her and stop. They'd really talk. That's all it would take.

You've got to be discerning, Matthew had told her. Her unleashed tongue seemed to be tied up again.

John gave his horse a *yup,* and she listened as he rode away, each hoofbeat trampling her heart as he went. Matthew was right. You couldn't take back words . . . the spoken or the unspoken.

She picked up her broom and went out to sweep the yard until every provincial speck of dirt was in its place. She would do it again tomorrow and the day after for as long as it took.

part three

Marilla's House
of Dreams

XXVI.

A CHILD IS BORN

November 1860

Afrigid but snowless November settled over the island, still awash in the bright golden-scarlets of autumn. The trees clung to their colors despite the bite and snap of wind. The sun was a mellow haze through the canopy of unseen ice.

Marilla sat alone in the kitchen, mending a pair of Matthew's wool socks by the stove fire, when Rachel's oldest son Robert came sprinting down the lane from Lynde's Hollow. He was built like a fox, short and spry, and he moved at a pace that made Marilla's knees ache. He reminded her of Rachel in their youth—had Rachel been born a boy and allowed to run as free as she wished.

"Marilla!" he called as he came closer. "Miss Marilla, the baby's here!"

Marilla untied her apron and hung it on the hook over the wood box so Matthew would see it when he came in from the field and know she'd gone out. Marilla had been up to Lynde's Hollow the day before to bring the family as many apples as she could salvage from their orchard. It still wouldn't be enough to fill all nine of the Lynde babies' bellies.

True to his word, Thomas Lynde had worked steadily until Rachel was eighteen and he had enough to buy a farm in Avonlea. There was a beautiful piece of property for sale at the end of the main road where most folks thought Hugh should've set his homestead but hadn't. It was the more sociable choice. And so, on Rachel's suggestion, Thomas purchased the acreage to the north of Green Gables, making the Lyndes and Cuthberts proper neighbors. It was a quick jaunt up the lane to arrive at Rachel's front door.

Before Robert had reached theirs, Marilla had her coat and mittens on. She was down the porch steps when, seeing her, he stopped, his face dewy and pink with exertion.

"Boy or girl?" asked Marilla.

Robert gulped to catch his breath. "A boy! Father and the midwife are taking care of him. Mother sent me to fetch you."

"And where's everybody else?"

"The littler ones have gone over to Grandmother White's."

"I bet she's fit to be tied about that. Your grandmother was never one for a rumpus under her roof."

He nodded in agreement. "No, ma'am. But they went on strictest orders not to set her temper off or there'd be Mrs. Winslow's instead of tea before bed."

Marilla bit back her smirk. "Well, you've got a tenth now. Let's hope he inherited your father's reticence and not your mother's affinity for opinionating."

He dared to smile as the two of them walked back up the lane at a proper pace. Marilla was never present for Rachel's labor. She understood that births were as natural and common as the rains, and yet one strike of lightning could change everything forever. Her mother and their family had been struck. By God or luck? After all these years, the answer had only become more ambiguous. Rachel had been through this twelve times, with nine children standing as a reward for her suffering and two buried in the Avonlea cemetery as a reminder of the risk.

A baby girl named Patsy died of influenza at age two. All soft curls and dimples, Marilla could still see her cherub face in Rachel's arms. An angel come to earth for a short time. The loss had nearly shattered Rachel, but she had the older children, and soon younger ones as well. Little by little, the split in her heart seemed to heal up. Then she had a stillborn boy. Marilla had thought it might be easier to lose a child that way, with less time to get to know the child's personality, no time to hear the pattering of little feet, and less love poured out all around. But Marilla had been wrong. It had been nearly worse than Patsy's death. Rachel couldn't even bring herself to name him. She simply referred to him as "my sweet son" and buried him beside his elder sister. Marilla had come to cook for the family during their mourning. Rachel's usual appetite was gone. She ate only meager bowls of porridge and grew so frightfully weak that Thomas worried she'd not live through the grief. But Marilla was determined. She baked more vanilla cakes and plum puddings than ever in her life, and Rachel slowly came round. It was one of the most sorrowful times Marilla had ever seen her friend through.

This twelfth child had surprised them all. Dr. Spencer had put Rachel on strict bed rest for nearly all of the pregnancy. Her body was weary, he warned, and if she wanted to mother the living, this should be her last. Marilla could only imagine how pregnancy and childbirth would exhaust the flesh. She'd not carried even one child, and yet the years had been like a vinegar in her bones, pickling her day by day.

Marilla liked children, but motherhood seemed outside her realm of possibility. She believed wholeheartedly in the "God giveth" tenet, and the good Lord had given her Matthew, Green Gables, health, and fields of harvest. She had more than many she knew. So instead of wishing for what she did not have, she was grateful that she'd not suffered like Rachel, or paid the ultimate price like her mother. The tariff for motherhood was too great when there was already so much depending on her. Besides, to bear a child one must first have a husband . . . on that account, Marilla could not deny the lingering weight of regret. She had hoped that Matthew would find a wife, but dared not say as much. They each held silent disappointments.

Matthew was forty-four years old now, and while his hair had
gone salt-and-pepper at thirty, his beard had remained a dark bushy
brown until that autumn, when it turned ash gray seemingly overnight. He'd begun having heart spells too—pangs in his chest that
took his breath clean out of him and left him twice as tired. Dr.
Spencer said Matthew needed to avoid heavy lifting, lay off the
pipe, and eat more beans. None of which he had done.

Dr. Spencer had been a frequent visitor to Green Gables over the
last few months. A summer cough had turned Hugh's handkerchief
crimson. Consumption. But even when he was so thin that his work
gloves fell off with a flick of the wrist, he'd gone into the barn at
sunrise to work the livestock with Matthew. Marilla couldn't stop
him even when she'd tried. So she too had gone on as if blind to the
evidence of his end: frying eggs for their breakfast, sweeping the
yard, feeding the chickens, harvesting the orchard, baking bread,
setting the table for the two men, and dishing out stews aplenty.
Life didn't stop grinding time, even when their mill wheels slowed.

On the morning of the first September frost, Marilla had gone to
Hugh's room with a fresh cloth and a warm basin of water. She was
shocked to find him still in bed, his sleep uninterrupted by the sun's
rise and the rooster's call. Dr. Spencer later said that Hugh's lungs
had frozen up in the night. He was gone. For two days, Marilla had
stayed in bed, her pillow wet with tears and her stomach gnawing
on nothing until Matthew dared to come into her room. He never
came up to the second floor after their mother's passing. So it had
surprised her to hear him softly knock and enter with a bowl of
potato soup he'd made himself.

"You've got to eat," he'd said, his eyes as swollen as her own.

The soup had been terrible stuff. Bland and overcooked to mush,
but it was good to have—to have *him* there as comfort.

"Everyone's gone but us," he'd said. "You're the only Cuthbert on
earth with me now."

It was true. They'd had one aunt who'd died in their youth, but no uncles to carry on the name. There were the Keiths, their cousins in East Grafton, and the Johnsons, like Aunt Izzy in St. Catharines plus more in Scotland, but there were no other Cuthberts as far as they knew. Of course, it was still possible that Matthew would take a younger bride to have children. But the only men his age she'd seen do as such were widowers. There was also the problem of his diffidence. Not since the hour Johanna Andrews spurned him had he so much as looked at a woman twice. Saying women made him nervous, he stayed as far away from them as possible. Marilla argued that she was a woman and he seemed fine enough talking to her.

"I dunno, it's different. You're my sister who just happens to be a woman," he'd explained, though Marilla still didn't see the rationale in it.

Soon enough, the months rolled into years, and the years coupled together in decades. The idea of anyone else coming in to change one sprocket of their routine was inconceivable. They were a well-oiled clock. But with Hugh's death, it seemed that they'd lost their pendulum. Matthew had always done the farming, Marilla attended to the house work, and Hugh handled all the commercial transactions. Matthew hadn't a mind for bargaining, and while Marilla was adept at numbers, she was a woman and unwelcome at the all-male farmers' meetings. Never mind that she couldn't leave Green Gables as often as the business end required. Who would cook, clean, launder, mend, tend the garden, stock the pantry, and do all the other innumerable chores that went into the upkeep of Green Gables if she were off in Carmody? Matthew could barely attend to the crops and livestock without his heart coming out of his chest. He needed her there. She'd made a promise to her mother, and she'd kept it.

Hugh had brought in a hired hand and his wife for a little while, but they'd moved to Nova Scotia after the birth of their child. Then there was that time John Blythe worked for them. But they'd all been younger, practically schoolchildren, and it happened so long ago, it was hard to remember how it'd all come to be.

"How old are you now, Robert?" she asked as they trudged up the lane.

"Fourteen."

She nodded. Maybe Rachel would let them hire him on while school was recessed. Robert was a smart boy and quick on his feet. However, the Lyndes had their own farm to run with ten children at the table. She dismissed the idea. It wouldn't be right, especially now when the eldest boy was needed most. She and Matthew hadn't much to pay him either.

In the Lyndes' house, Robert waited downstairs while Marilla went up to the bedroom. The midwife was just laying the wrapped bundle in Rachel's arms.

"Marilla! Come, see, it's a boy—a boy!"

Marilla came to her side and pulled back the blanket from the flushed little face. "Another fine Lynde in the world. Congratulations, Rachel—Thomas."

In the corner, Thomas blushed, bashful at the compliment.

"Well, don't just stand there, Thomas. Get Marilla a chair!"

He went out to fetch one with a dazed grin.

Rachel shook her head. "Twelve times and still the man faints at a drop of blood. You'd think he'd know by now that babies don't come in neat packages. But Thomas seems bent on being unconscious to the truth. He just woke up right before you walked in."

The baby gave a sigh and drew both women's attention. He had the finest skin of pink gossamer. His lips were a perfect bow, and each finger seemed a miniature masterpiece, flexing and releasing at his mother's breast. There came a flutter in Marilla. She'd felt it with Rachel's other children too, but it inevitably grew fainter as the newborn dew cooled to sticky toddler.

"It was the oddest thing, Marilla. He was born hiccupping. Not one cry. What kind of child is born without hollering out, 'I'm here'? But then I heard the steady chirping, so I knew he must be well."

"A quiet spirit," said Marilla. "I understand that sort."

"Must be. That's why it's ever more fitting that you should name him."

Marilla stepped back. "Name him? Oh no, I couldn't. He's your son. A name is too important a thing. It belongs to the mother and father."

Rachel frowned. "You are my oldest, most trusted friend. Please don't argue with me. I spent months trapped in this bed followed by hours of suffering." She drew her chin down dramatically. "Won't you do me the honor of naming the very last child I bear forth?"

What was she to say to that? Rachel had never been above using sentimentalism to get her way. Marilla was on the spot with hardly a minute to think.

"Well, I haven't any idea . . ."

Rachel sighed, a blustery thing quite unlike her son's. "Marilla, I've named ten children, and I simply don't have any more to give. *Please,* just think of a name—whatever it is will be a gift. Save my tired head from the pondering."

"Well, I . . ." Marilla's mind jackrabbited about. A handsome baby boy, not given to fuss . . . "I suppose the only name that comes to mind is my father's. How does Hughie suit?"

"Hughie Lynde?" asked the midwife.

Rachel adjusted the baby so his head sat up as best as possible. "Hughie Lynde. A good name in honor of a good man."

The midwife penned it in neat cursive. Thomas returned with a chair.

"That took long enough. Marilla's already given us a name."

"Oh?" Thomas set the chair beside the bed.

"Meet our son Hughie."

Thomas smiled and nodded. "Much obliged to you, Marilla. No better namesake."

Marilla felt hot tears well up, though she thought she'd run out of them years ago. Taking a seat beside her friend, she drew her finger gently over the baby's brow.

"Hello there, Hughie. Welcome to the world."

XXVII.

A CONGRATULATION,
AN OFFER, AND A WISH

The next day Marilla was embroidering the initials *HL* on a baby smock when she heard the steady plunk-and-roll of a horse and carriage.

She thought it might be Dr. Spencer stopping in after giving Rachel a final examination. A number of guests had already been to Lyndes' Hollow, with more to come. Marilla reckoned her eyeglasses were playing blurry tricks again when she saw that the driver coming down Green Gables lane seemed to be none other than John Blythe. While Matthew and John had remained friends, John had rarely come to call, and never without Matthew giving her forewarning. Then she'd made sure to set off for the post office, climb up an orchard ladder, or pluck every last string bean from her garden to avoid an awkward encounter. It was easier than one would have thought to steer clear of a person in a small town like Avonlea. All you had to do was keep busy looking the other way. So long as things stayed the same, nothing changed.

Now John came riding up to their front door as if it were any normal Friday afternoon, which it had been until he appeared. She made herself sit very still, concentrating on perfect stitches to form the smock's *L*. She counted his footsteps, one-two-three-four, up the porch stairs. Then one-two-three-four to the door. A knock. She inhaled, counted one-two-three-four, then exhaled and rose all in one motion.

Hand to the doorknob, a moment of déjà vu: wasn't she just
here? While her eyesight might've been prematurely receding, she
prided herself on having a sharp mind. Memory, however, was a
slippery thing. Like a dawn mist that vanished by midday.

The knob turned. The door practically opened itself.

"Hello, John Blythe."

He took off his hat, hair still a flap of curls, though lighter in
shade. Or maybe it was Marilla's eyes dulling the coloring.

"Hello," he said as an inhalation. "I didn't mean to intrude."

"You aren't." She gestured for him to come in. "Please."

Time had taught her to siphon emotion: hold back the hard and
let through the soft. Curiosity was as much as she allowed herself
to feel. Anything more and she'd have to feel it all again.

"May I offer you something to drink?"

"No, thank you kindly." He stood in the parlor.

The November light filtered through the windows like pond
water after a storm. Dust that she hadn't noticed before eddied at
random.

"I've just come from visiting the new baby at the Lyndes'."

"A healthy boy."

"Yes, and Rachel well too."

Marilla nodded. "Thank God."

"Yes." He looked down at his hat in his hand. Clara's memory
filled up the space between them.

Marilla smoothed her skirt and had a sudden pang of longing. Not
for her mother—no, she'd long ago learned to dam that stream—
but for their old, cranky cat Skunk, who'd had an instinct for making his presence known at just the right time to turn an awkward
conversation. She'd never had the heart to bring in another cat. She
would've, she told herself, but they'd never had another feral kitten
come around the Gables. Skunk had been gone some nine years
now. He'd died the year after John's parents. Mrs. Blythe passed

away, and less than a month later Mr. Blythe followed. Everyone said it was the pull of the soul after its other half. She'd wondered if such things were true. Moreover, what happened if your soul never had another half?

That was the last time she'd been this close to John—at Mr. Blythe's funeral. He'd barely looked up to nod when she'd paid her respects. So lost in the loss. She understood that more than she understood love. It had softened her to him, and she'd told herself that if he ever returned to Green Gables, she wouldn't hold the past against him. Little did she know it would be ten years before this day—on the occasion of the birth of the tenth living Lynde child. $1 + 2 + 3 + 4 = 10$. The tetraktys. It had been a geometric favorite of hers. Ten was the number of completion.

"Rachel and Thomas tell me that you named the child."

Marilla nodded. "After my father."

"Yes." He frowned. "I meant to send my condolences."

Hugh had requested a quiet private burial, as was his nature. It had been only Marilla, Matthew, and the new minister, Reverend Bentley, round the newly engraved tombstone. The smell of chiseled stone had salted the air:

In Affectionate Remembrance of
Matthew Hugh Cuthbert
and Beloved Wife
Clara Johnson Cuthbert

They'd laid Hugh's coffin atop Clara's. Seeing the warped wood against the new, the deadened heartache returned with the gnawing desire to touch her mother's hand. Marilla had balled her fists against the pain and taken comfort in knowing her parents would rest together, lulled by the murmur of the sea and reunited with the babies they had lost.

Back at the Gables, she had immersed herself so deeply in the day-to-day chores of grieving that she'd barely stopped to think on who had or hadn't offered words of sympathy. Avonlea had always been good to her father, and her father to Avonlea. That was more than enough.

"Very kind," she told John.

"Had I been here, I would've come immediately." He lifted his gaze to meet hers. While his coloring might've dulled with age, his eyes had not lost one ounce of luster. "I was in Rupert's Land."

"Oh?"

Marilla recalled the rumors. She hadn't dared to inquire, not even of Matthew. Whether John was away on business in Charlottetown or off in the Canadian wilds, it didn't change anything. He was absent and she was present, and there was no meet in the middle of that equation.

"Yes, your mother's family is there. Your Uncle Nick and cousins, correct? You once told me of them. Were you there to visit again?"

"Yes." He grinned, pleased at her mention of their old talks. "And to take in fresh air."

She pictured him in the midst of great mountain peaks and glacial lakes and had to turn her cheek away to hide her own wistfulness. In all these years, she'd not ventured to the west. How could she without thinking of him?

"Did you get your fill?"

"I didn't."

She looked up, surprised by his candor. He smiled.

"But I'm glad to be back. Mr. Bell was good enough to look after the farm for me. I wasn't sure if I'd return. My Uncle Nick had hoped that I'd stay on to join the family trapping business, settle down with someone, and make a home nearby."

This was news to Marilla. She frowned. She couldn't imagine anyone abandoning the land and livestock they'd grown up tending.

"Make a home? But you have one here."

Matthew came through the foyer from the kitchen.

"Is that my old friend John Blythe I hear?"

"Is that my old friend Matthew Cuthbert I see?"

The two shook hands of welcome.

"You've gone silver as December—only without the holly berries and bows."

Matthew gave a laugh and stroked his beard. "And you disappeared like a hibernating bear, so I guess we're both of a wintering season. How's everything?"

John shrugged. His eyes moved from Marilla to Matthew. "Better than before. Not as good as the old days. But no complaints, which is wholesome ground to grow in, right?"

"Can't argue with that. How long have you been back?"

"Three days. I've just come from the Lyndes' and seen the new boy, Hughie." He cleared his throat. "But Rachel was bent on filling me in on all of Avonlea, more than on the child. She mentioned that in the wake of Mr. Cuthbert's passing, you were looking for some extra hands."

Matthew scratched his neck beneath his beard. "Reckon so. Father did most of the buying and selling. I do all right at the farmers' junctions, but then, if I go, who'd be here to keep up? Marilla's got enough with the house . . ." Matthew looked to Marilla.

"Thought about getting a local boy to work for barter when Matthew goes off." She cleared her throat. "But a farm boy would need looking after. Hiring on a full-time runs a pretty penny, and that isn't a purse we've got at the moment."

Money talk always felt like putting her hands in a bucket of tallow. No matter how many times she washed after, her fingers stayed too greasy to be comfortable.

"Yes, that's about what Rachel told me."

The muscle between Marilla's shoulder blades twinged. After all these years, Rachel's capacity for speaking as if she knew what she did not had only matured from bad habit to stubborn constitution.

"Well, being that you seem to know all the details, might you have a suggestion for us?"

"In fact, I do," said John. "I offer myself."

Matthew gave a shy smile and stroked his beard to hide it. Marilla's heart fluttered, and it took all her composure to keep her breath steady.

"Yourself?"

"Yes. Now that I've returned, I plan to resume all of my family's dealings. Our dairy cow stock continues to profit. I've been able to take on a couple of Mr. Bell's seasonal laborers for permanent work while I conduct the trades. I'd be happy to be of service on your behalf in that way too. Matthew can stay on the farm and you in the Gables."

"Well, I'll be." Matthew grinned. "Mighty good of you, John. *Mighty* good."

Marilla was less quick to accept the offer.

"So you would speak on our behalf at the farmers' meetings in Carmody and negotiate our seed and sell prices. How would we know you were doing right by us? The fate of our livelihood would be on your word."

He stood straight, chin raised, and eyes locked on hers.

"You may not have liked some of the things I've said in the past, but I have never done wrongly by you. Not one day of my life."

Marilla's throat closed up with shame. She swallowed over and over, but could not find air to reply. Thankfully, Matthew did.

"Certainly we trust you, John. You're like the brother I never had."

His words hung in the air between the three of them.

Matthew patted him on the back. "Have a smoke with me?"

They went out to their old haunt on the back porch.

"Dr. Spencer says you oughtn't smoke," Marilla whispered, but only her parlor window reflection heard.

❦

When Marilla returned from the evening milking, Matthew was seated alone in the kitchen, oiling his leather horse tack.

She tied on her apron and pulled down a dried ham hock from the pantry. "John leave? I would've offered him some pork and pea soup for his troubles."

Matthew set aside his cleaning rag. "You don't exactly have a hospitable air, you know."

"In fact, I *don't* know. I would've offered him supper. That's as hospitable as it gets!"

Matthew sighed. "You and he have let too long go by. It's got to a point where you don't even remember what it's like to not act affronted."

She filled the pot with water and tossed in the ham with a *plunk*.

"I know exactly why I act the way I do toward John Blythe, and so do you."

"No, I don't. Not anymore. Mother is gone. Father is gone. The past is past. Can't bring any of the old back. So let go of what was and put a kindly hand out to what's right in front of you, Marilla."

She picked up a wooden spoon.

"I'm not mad at John Blythe. We simply don't see eye to eye."

"You don't got to see eye to eye with people to love them."

She looked over her shoulder with a scowl, and he held up his hands in defense.

"I'm just quoting scripture—love your enemies, it says."

She had never said John was her enemy. She went back to stirring her pot.

Matthew continued. "No matter what your difference of opinion may be, we can agree that it's a testimony to John's character that he'd step in to help like he is without one advantage for himself."

"Oh, you don't think there are advantages?"

Matthew tossed his harness on the table. "Tarnation, Marilla . . . when did you become such a cynic?"

She put down her spoon and turned to him. "All right, yes. John Blythe is a good friend to us. We're beholden to him."

Matthew shook his head. "Got nothing to do with beholden. You're looking at the thing all topsy-turvy."

"Care to put me straight then?"

He hesitated, taking stock of Marilla. Coming to the conclusion that what he had to say was worth her temper, he nodded. "All right. Been on my mind for years. John's not a young bull anymore. He should've married a long time ago. But he didn't, and hasn't, and I know you're wised up to the feelings between men and women. You're lying to yourself if you won't acknowledge the obvious between you and John. I've held my tongue on the matter. God knows, I haven't the experience or business to speak on such things. But Marilla, as your older brother, it's high time you stop looking at a table and calling it an elephant."

"You mean the elephant in the room?"

"I mean, recognize what is!"

Matthew hardly ever raised his voice, and never at her. Instead of inflaming her anger, the truth shushed her. She wiped damp hands on her apron. The cold had turned her fingers purple-blue at the nail beds.

"Don't you think I pray every night for John to find a nice young woman to marry and give him sons and daughters to carry on the farm? Don't you think I know how good a man he is?" *Don't you think I know what love is?* She balled her fists. "I do."

Matthew said nothing, leaving Marilla with her own words

echoing back in the silence. They ate separately. He left his empty dish on the table. A dusty rose light bled out from beneath his bedroom door. She didn't bother with the parlor hearth. Instead, she took a bed warmer full of hot water up to her room, but it did little to thaw the chill.

The next day Matthew rigged up the buggy to drive Marilla to her Ladies' Aid Society meeting at Mrs. Irving's. After Marilla served as president for nearly ten years, the baton had been passed to Mrs. Irving. Rachel had been vice president for a short year but had to resign to take over for her mother in running the Sunday school and the Foreign Missions Auxiliary, in addition to the sewing circle, the Avonlea School committee, and her own farmhouse of nine, now ten. Marilla thought it best to do one thing and do it well, so she continued on as a board member of the Ladies' Aid Society.

Women trickled through the picketed front gate as Matthew put the carriage wheels to park. Marilla straightened her hat and the fur collar of her coat.

"We won't be but a couple of hours." It was the first time she'd spoken to him since the night before.

"All right. I'll be here to fetch you."

She gave him a conciliatory grin. He was the last person she wanted strife with.

"Thank you, Matthew."

He held her hand to help her down. When her boot hit the ground, she felt his hand stiffen. Turning, she came face to face with Johanna Knox and her sisters coming across the sidewalk.

"Well, hello, Miss Cuthbert." Johanna pushed back the feathers of her cap and nodded up to Matthew in the buggy.

"Mrs. Knox, what a surprise," Marilla greeted. "I'll see you later, Matthew."

Thank goodness for Matthew's beard, which hid the majority

of his face from the former Miss Andrews. Marilla alone noticed the reddening of his nose tip. He gave the reins a joggle and off the horse went.

Marilla turned back to the ladies. "What's brought you back to town, Mrs. Knox?"

Johanna had gone to White Sands and married the son of the First Savings and Loan president, Mr. Joseph Knox. It was whispered across Avonlea social circles that she'd always had her heart set on marrying up.

Marilla thought Johanna awfully pretentious. A man ought to be judged by the richness of his heart, not his pockets. Despite Johanna's rebuff and marriage to Joseph Knox, Matthew refused to speak one harsh word against her. But he still winced whenever the old wound was grazed. Seeing her face to face was like having salt rubbed in that wound. Marilla wasn't sure whom to be most frustrated with: Johanna for showing up unexpectedly, or Matthew for continuing to pine for her.

She understood her brother well enough to know he wasn't covetous. He didn't yearn for the married woman Johanna was now, but for the girl she had been. That person was fixed in the broken mirror of his memory, and Marilla was hard-pressed to make him see the present-day reflection.

"My husband has business in Avonlea. I came along to see my sisters." Johanna's speech had taken on a strange British lilt. Marilla could only assume it was her new Mrs. Knox of White Sands voice. "Franny mentioned the society meeting, and I thought I might join you. See if I can aid somehow." She ran her hand over the beaded purse dangling at her elbow. "Funds in a provincial place like this can be difficult to procure. I'd like to do my part—give back to the community that raised me."

There were few things that rankled Marilla as much as backhanded goodwill.

"The return of the prodigal," she said. "We welcome you with open arms."

She didn't wait for Johanna's reply. Instead, she moved out of the cold and into Mrs. Irving's warm tearoom smelling of baked sugar shortbread and maple creams.

XXVIII.

A CHRISTMAS PARTY

All anyone could talk about going into December was the Blairs. After having their shop for as long as Marilla could recall, they decided to close up the one-room depot in Avonlea and allow their son William to expand the business to a larger, bona-fide store in Carmody. The roads had been vastly improved since Marilla's childhood, making it a far faster and easier journey than before. She could harness up the buggy and ride into Carmody in under an hour. Besides, the Blairs were too old to be carrying parcels and climbing stools for products in the store. William had joined the family merchant business with two grown daughters, a son, and three grandchildren.

"Blairs' General Store in Avonlea Closing" read the notice on the post office bulletin board. It caused quite a stir with a number of Avonlea's older set, moving some nearly to tears as they wondered where in the world they'd get their lye soap, paraffins, and milled oats. The following week the report was amended: "New, Bigger Store Opening in Carmody under the Management of William J. Blair." So while they grumbled at not being able to walk to the shop, they were relieved that the Blair family would continue on in their trade.

To celebrate the occasion of the Blairs' townhouse being restored to a home, Mr. and Mrs. Blair were hosting a holiday party on the first Saturday of December. A passing of the torch: William and his family would be there to toast his parents' legacy and pledge fidelity to the Blairs' loyal patrons at the new Carmody site.

The announcement made Marilla think of Izzy. She'd become a prosperous dressmaker running one of the Underground Railroad's safe houses in St. Catharines. At over sixty years old, she was doing much *more* than most women her age, and that would never have been possible had she wed William J. Blair. Izzy was happy, and so was Marilla . . . and Matthew, the Sisters of Charity, and Queen Elizabeth I of England. History held plenty more examples of the unmarried being happy. Who said a man or a woman had to be a husband or a wife? Maybe they could simply be, unto themselves. Besides, there were bigger issues in the world than love doves and wedding bells.

At that week's Ladies' Aid Society meeting, they were set to vote on what product to sell at the Avonlea Christmas market—fruit jams versus needlepoint handkerchiefs—when Mrs. Sloane brought up the subject of colored thread prices.

"Exorbitant!" she bemoaned. "The highest I've ever seen. They might as well be spun of silk not cotton."

"It's the trouble in America," explained Mrs. Barry. "Cotton's gone sky high, from thread to fabric."

"I hope their President Lincoln does something about it."

"I'm afraid he may be the cause. The states are on the verge of mutiny."

"Maybe it'll do them good—like our rebellions. Look at Canada now? United!"

The women erupted in chatter, ignoring all of Mrs. Irving's calls for order. She finally gave up trying to steer the discussion back to jam and hankies and joined their debate.

"I have a third cousin down in Wilmington," she told Marilla. "She says it's even more severe than the papers report. The slaves are rising up, murdering, thieving, and running off north. Madness. She put her thirteen-year-old son Heyward on a boat and sent him to relations in Scotland. They're after blood in the southern states. I just pray it doesn't come to that."

Mrs. Irving went on about her distraught cousin in North Carolina, but Marilla's mind was adrift. She worried over Izzy and those she sheltered.

At home that night, Marilla wrote to her. They'd kept up their correspondence through the years. The letters arrived in spurts, more in the colder months when they were both locked indoors. They'd developed their own kind of code regarding the runaways. The slaves were called "distinguished guests" who visited Izzy's dress shop in search of "modified costuming" for their "specific line of work" or "special occasion." On those pretenses, Izzy wrote of the nervous girls who gained confidence in a well-tailored dress. The cook who said she felt like a queen under a bright peony bonnet. The mothers who grinned with pride at their children dressed in new petticoats and pantalets. It did her heart good, Izzy wrote, to service such appreciative clients.

Marilla knew it was much more than that. Their costumes were their salvation, transformative as Cinderella on the night of the ball, and Izzy was their fairy godmother. Izzy hadn't returned to Green Gables since Clara's death, but somehow it felt like she'd always been there. Magically. If one could be of practical mind and believe in such.

༄

On the eve of the Blair Christmas party, their cow Bonny-D, Darling's granddaughter, caught a nail in her hoof.

"I can't leave her," Matthew argued. "Got to make sure the wound doesn't fester."

Despite Matthew's pretense of regret, Marilla saw his relief. His preference for avoiding group gatherings had grown ever more pronounced as the years went on. She hardly blinked when he said he wasn't going to the party and realized that she'd known all along something would prevent him from attending. Matthew's ways were set and she accepted them, just as he accepted hers.

The temperature had risen above freezing. While the roads were dry, the wet of unseen snow lingered lightly on the breeze, smelling of pine and winter sea.

"I think I'll walk to the party," she told Matthew. "Won't be very many days like this left. There's roast beef and turnips on the stove. I'll give your apologies to everyone."

And off she went with a crock of marmalade and a bottle of red currant wine tied up in colored tissue paper. She reached the Blairs' as the last shard of blue daylight turned plummy. What had been the old storefront window was now lit with candles. A woolly fir tree stood tall in the middle, its needled boughs drooping ever so slightly under the weight of twinkling glass ornaments, candy canes, and small pears balanced on top of them. An army of guests' presents, in every color of paper and ribbon, had been stacked beneath. One of the little Pye boys stole a peppermint off the tree and raced to the corner to devour it. A fiddle and a fife trilled out carols, and from the sway of the crowd inside, Marilla knew they were already dancing.

She took in the night: home and friends and all that she cherished. She wished she could stay right where she was, comfortably watching the festivities unfold like a storybook. The problem was, the minute she entered the page would turn.

"Marilla?" said Mr. Blair from the door. "Come in, dear. Mrs. Blair has been asking after you—is that there a bottle of Cuthbert wine?"

She pulled the gifts from her basket. "Wine and fruit. Spirits and sweetness to celebrate William's new business in Carmody and your home restored."

He patted the door frame like a living thing. "What was old is new again. Life's seasons never cease evolving. Makes a person want for two lives to spend, eh?"

She smiled. If only.

She entered the party, gave her apologies for Matthew's absence, and took a cup of rum punch. On Mrs. Blair's insistence, she sang half a dozen carols, played a game of Lookabout, and did a jig with Reverend Bentley—who stepped on her foot thrice—before retiring to the side with a slice of fruitcake. Only then did she see John, gallant as ever: he wore a dark vested suit, his hair was slicked back, and the wisps of silver at his temples winked at her under the gas-lit sconces. Age had only refined him. He caught her stare and grinned while Mrs. Bell and Mrs. Sloane buzzed around him. Maybe it was the punch or the heat of the fire, the fiddler's bow or the season at large, but she let herself feel loving toward him.

As quickly as the fondness lit, she snuffed it out.

"I must get home," she told Mrs. Blair.

"Must you?"

"Yes, Matthew will be waiting up for me."

"Thank you again for the gifts." Old Mrs. Blair had softened too with age. She embraced Marilla. "You and your brother don't be strangers. The store might be closed, but our door's always open."

Marilla promised. Then, feeling John's gaze burning across the room, Marilla slipped quickly through the crowd and out. The cool night sobered her senses, and she was glad for it. In a short walk, the main road gave way to pastureland. The town lamplight dwindled, and the starless night cast a violet shade. In the distance were the gulf's crashing waves. The wind blew in one steady gust, and then held its breath to allow a single white speck to drift. Marilla put out her mitten to catch it, but it disappeared before landing. Another followed. Then another. And all at once the air was a latticework of falling snow. She leaned her head back and let it knit across her eyelashes, nose, and lips. Beautiful, but by the velocity of descent, she reckoned it could be a foot high by the time she reached Green Gables. She picked up her pace while the roads were still solid to the boot.

There came the vibration of the horse hooves before she saw the carriage behind her.

"Whoa now!" called the driver.

Marilla could only make out his silhouette. The snow had accumulated around the carriage top like the brim of a fur hat.

She shielded her eyes from the snow as she would from the sun. "Who's there?"

John leaned out of the shadow with his hand extended to her. "Save your feet from freezing . . . that is, if you don't mind riding with an old Grit like me."

She hadn't time to wince at the quip; her heart was too busy pounding up her throat and out as a laugh. She was more surprised by it than John. Therein lay the nub of their friction. He'd always been able to vex her.

The snow picked up even more. She could hardly see six inches in front of her face, never mind the quarter of a mile to Green Gables. It would've been foolish to continue on foot, so she took his hand and climbed into the warm seat beside him. He pulled the coverlet over both of their laps and gave the reins a flick. The horse took to a trot, and she had to hold on to John's arm to stay clear of the snowdrift.

"It was a nice party," said John.

"Very."

"I must admit, I've never been to a place with indoor gas lighting. I felt like a bumpkin staring at those flickering flames. Bright as day in the middle of the night."

Marilla had thought the same when the Blairs put in the lights, but that was over six months ago, when the store was still open. "You've been gone a while."

"First time the Blythe fields hadn't brought seed to harvest." He frowned. "Didn't feel right."

Marilla understood. No seedtime, no harvest; empty fields, empty cellar. She shuddered to imagine. "Must've been hard to go."

"Even harder to come back."

"Rupert's Land must be some kind of wonder—to make a man leave his farm, his town, and all."

He cleared his throat. "Remember when I told you I'd take you there?"

How could she forget? She looked down at the reins in his hand. He always smelled faintly of leather straps and pinewood. She let herself lean in closer. Not enough to be noticed, but enough.

"I do."

He put one cautious hand on hers beneath the coverlet.

"I did a lot of thinking while I was away, Marilla. I—I wondered if we might make amends."

Finally. She loved John, even when she couldn't say it, even when they were parted by discord.

"I've done my share of thinking too."

He let the reins slacken in his left hand and tightened his grip on hers with his right. The horse slowed to a *clip-clop*.

She'd kept her promise to care for her father, her brother, Green Gables . . . maybe it was time to let someone care for her. They could make it work: the Blythe farm on one side of town, Green Gables on the other. Nothing was impossible if they put their two heads together. She remembered the steady *click* of chalk sticks against their school slates and the warmth of John's embrace those many years ago. It had been spring when they first met. Spring when they first kissed. Spring. As Reverend Bentley preached: so long as the earth endured, there would be day and night, cold and heat, winter and spring. Sometimes one winter could last longer than another.

She'd been in a wintering way for twenty years. John's return could be her turn of season. Her spring.

Softness blossomed in her chest even as the snow blustered between them. His gaze was a fire of hope. A happy chill went through her.

"I think we can," she said.

John nodded. "This thing between us has gone on long enough."

"Indeed." It was exhausting to be perpetually defensive. Like a boat anchored against the pull of the tide.

"I'm glad we are to be friends again," he said with a wink.

Oh that devilish wink, how she'd missed it! She wanted to kiss him right then but didn't know how. Her lips burned for him even as he let go of her hand to take up the reins. The road banks were beginning to pile up with snow. He gave the horse a double-snap to move along.

They sat for a short while in silence, and for one of the first times in her life, she wished desperately for conversation: to tell him all the things he'd missed over the years, to hear all that she'd missed in his travels, to know him again, and for him to know her, so that not one scar would remain hidden. They would know all.

"Marilla?" She turned eagerly at his call.

"Yes, John?" How good it felt to say his name again without bitterness or guilt or remorse.

"I wanted to talk to you about something else too."

His Adam's apple bobbled, and she smiled at the old trait—glad to see it hadn't gone away.

"There's a girl—well, a woman—the daughter of a veterinarian I met out west."

It came out of nowhere and jolted her so fiercely that she nearly fell out of the moving buggy. She'd prayed for such a thing, said it time and time again, but to have it come to fruition now . . . her heart broke all over again. The rest of the ride home, she counted out her breaths: one-two-three-four in, one-two-three-four out, one-two-three-four in, one-two-three-four out.

Green Gables was a beacon in a sea of white by the time they reached the front yard.

"I'm glad we talked," said John. "I needed to right things between us."

She smiled through the salty snowflakes in her eyes. It was all she could do. She hid her crumpled face beneath her bonnet and raced up to her room before Matthew could ask how the party had gone. As quietly as possible, she emptied herself of tears, and then berated herself for being an emotional ninny. He'd merely mentioned the other woman, and she was far off in Rupert's Land. He couldn't foster a relationship at such a distance, could he? She'd never experienced a traditional courtship, so she couldn't say for sure. All she knew of love was him.

XXIX

A TELEGRAM

When Marilla went to pick up the Monday mails, she was surprised to find a telegram:

THE MONTREAL TELEGRAPH COMPANY
TO MISS AND MR. CUTHBERT

RECEIVED AT AVONLEA, P.E.I.
FROM MISS ELIZABETH JOHNSON, ST. CATHARINES, CANADA
WEST

MY DEARS, IT'S BEEN TOO LONG SINCE I VISITED. CHRISTMAS SEEMS THE PERFECT TIME TO BE IN THE SAFEKEEPING
OF FAMILY. I'LL BE ARRIVING DECEMBER 24 WITH MR. MEACHUM, MY BUTLER, AND TWO HOUSEBOY SERVANTS. I KNOW
GREEN GABLES WILL WELCOME DISTINGUISHED GUESTS.
MY LOVE, AUNT IZZY

"A butler and houseboys?" asked Matthew while moving two pallets up to the hired hand's room.

Marilla was tying tartan bows on the pine garlands she'd threaded through the stair balusters.

"A person slows down quite a piece by her age. If you don't have family nearby to help you along, then you'd have to bring help in from somewhere, right?" She straightened the loopy ears of the bow.

"Suppose so," said Matthew from the upper landing. "Age and health do change a person. Izzy's made a big name for herself in St. Catharines. Perhaps it's the way of the well-to-do."

Marilla stuck a pin in the bow to hold it in place, wishing she had one for her nerves as well. Their code was clear: "distinguished guests" meant that Izzy was coming with runaways. What she didn't know was who exactly they might be—Mr. Meachum, the servants, or unmentioned others. She'd read the telegram backward and forward to decipher it but still couldn't say for sure. So she funneled all her energy into decorating the Gables.

They didn't usually do this much. Marilla set a balsam wreath on the table to bring in the scent, with a candle in the center to shed light. She would also make a batch of gingersnaps, and they'd have cups of mulled currant wine. A church service on Christmas Eve would be followed by quiet reflection on Christmas morn. That's how they'd done it for the past too many years to count. But that wouldn't do with guests of any sort, and certainly not when two of them were children. Family, servants, or escaping slaves, children were children. And if on no other day of the year, impartiality should be celebrated at Christmas.

She'd gone over to William Blair's new store at Carmody to pick up the tartan ribbon, ginger, cinnamon, coffee, a store-bought holiday card for Izzy, the new *Harper's Weekly* for Matthew, and peppermint candies for the little ones. They'd stopped bringing in a tree years ago. Such a cumbersome chore. Marilla hated cleaning up the dry needles. But now, with company coming, a tree was essential. It'd be un-Christian to go without!

"On my way home from William Blair's, I drove the sleigh the back way," she called up to Matthew. "Spotted a nice five-foot fir along the wood line. I don't want anything taller. Too hard to decorate."

"Aye," said Matthew. "I'll take my ax out as soon as I'm done with these sleepers. Where do you want 'em?"

"Under the bed for now. Mr. Meachum can pull them out at night for the lads."

She listened to the tick mattresses being pushed across the floorboards overhead. She hated keeping a secret this big from Matthew, but she'd been keeping it for so long that she hadn't a notion of where to even start.

"Do you think I ought to get Mr. Meachum and the houseboys gifts for Christmas?" she fretted. "I reckon they're being paid for their time, but I feel poorly not offering something." She stood at the bottom of the stairs inspecting her cascade of banister ribbons. "We've never had house staff here. What *does* one do with a butler and servants in another's home anyhow?" She pulled the tail of a bow so that it sat straighter.

Matthew put a hand on her shoulder. "You're giving them the gift of hospitality—you're giving us all that, Marilla." He looked up the stairs with a smile. "The Gables haven't looked so well since Mother was alive."

"I probably should've done more to make it special all these years." She leaned into his side. "It feels good to make a home so pleasing."

"You've always made it pleasing. Just by being here." He kissed the crown of her head then pushed off toward the kitchen, where his ax lay inside the wood box.

"I'll have hot potatoes and curds for supper when you get back."

He put on his coat and cap, slung the ax over his shoulder, and inhaled sharply at the chill of the open door. Marilla put the potatoes in the stove, then went around setting lantern candles in each window so that the Gables winked brightness into the night. Soon enough, Matthew returned with a pert blue-green fir strapped to his pull sleigh, not a breath over five feet.

"It's perfect."

While Matthew ate his supper, Marilla spread the bristled branches in the parlor and decorated the boughs with fat walnuts, candied fruits, colorful bits of broken glass and seashells, tartan ribbon, and strings of cranberries that she'd needle-threaded herself. On the top, she placed a star of Bethlehem made of copper. It glistened in the candlelight. She couldn't remember a prettier tree.

Matthew was no musician, but William Blair had sold him a harmonica, calling it the "newest instrumental rage of the century." Matthew had learned to play a handful of tunes. Marilla was a proponent of anything that kept his hands off the tobacco pipe. His heart was already an issue, with his lungs not far behind. Dr. Spencer said Matthew needed to exercise them more regularly, so she considered the French harp medicinal.

Seeing the parlor Christmas tree, Matthew sat down in the winged-back chair and put the little instrument to his lips. Slowly, he played "Silent Night," a longtime favorite of Marilla's. She took a seat across from him on the divan and leaned her head back to rest a moment.

Silent night, holy night,
All is calm, all is bright.
Round yon virgin, mother and child,
Holy infant so tender and mild.
Sleep in heavenly peace,
Sleep in heavenly peace . . .

The song brought on a tear, and Marilla didn't tense a muscle to stop it. Tears were misunderstood, she thought, and used inappropriately most often. They were designed as a private response of being. Because sometimes life filled you to the brim and spilled over. Tears were the body's way of cleansing the overflow of emotions, from sorrow to joy and so many others that couldn't be described. Like now. Marilla felt an overwhelming relief that a silent night was holy, that a calm could be bright, that a virgin could be a mother, and that death and sleep were two kinds of the same heavenly peace.

"Sleep in heavenly peace, Mother," she whispered to Matthew's tune. "Sleep in heavenly peace, Father."

The next day Matthew came back from town in an anxious fluster. Marilla was in the kitchen mixing up a new bread sponge, her hands covered in flour. He held the newspaper up in front of her nose, but she didn't have her spectacles on, so all she could see properly was the date: December 20, 1860.

"What is it, Matthew? Can't imagine anything causing such distress so close to the Yule." She waved him toward the wood box to take off his boots. He was leaving slushy footprints across her clean kitchen floor.

"South Carolina seceded from the United States. The other southern states will join it. America is about to crack in half. It means there's probably going to be a war at our doorstep."

Marilla's mind immediately went to Izzy and the "distinguished guests." Thank goodness she was coming to Green Gables, away from the border.

"All of this to keep their slaves in bondage?"

Matthew pulled off his boots. "That's not the only reason—or at least, so they claim."

Marilla frowned and wiped off her hands. "Let's not bring up politics while Izzy is here. Turns my stomach sour. Izzy's been gone all these years. I want us to have a happy Christmas without sully-ing it with war talk. Let the Americans handle their own business, and we'll handle ours."

"Discord doesn't end at a line in the dirt."

Yes, she knew that to be true, and yet she hoped that a line in the dirt could protect the innocent just the same.

"If that line is the Northumberland Strait, I don't see why not," she said and put the yeasty sponge above the stove to rise.

While Matthew added kindling to the parlor hearth, Marilla pulled on her eyeglasses to read the newspaper article.

Special from the London Times: This is the result of slavery. It began as tolerated. It is now an aggressive institution that threatens to dissolve the American Union and spread like a virus throughout the world. It must be inoculated for equality to root itself in our modern era. Negro or white. The color of a person's skin must not predicate freedom . . .

Matthew returned, so she quickly went back to cleaning her baking board, dusted over with brown-white speckles. The idea of bigotry based on color seemed foolish, laughable even, if it weren't so horrific. But people were killing and dying because of it. Red bled from all.

XXX

AUNT IZZY AND THE THREE MAGI

As dusk turned everything to blue velvet on Christmas Eve, a covered buggy trundled its way down Green Gables lane. The horse's jingle bells stilled when the buggy came to a halt at the front porch, and Matthew and Marilla hurried out to welcome their guests.

"You folks must be the Cuthberts." The driver stood and took off his hat with a bow. "I'm Martin Meachum."

An older gentleman, he was as tawny and tall as one of the Frenchmen from the West Indies. His eyes sparkled hazel against the bleak land. But there was no mistaking the curl of his hair or the pink underside of his palms.

For all her talk and advocacy, Marilla had never had a black man as a guest in her home, and she wondered why ever not. There were families of African descent in Avonlea, in Nova Scotia, and across the Canadian provinces. But they kept themselves apart from the broader white community, for reasons she understood were closely tied to the American unrest.

Mr. Meachum gave a magnetic smile and called, "Mademoiselle Izzy!"

His tone was so warm, Marilla found herself leaning in like a potted geranium toward the window.

Izzy's head popped through the curtained carriage window. Her hair had gone gray as a dove's breast, but she was beautiful as always. Marilla's heart stammered at the sight of what her mother would've been. Her vision tunneled at the peripheries, but she forced her eyes wide to the cold until it moored her.

"Is that my flower girl and Matthew?" Izzy swung the door open. "You've aged about as many days as I have—which I count as none!"

Mr. Meachum helped her down from the cab. Marilla noticed a slight sway and give of Izzy's body, like a beach reed. Another five inches of snow had fallen overnight, concealing the ice beneath the powder. It was easy for a boot to slip, so Mr. Meachum stayed close to steady her.

"Come on, boys," Izzy called into the carriage. "Meet my niece and nephew. No need to be bashful."

Marilla looked to Matthew, thinking it strange that houseboys should need coaxing. Two nut-brown faces peeked out, the younger from below the older.

Izzy introduced them: "This is Abraham and that's Albert."

Matthew grinned. "Welcome. It'll be nice to have more men about the place. Between Marilla, the dairy cows, and the hens, a fellow can feel lonesome for others of his kind."

The younger boy, Albert, dared to step out. The snow came to his knees. He ran a hand through it and marveled.

"So much," he whispered back to his brother. "Like a sand pit, only softer and cold."

Mr. Meachum cleared his throat. "Al's never seen this much snow."

"I seen seven winters, but I only remember the last three. Snows be like dandelion seeds in the harvest time, moving with the wind. Not like this—staying in one place and piling."

He turned to Abraham, who frowned and shushed him.

By their look and speech, these boys could only be from the American South. Marilla put a hand on Matthew, not for his sake but for her own.

"We got plenty more coming. Best get you settled," said Matthew. "I'll help Mr. Meachum with the luggage."

"There's hot tea and gingersnaps inside," said Marilla.

Abraham wore an old military cap with tassels that he pulled down low on his forehead. At the mention of gingersnaps, he raised the brim with a flinch of a smile, which he bit back between his teeth.

"Yes, let's get within. Don't look behind us or we'll turn to pillars of ice!" said Izzy.

Matthew helped Mr. Meachum unload the carriage while Izzy brought the boys up the porch and into the foyer.

"My Marilla," she said when finally embracing her niece.

Marilla closed her eyes and let herself fold into it. Lilacs. Time returned and rooted itself between them. She felt her mother's heart beating again; her father's quiet presence; the Gables sentient as spring; life and love muddled under a canopy of unseen possibilities. She was so wrapped up in the memories that she almost missed the wide gazes of the two boys.

The fir tree stood gigantic to their statures, each branch festooned with treats that glowed under the light of the purring hearth.

"I forgot it be Christmas."

It was the first time Marilla heard Abraham speak. Catching himself, he put a hand to his mouth.

Al swathed himself in the hem of Izzy's blue cape, then tugged on it to get her attention.

"Miss Izzy." He was quiet as a nesting sparrow. "It be just like the house in my dreams."

Izzy cupped his fawn cheek. "It's Marilla's house. Safer than dreams."

Marilla dared to give Izzy a look, but then Mr. Meachum and Matthew came through the front door with the trunks. They all proceeded upstairs to settle.

Marilla made up Izzy's old room in the East Gable, neat as a pin with its whitewashed walls and braided rug. Years before, she'd found one of Izzy's sewing cushions: red velvet like an apple off the bough. Marilla had set it on the three-corner table where the mirror hung so that the color refracted across the room. She brought in Izzy's yellow chair that had been by Clara's bedside and hung one of the muslin frills they'd made together across the window.

Izzy went to it, fingering the tatting at the edge. Then she held it aside to look out at the cherry tree, grown tall and thick with branches that tapped lightly against the house. Each spring it blossomed so fully that Marilla feared opening the window would give bridged access to every squirrel in Avonlea. In the flower garden that bordered the Gables bedrock, she'd planted lilac trees beside her mother's white Scotch roses, specifically for her aunt. Marilla knew Izzy would return one day.

"We made the North Gable, Mother and Father's room, into a spare. It's bigger, but I thought you might like this."

"It feels the same, even though they're gone. I thought I would feel differently." Izzy turned to kiss Marilla's cheek. "It's just as it should be—life keeps on."

Down the hall, Matthew showed Mr. Meachum and the boys into the hired hand's room.

"Hope you'll be comfortable."

"More than. We're grateful for a place to rest."

"It's hard to sleep during the day," yawned Al.

"Have you been night traveling?" asked Matthew.

"Miss Izzy wanted to be here in time for Christmas," explained Mr. Meachum. "Had to keep apace."

Marilla looked to Izzy, and Izzy seemed to read her thoughts. She took Marilla's hand and patted it. "It's the eve of our Savior's birth. Let's leave it at that. My heart's full of peace and joy to be here."

"Marilla?" Matthew called from the hall. "I think our young guests might be hungering for some of those snaps."

"Your belly be talking," said Al to his brother.

"No, it ain't," defended Abraham. "That's my shoe."

"Maybe it be mine then. Whenever I'm cold, I feel something emptier."

Izzy started toward them, but her knees gave a quiet buckle that only Marilla noticed.

"Let me," she said. "You change out of your traveling clothes. I'll take the boys down for a nibble while Mr. Meachum unpacks."

Izzy gave an appreciative smile. Her dimple had deepened under an eddy of wrinkles.

"Hot tea waiting for you when you're ready." Marilla closed the East Gable door and went out on the landing to Matthew and the boys. "Our cow Bonny-D's just done her night milking. I imagine it'd be a perfect pairing with the gingersnaps. Don't you think, Matthew?"

Matthew pursed his lips in consideration. "Well, I tend to think so, but warm, sweet milk from one of the island's best cows isn't to everyone's liking." He turned to Abraham. "How old are you?"

"Ten, suh."

Matthew nodded slowly. "Old enough to make up your own mind about such things. What's your opinion?"

Abraham gulped and when he did, his stomach gave up a little groan. Al cleared his throat in an I-told-you-so and Abraham elbowed him.

"I—I like fresh milk plenty, suh."

"Me too!" said Al.

Matthew stroked his beard. "Then it's settled. Three Christmas milks."

Marilla led them down to the parlor, where the boys dipped their gingersnaps in warm milk by the log fire. The combination had a soporific effect. They were half asleep by the time she led them back up to their room. Mr. Meachum had laid out their pallets.

"Dream sweetly, lads," said Izzy. "I'm away to bed too, dear." She was in her night robe, face washed dewy and hair neatly plaited. The only adornment was her quartz pendant—the wishing stone—glinting like the snow's shadow on the window sash. "Today was quite a journey. I have the utmost admiration for the Magi follow-ing the star." She winked. "Like them, what I've found at the desti-nation has fulfilled my hopes and dreams. You've done a beautiful job with the Gables. Clara would be so proud." She kissed Marilla's forehead.

"Good night to you," said Mr. Meachum. "And thank you again, Miss Marilla."

The footsteps in the hired hand's room soon went still. The light capped.

Only Matthew remained down in the parlor, reading.

Alone in the upper hallway, Marilla put a hand to each wall, north and south. The house was filled up with people. She closed her eyes to feel the warmth of breath and bodies through the boards. How good it was. Green Gables was built for family, and she delighted that the rooms were full. Her father had built them for a purpose.

It was a night when they believed in miracles. A virgin mother. The son of God. A star to guide the shepherds. So right then, with arms bolstered by each wall, she prayed for one: *Let life and love runneth over here.*

Instead of preparing the kitchen for the following morning, she went up to the attic. By a short wick of candlelight, she opened the cedar chest where she'd stored the extra scarves and mittens she knitted with her mother but outgrew before she'd had a chance to wear them. She'd chastised herself many times for hoarding them in the hope of "maybe one day." She never could decide what that one day might bring. So year after year she made extra items for the Hopetown orphans as penance for not being more willing to give and give up. Now it surprised her how eager she was to see them on Al and Abraham.

Marilla lifted the little mittens and ran her thumb over the finely crafted cables. What skill her mother had lacked in needlework she made up for in knitting. Marilla held the items to her lips, remembering the graceful movement of Clara's hands as she threaded and knotted the strands of wool together, the clicking of her needles like music. It was time these were put to use.

She wrapped two sets of gloves and scarves in brown paper with big bows made from the last of the tartan ribbon and placed them under the Christmas tree with peppermints.

"Happy Christmas to all," she whispered, then snuffed out her candle.

XXXI

A GREEN GABLES CHRISTMAS

Early the next morning the sky opened like the seam of a sugar bag, powdering the land and filling in the tracks with fresh snow. The timber in the hearth threw cheerful sparks. The boys were giddy, and it was catching. For the first time in many years, Marilla could think of no chores to be done. She was happy just to *be*.

"For us?" asked Al.

Marilla nodded. "Father Christmas knows where every child dwells."

Out of the corner of her eye, she saw Abraham flinch, then cast his gaze far out the window.

"Come," she said and pulled him close.

Gathered in the parlor, Matthew read a passage from their father's Bible: Luke 2. Izzy and Mr. Meachum bowed their heads in prayer while gusts of white flapped gently against the window-panes like angels' wings. The boys unwrapped their gifts, then ate their bellies plump on buttermilk biscuits studded with sweet currants, sprinkled with cinnamon, and drenched in maple syrup. Afterward, Matthew laid out the checkerboard on the three-legged table and the brothers set to a tournament.

While they swapped moves and good-natured jibes, the adults convened in the kitchen. Marilla brewed coffee, and Izzy ate her plain buttered biscuit. She hadn't changed in her predilections. She cozied up in her same spot at the wooden table, with Mr. Meachum by her side and Matthew across.

"My niece is a famous cook."

"I can see why." Mr. Meachum took another biscuit from the plate. "Mighty grateful for the sustenance, Miss Marilla. My boys, especially, could use it."

Marilla caught the pronoun: "my"? Mr. Meachum seemed too old to be their father, but then, she was unfamiliar with how those things might go. It was obvious that he was some relation. She poured steaming coffee into cups.

"Abraham and Al are solid lads," Izzy said. "Just need a bit more meat on their bones for the kind of winters they'll see in Canada."

"Are they to be staying in St. Catharines with you now?" asked Matthew.

Mr. Meachum cleared his throat, but Izzy put a hand on his before he could speak. The intimate gesture surprised even Matthew, whose query showed on his face.

"Marilla, Matthew," said Izzy. "You're my family, and I've never feared truth between us. We've shared much."

Marilla sat down at the table.

Izzy looked to Mr. Meachum confidently, and he turned his hand over so that it grasped hers.

"Martin is not my butler," said Izzy. "He is my truest companion. We met ten years ago, through the Reverend Mother at Hopetown. Martin was a contact for the orphanage, helping to bring children up from America by way of the Underground Railroad. We had a friendship based on admiration and common mission. Soon enough, however, it became much more."

She squeezed his hand and something in the gesture made Marilla's stomach tighten: the memory of her own hand in John's.

"I offered Martin a job as my dress shop assistant and butler so we could continue our work with the runaways. It's an effective disguise. No one suspects an old spinster dressmaker and her shop butler of anything. It has allowed us to be together, unconventional as it may be."

Marilla had stopped breathing at some point. Now she drew in a deep breath. She wasn't sure what to think. Her aunt was in a relationship with a man, a black man—and a former slave? She looked to Matthew, who'd taken out his pipe. For once, she would not admonish him for smoking.

"So . . ." She rubbed the twinge in her forehead. Where to begin? With the most pressing question, she decided: "Are Mr. Meachum and the boys runaway slaves?"

"I am free," Mr. Meachum answered. "The boys are my grandsons. When my wife passed away of sickness, our five children were sold to various plantations across southern America. My master promised me that I could buy my freedom, which I did lawfully, and then I moved to St. Catharines. There I was introduced to Mr. Jermain Loguen and the Underground Railroad while attempting to learn the whereabouts of my children. Nothing could be found. So I pledged myself to the Railroad's mission. I worked with the nuns in Hopetown and, through them, met Izzy." He squeezed her hand. "We've been able to secure safe passage for hundreds through the years."

"And then Martin received word of his own kin," said Izzy.

"My daughter in South Carolina tried to run. Her master caught her and cut off the toes of her right foot so she couldn't escape again—she can hardly walk now. When the South Carolina General Assembly stated its intention to secede last month, she knew it was then or never to get her boys out. She'd learned that I was in St. Catharines, and so she gave over her children to an Underground Railroad conductor bound for the border. The day I received word of their impending arrival, your aunt sent you the telegram. Izzy's is a safe house, but not a permanent stop. Every slave-catcher from America searches our city. We provide the resources to keep moving to delivery locations, but this was the first time that *we* were that location."

"To protect the boys and our operations, we had to get out of St. Catharines as quickly as possible," Izzy explained. "Thus, my hasty telegram. I apologize for that. But the safest and most plausible place for us to journey without suspicion was Green Gables."

"Christmas with family," said Marilla. "No apologies or explanation needed."

Izzy smiled. "I knew we could trust you."

Marilla had long been aware that a quiet but powerful force was at work between Canada and America. She'd seen a glimpse of it as a girl and watched it grow over the years, but she'd never discussed it with Matthew. She looked to him now to gauge his reaction. He puffed on his pipe. The smoke wreathed his head. He sucked once, twice, then a third time before taking it out of his mouth.

"These boys brought you home and we're grateful. You're our family. So as I reckon, if you call Mr. Meachum family, then he and his are ours too."

Marilla palmed the table in agreement, and the coffee in all four cups rippled dark.

"You're welcome to stay as long as you need," she said.

Izzy leaned forward and kissed her cheek. "Bold and beguiling. As always."

Mr. Meachum shook Matthew's hand, then took Izzy's again, and there passed between them a gaze that Marilla could only describe as love. It gave her hope that a person could find it anywhere and at any time. The heart was a limitless territory if one was willing to risk it all.

❧

Three days after Christmas, Rachel came for a visit.

"When I heard Miss Izzy Johnson was in town, I told Robert

to hitch up the sleigh and take me over to Green Gables so I could show off the Cuthberts' godchild."

Mr. Meachum and the boys were helping Matthew with the barn chores. Robert had taken the horse there to keep dry and warm away from the snow while the women did the same by the kitchen stove. Izzy held the sleeping baby Hughie.

"He's perfect."

"He takes after his namesake. The quietest of all my children. I've only heard him cry but the once, and that was on account of his sister dropping a shoe on his face." Rachel ran her finger over his cheek. "He's a sweetheart, this one."

"Well, I'm honored to meet him, and I can say with all certainty that Hugh would've loved him too."

"He's lucky number twelve."

"Like the apostles," said Izzy.

"Ten living children plus me and Thomas, that does add up to an evangelical dozen." Rachel beamed. "It's good to have you back with us, Miss Izzy."

"Please tell your mother hello for me. It's been too long. How is she?"

"Oh, you know Mother. Since Father's passing, she's done nothing but dote on the grandchildren . . . and clean up after they visit!" Rachel laughed.

"Mrs. White hasn't changed a day," said Marilla. "Ella is still working for her too."

"How's that sweet girl?"

"Mighty fine. Got five little ones of her own now," replied Rachel.

"My, my . . . a gracious plenty." Izzy gently rocked Hughie. "We'll move over to the parlor so you girls can have your tea talk without waking him."

"Oh, no worries. That child sleeps through nine brothers and sisters jumping rope. A little kettle whistle won't be a thing."

"Just the same. We'll go settle in by the Christmas tree. Something about a Christmas tree and a sleeping babe rejuvenates the spirit." And off she went before anyone could argue.

"She's going to the cushioned sofa," said Marilla. "Her bones ache her."

"Is it the arthritis?"

Marilla nodded. "I think so. Of course, she never would mention it, but I've seen the way she bears down when she moves."

Rachel shook her head. "The body is a fair-weather friend. Loves you when you're too young and stupid to appreciate it, then grows ever more petulant with each passing year until finally"—she threw up her hands—"the gears halt, whether you're ready or not."

Marilla set the leftover Christmas biscuits on a plate and put the water kettle on the stove. "Rachel Lynde, I never thought you to be one of those fire-and-brimstone, death-is-coming sorts."

"Well the end *is* coming, isn't it? We spend our entire lives running from it. No speaking of it allowed. Fearing it for our loved ones." She shook her head and folded the burp cloth in her hand. "But after all we've seen of the world, I decided I'll get more joy out of the days I have left if I just acknowledge that death is part of life. The leaves on an apple tree blossom yield and fall. No use fretting over the sweetness of the fruit. Got to pick it when it looks ripe and move on. It's the fool who's forlorn over what he imagines he's lost. I'm sure that's in the Gospel somewhere."

Even if it wasn't, Rachel would amend the text to her liking. The Word according to Rachel, as some complained. Not Marilla, of course. Rachel was her closest friend, so she kept quiet, in Cuthbert fashion. He that hath knowledge spareth his words—that was from the Proverbs, and underlined by Hugh in their family Bible. She exercised that restraint now, not knowing exactly where her friend was going with this sermon. Sometimes Rachel got off on a relatively everyday idea and wouldn't stop until she'd turned it into a homily. A change of subject would nip it in the bud.

"Lucky for us, we have a generous orchard and more in our harvest baskets than we know what to do with. The cellar is full up on jammed fruits. Might your young'uns like some jars of applesauce or plums to start the New Year? We got plenty for the eating." The kettle whistled, and Marilla poured the water over a batch of black Assam leaves in the teapot.

"Best orchard on the island is here at Green Gables. Thomas is partial to your famous blue plums."

Rachel too, Marilla was well aware. She started in the direction of the pantry.

"I'll fetch a few jars."

Rachel put a hand on her wrist to stop her.

"Marilla, I got something I need to get off my chest. It's been hounding me. I've barely slept for it."

A hot flash of concern: had their secret about the boys gotten out? Avonlea was a little town. But none of them had left Green Gables since their arrival. The snow had kept on, only stopping the night before. Rachel was the first person she'd seen on the road, and only because she lived so near.

"Whatever it is, please unburden yourself. I hate to think you're losing rest on my account."

Rachel gave a sad sort of face. "I said to Thomas, I know it don't matter, but I know it *do* matter. He said I ought to bring it up after Christmas. As soon as I could get you alone from your company. I didn't want it to come as a surprise from someone else and . . ." She shrugged.

"You're starting to frighten me, Rachel."

Steam rose from the teapot spout on the table.

"All right. I won't sugarcoat it." Rachel gave a resolved nod. "John Blythe married a girl. She's not from these parts. A veterinarian's daughter, so I hear. It was a modest ceremony with only John, the bride, and her parents. No friends at all invited. They exchanged vows in the Charlottetown preacher's living room. Guess it happened after the Blairs' party. They've spent the holiday in Boston as a kind of honeymoon." Rachel shook her head but did not meet Marilla's gaze. "Scandalous. A girl from Rupert's Land? A honeymoon in Boston? America is on the verge of war, and there they are, romancing through the streets!"

The room swayed. Marilla steadied herself against the ledge of the table.

Sensing upset, Rachel babbled on: "She's ten years his junior, mind you. Appalling! What does that make her—thirty? Well, I suppose that is rather long in the tooth. But an impromptu wedding over a fortnight ago with no invitations sent out, no wedding march, no formalities at all? They probably didn't even have a cake—good heavens! Hardly a real nuptial at all. I wonder if the preacher was even ordained."

A shrill ringing began in Marilla's left ear. She pulled at her earlobe to try to make it stop, but it continued, piercing into her neck and up the side of her cheek.

Rachel's hands moved nervously. She gave them the task of pouring the tea Marilla had neglected.

"Here. Drink this, Marilla. You're pale as a gilled mushroom."

"I haven't eaten much today," she lied, immediately feeling guilty for it.

She should be happy for John. But years of righteous sentiment had vanished in a blink. All she felt was regret. Marilla was not the kind to spend a long time musing on her feelings, but now she was incapable of thinking of anything else. Rachel was wrong. A person was a fool, not for being forlorn, but for not having the good sense to take a bite when the fruit was in her hand. The problem was, she hadn't realized until now that she was starving.

She ate a biscuit without tasting a thing and washed it down with her tea. That momentarily pacified her nausea.

"I'm glad you told me, Rachel. I'm glad for John. I . . ." She got up. "Let me get those plum preserves."

In the pantry, with only the army of jarred fruits and vegetables to witness, she covered her eyes with a hand. It was all she could do against the bedlam within.

Footsteps thudded the floorboards from the back kitchen door.

"Marilla?"

Matthew with young Robert and Mr. Meachum.

She swallowed hard, pulled the jams from the shelf, and turned with as untroubled a countenance as she could manufacture. She'd think about John tomorrow. There was enough for today. *My cup,* she thought, *runneth over.*

XXXII.

INTRODUCING MRS. JOHN BLYTHE

A leg of mutton was to be supper for Hogmanay—New Year's Eve. Early that morning Marilla took up her shopping hamper and started out across the fields to the butcher's.

The sky was a glaze of bright blue, with not a cloud and the sun so bright, she might've thought it was June if not for her frostbitten nose. The warmth on her shoulders and the steady push of her feet through the snow were comforts. Nature cleared her mind.

Entering the butcher's shop, she saw only shadow figures. Her pupils were slow to release their contraction from the light. For a long minute, she thought one of the hanging ham hocks was a set of eyes and grinning mouth. She might have said good-day to it if Theo Houston hadn't come out from the back carrying two plucked chickens that very moment.

"Miss Cuthbert, happy Hogmanay to ya!"

She widened her eyes so that the shadows fled and her vision returned to normal.

"The same to you, Theo. I've come for a leg of mutton for our New Year's roast."

"Lucky you, only one left! Everything else has been sold. Busy during the holidays." He hung the chickens upside down on hooks, then wiped his hands clean on his apron. "I hear you got company over at Green Gables."

"My Aunt Izzy." She nodded. "You were still in pantalets when she last visited. Doubt you remember her."

"Lots of new faces these days. Town's full up on folks."

"And I guess they all have a taste for mutton."

He laughed. "So it seems. Let me grab the last for you."

He went back through the curtain, and the bell over the front door jingled. Voices spilled in.

She gave a glance over her shoulder to a couple silhouetted against the light. The man quickly took off his hat and turned to the woman. Marilla's eyes alighted on a little shadow indent just below the peppered hairline.

"John?" She hadn't meant to speak; it'd been a thought that slipped over her lips.

On his arm was a woman with doe eyes, peach cheeks, and a smile as wide as the day's sky. She looked far younger than Marilla had at thirty years of age. One could always tell those who'd grown up in the Maritimes and those who had not. The island winds left their mark on a face, raw and unmistakable. This woman had hardly been kissed by a breeze.

"Marilla—I—that is . . ." John's tongue knotted. "I've been meaning to call on you and Matthew—to make introductions—but I heard you had family in town and we're just back from America."

His breath gave out. His Adam's apple bobbled on the intake.

"This is Katherine. Katherine Blythe."

Marilla looked to his wife, an unknown, friendly face that carried no memories in its fresh curves.

"Marilla Cuthbert." She held out her hand.

The woman let go of John's arm and stepped closer. "Please call me Kitty." She took Marilla's hand. "I've heard so many good things about you, Miss Cuthbert. John says the Cuthberts are practically family. So I'd be honored if you'd do me the kindness of calling me family too. I have much to learn about Avonlea. All I know are the stories John's told me."

"Marilla. Just call me plain Marilla. The 'Miss' makes me feel . . . old." She did her best to smile.

"Marilla," Kitty repeated, and it did sound a soothing tone coming from her.

Kitty's nut-brown hair was gathered in dainty coils held at the back of her neck with a comb. When she turned her head, the light caught the gems in it, winking violet.

For want of something neutral to say, Marilla ventured, "Your comb is lovely. Amethyst is my favorite."

Kitty put a delicate hand to her head. "John bought this for me in Boston. A honeymoon present." She looked to him admiringly, and the comb glimmers danced across Marilla's cheek. "I like colored stones more than diamonds. They're so much more interesting, don't you think?"

Before Marilla could reply, John intervened: "We came to see about Theo's mutton."

"So many sheep here," said Kitty. "John says the livestock is the best in the Maritimes. Something about the soil?"

"It's iron-rich," explained Marilla. "The animals graze on the grass, so the meat is more nutritious."

Kitty blinked her long dark lashes. "How wonderful."

Hearing his name, Theo came from the back carrying the leg.

"Mr. Blythe and . . ." He looked to Kitty curiously.

"The new Mrs. Blythe," said Marilla. "She's just come to Avonlea. You'll be seeing a lot of her." She turned to Kitty. "This is Theo Houston, our butcher."

Theo's eyes darted between the three. "Yes, of course! I heard of your recent nuptials, Mr. Blythe. Congratulations and a pleasure to meet you, Mrs. Blythe."

"You too, Mr. Houston." Her eyes registered the leg he carried. "Is that mutton?"

"It is. The last bit in the shop."

"However did you know—you must be a prophetic butcher!" She clapped.

Theo frowned with confusion, and Marilla thought it best if she stepped in to keep the awkwardness at bay.

"Indeed, he has a gift for intuition." She gave him a solid look. "Now, Theo, you go on and wrap up that leg for Mrs. Blythe. I think I'll take some of your smoked ham."

Theo nodded slowly. "Whatever you say, Miss Cuthbert."

She turned to Kitty. "That mutton would be excellent with a little garlic, rosemary, salt, and pepper if you have it."

"I believe so," said Kitty.

"A leg that size, I'd roast it over the hearth slowly for two hours. A little longer if needed. Until the juices run clear. Should be enough to feed you both for a few suppers."

"Oh, thank you! John tells me you're a famous cook, so I'm ever so beholden to you for sharing your secret recipes."

Marilla shook her head. "Nothing secret about a recipe. It's how you put it together that makes it yours."

"Well, I hope I do you proud, Miss—Marilla."

A sweet girl, gracious and genuinely pleasing: Marilla understood the attraction. John had chosen wisely, and so long as she kept her eyes on Kitty, she could tolerate the heartache. Every time he started to edge into her vision, she busied her mind with just what to do with the ham tomorrow. She'd already picked out all the sides for the mutton.

"John and I will have to come calling on you soon."

Maybe a brown sugar and vinegar dressing.

"Yes, that'd be fine."

"After your company has gone, of course. Wouldn't want to be imposing ourselves, though I am envious of your hospitality. I bet they're eating like royals!"

Side of green peas. Two jars in the pantry.

"We're eating simple and good like Avonlea folk do."

"Well, I'm of a mind to learn to cook like you. John can't talk enough about your baking."

Nothing too sweet for dessert. It wouldn't digest well with the ham. Tart apple turnovers.

Theo finally handed Kitty the wrapped mutton leg, and John paid him.

"Thank you again, Marilla. It was a true delight meeting you. I know we're to be good friends."

Marilla nodded. "Good luck with the mutton roast."

"Who needs luck when I have the blessing of Marilla Cuthbert!"

John steered Kitty toward the door, and Marilla turned away so that she only heard him say, "Good-bye, Marilla."

She walked home with her bundle of ham, not remembering a tree or stone. Matthew was in the kitchen cleaning his harness bridles.

"I got ham for supper instead."

"Ham? We got a smoked rump in the cellar already, don't we?"

They did, but she wasn't in the mood to be reminded.

"One isn't enough for six mouths," she snapped.

Matthew set down his halter. The metal bindings made a quiet *click* on the table.

"You're right."

He sat, waiting. They'd spent too many years together. He knew her well.

"I met John Blythe's wife today." She pulled the butcher paper off the ham. "A fine match for him. Bright, cheerful, beautiful, and young." She scored the ham flesh over and over into a neat hatch pattern for the dressing.

Matthew said nothing. When she turned back from fetching the brown sugar and vinegar from the pantry, he'd left.

In the parlor, Abraham and Al played the quietest game of checkers she'd ever seen.

"Where'd everyone go?" she asked.

"Miss Izzy and Pa Meachum went on an errand," said Abraham.

"Told us to stay right here and not make a sound," added Al.

It was unnerving to see two boys so still.

"Ever trussed up a New Year's ham before?"

They shook their heads.

"Come on then, leave those checkers. Win or lose, everybody's got to eat."

XXXIII.

FUGITIVE SLAVE HUNT

A week later, Marilla sat knitting by the fire. Her eyes ached her. She rubbed them to regain focus, but her vision remained soft and smudged like butter on a knife edge. She thought about having Dr. Spencer give her a tonic to help. Rachel had said something about an elixir of ginkgo and bilberry that eased Mrs. White's cataracts.

The parlor was dim. She hadn't the energy to light the lanterns, so she and Matthew huddled by the fire, as close to it as they could get without scorching. Izzy and Mr. Meachum joined them after putting the boys to bed. Marilla thought it endearing how Izzy doted on Abraham and Al as if they were her own. Each night she and Mr. Meachum tucked the boys under their pallet covers and said a prayer with them before sleep. Part of Marilla envied the intimacy of that ordinary tending.

"Marilla, Matthew, we have news," said Izzy.

Matthew put down his *Harper's Weekly* and Marilla her knitting.

"We've heard from our Underground Railroad contact in Charlottetown. He's agreed to make free papers for the boys. He has a route mapped out from Prince Edward Island to Newfoundland. There's a couple there who've offered to take the boys for as long as needed. Until Mr. Meachum can reunite them with his daughter, of course."

"*If* they can be reunited." Mr. Meachum didn't flinch when he said it, though the rest of them did. "I'm not purblind to the reality of our situation. No one has heard from my daughter in South Carolina since she dispatched the boys. Slave masters don't deal kindly with having their property disappear. An ad has already been placed for Abraham and Albert's return—at a significant bounty too."

He looked away to the fire, crackling and spitting at the log. Izzy took his hand. Her eyes glinted worry.

"The farther north the boys go, the safer they are from being found," he continued. "We've got to move them. We can't stay hidden at Green Gables much longer. Visiting relations over the holidays is one thing, but folks will start suspecting soon. We've got to get the boys to Newfoundland and then return to St. Catharines."

"From St. Catharines, we can do our best to prevent the fugitive-slave hunters from following the trail," said Izzy.

Marilla understood. She hated to think of them leaving, but it was the only way to ensure the boys' protection. Prince Edward Island was too close to the mainland. It was only a matter of time.

"What can we do to help?"

"We must get papers in Charlottetown first. Then go to the coast. There's a safe house there with a boat ready to sail for Port aux Basques."

"I'll drive you," said Matthew. "No one would think twice about me and Aunt Izzy with Mr. Meachum accompanying us. But you two alone . . . people would talk."

Mr. Meachum nodded. "True."

"It's a full day and night to Charlottetown and back," said Marilla. "With the livestock bedded down in the barn, there are only the indoor chores to be done. Abraham and Al can help me."

"Thank you." Izzy gave Marilla's hand a warm squeeze. "So we leave at first light."

All in agreement, they said their good-nights and went to bed, anxiety gnawing on the hems of their dreams.

Marilla was up well before sunrise, wrapping oatcakes and cold bacon in knapsacks. Matthew finished his coffee in three gulps and was out the door preparing the horse and wagon. He thought it best if they took theirs so that Izzy's charge would be rested for the journey to the coast. They left at dawn.

The boys hardly made a peep at breakfast. Abraham forced down a bite of hotcake, while Al forked his over and over until it looked like a tilled field.

"I don't blame you for not being hungry," consoled Marilla. "But no matter what, you've got to face the day. Air to breathe, ground to walk, chores to do. You need sustenance for that."

She drizzled maple syrup over the cakes, and before she'd returned from the pantry, their plates were clean.

"That's the way, lads. Everything looks better with a full stomach."

They helped her do the dishes, and afterward they went to the barn for the morning milking and feedings, mucking the stalls, and refilling the animals' water buckets. The boys had quiet, peaceable spirits—eager to lend a hand where they could, without dawdling off to daydream as children were wont to do. At ten and seven years old, it was as if they were grown-up men in boy disguises. Marilla admired them while simultaneously grieving for their abridged childhoods. Losing a mother irreparably aged a person, she knew, but she'd never feared someone would come to take her life too. That kind of ceaseless terror was unimaginable at any age. Yet these two bore it as nobly as princes. It softened her toward them, and for the first time she felt the bud of something she could only assume was a kind of mothering.

"Bonny-D favors you both," she complimented them. "She never gives me or Matthew this much milk on the day to day."

By noon, the boys proudly stood in the kitchen with the pail full of milk, the firebox restocked, half a dozen eggs collected from the henhouse, and their Christmas mittens drying by the stove.

"I know Matthew introduced you to the simple goodness of

Bonny-D, but when hard work earns extra measure, I like to add a bit of cocoa and sugar. Keen on a taste?"

Al's expression broke into a smile. "Yes'm! That's how our momma makes it when Missus gives her a special chocolate. She boil it down in milk for us."

"I told you not to talk about Momma!" Abraham hissed.

Al nearly came to tears. His bottom lip stuck out so far, Marilla was afraid he might've swallowed the top.

"Now, now," she put her arms around the brothers so that they were three in a circle. "Why can't Al talk about his mother? She was a good woman, and she done right by sending you boys to your Pa Meachum. You should tell each other happy memories of her. That keeps a person with you no matter how far away or how long it's been since you saw each other. Not even the grave can take that from you. I know. My mother's been gone since I was a little older than you, Abraham."

She didn't know how she'd come to say so much—like a honeycomb, once pressed, she couldn't stop the flow.

Abraham's eyes widened, tearful. "Your momma's gone to Glory?"

Seeing his emotion brought out her own. She had to gulp hard to keep it in place. "Yes."

It stuck her like a pin: the hypocrisy of what she'd just said and what she didn't do. Matthew and she never spoke of Clara, and hardly of Hugh since his passing. She suddenly wished Matthew were there so they could.

"Do you miss your momma?" asked Al. A tear wormed down his cheek.

Marilla cupped his face between her palms. "Every bit as much as you miss yours."

She came close to kissing his forehead but restrained herself and wiped his tear away with her thumb instead.

"Now, how about you two play checkers while I simmer the milk and cocoa."

"Yes, ma'am," they said and went to the parlor without making another sound.

Darkness came on too early in winter. She'd barely ladled the hot cocoa into cups when her eyes began to smart for squinting. Probably best. Night was a comfort when one wanted to remain hidden. She hoped Izzy and Mr. Meachum had accomplished their mission and were resting comfortably under the roof of the Charlottetown Inn. They'd be back soon enough, repacking their wagon and heading north. Then her Gables would be emptied.

In just a short time, she'd grown used to having them all there. It was hard to imagine the house without them. But tomorrow was a new day, with no memory or sentiments of yesterday. *How wonderful*, she thought. *How tragic*.

She lit a lantern and put it on the tray with their drinks.

"Here we are." She set the tray on the parlor table beside the checkerboard.

Just as each boy was taking a cup, there came a distant thudding. Horses. Riding toward them at a pace.

The boys heard it too, and their eyes looked to her wide.

"Go!" Marilla directed. "Into the West Gable sewing room. There's a black horsehair trunk with brass nails for fabric bolts. Get inside and cover yourselves. Don't come out no matter what you hear."

Their cups sloshed over as they fled.

Marilla was glad she'd only lit the one lantern light, and now she blew it out. She went to the parlor window and willed her eyes to see as best they could: a line of black bees winged their way closer and closer; giant locusts set upon the Gables. All she could do was wait as calmly as possible. Her mind raced. Her heart pounded. Fear hammered her skull. Do what you would on any given night.

Do what you would alone, she told herself. Quickly, she went to the kitchen, refilled the pot with water, carrot, turnip, onion, and set it on the stove. She picked up her knitting and held it in her lap for what felt like an eternal purgatory. And still she jumped at the bang on the front door.

"Who's there?" she said loud enough for the boys to hear upstairs. "Just a moment!"

She put down her needles and slowly, calmly unbolted the front door.

The men did not surge inside as she'd anticipated. A foursome stood across the front lawn with rifles in hand and horses flicking dark manes. The leader greeted her on the porch.

"Good evening, are you Mrs. Cuthbert?"

"Miss Cuthbert," she corrected and raised herself high to conceal her shaking knees. "And who are you coming onto my property in the dark like this?"

"Miss Cuthbert, I am Mr. Rufus Mitchell of the Runaway Slave Patrol." He flashed a metal badge pinned lopsided to his vest.

Marilla squinted. "Never heard of you."

He laughed a sharp, tinny sound that reminded her of a plow blade hitting bedrock.

"Pardon me," he bowed. "Of course you haven't. Never been to this part of Canada. An island is an unusual place for Negroes to be congregating, don't you think?"

"Not so unusual," she dared. "Nova Scotia has many. Whole families. We have some working on Prince Edward Island."

"So you do have Negroes around." He raised an eyebrow high. "Any staying with you here?"

She held her tongue a beat, not knowing how much to say. Only Rachel and Robert had seen the boys. The rest of the town was of the mind that Izzy was visiting with her butler Mr. Meachum, a free servant traveling with her of his own accord.

Mitchell took her pause as an indictment. He stepped forward. "You wouldn't mind if we take a look. Nothing to hide, right?"

His companions came up the steps behind him.

Marilla barred the door with her arm. "You have no right."

"Property laws say otherwise."

"This is *my* property, and I object."

"If our employer's slave property be within, then I must insist."

He pushed past her into the house.

She pulled at her collar. "For the sake of propriety then—if you do believe that there is anyone fitting your description here. I live with my brother, Mr. Matthew Cuthbert, and he is away. It would be *indecent* for an unmarried woman such as myself to have men in the house. I'm told the people of the South have the utmost honor. Are you the outlier, sir?"

Mitchell put both hands up innocently, though she saw the bulge of his gun against his side. "I'm not going to lay a finger on you, Miss Cuthbert. You have my word as a gentleman of the Confederate States of America."

"What country is that?" she asked. "I've never heard of it either."

"Oh, you will," said Mitchell. "You surely will."

His guardsmen entered. Snow-muddied boots clomped across her floors. One of them went to the parlor, pushing past the Christmas tree. Needles fell to the ground. The other three men went into the kitchen, Matthew's bedroom, and the barn beyond. Marilla had to keep them from going upstairs. The man in the parlor picked up her father's Bible, flipped the pages as if looking for hidden messages. She hated his impertinence—and his filthy hands on her private things.

"'Lying lips are abomination to the Lord,'" he sneered at her. "Proverbs 12."

The truth will make you free, she thought, *but how?* Then it came to her.

"Mr. Mitchell, please." She took the Bible from the guard and gestured to the mess on the floor. "I would appreciate if your men respected my home. If you would simply *ask* if I've had any slaves under my roof, I would tell you truthfully."

Mitchell sucked his teeth, then gave the signal for his man to move aside.

"All right, Miss Cuthbert. I'll give you one chance to tell me the truth."

She forced herself to take two steps toward him so that she could see every hair of his beard. "I've provided accommodations for my aunt's butler, a *free* black man with papers. She was here for the holidays. They've gone to Charlottetown on an errand. That's where my brother is too."

The men came from the kitchen. "All clear. Want us to go upstairs and look?"

Mitchell stared hard at Marilla. She held her breath to keep from trembling. "Mr. Mitchell, I cannot abide . . ."

"I take you for an honest woman, Miss Cuthbert. I do indeed."

He set his hands casually on the back of Matthew's sitting chair, and she'd never been gladder for an antimacassar.

"Do you swear to me that there is no reason we need look through your bedrooms?"

She met his gaze with narrowed determination. "Absolutely none."

He turned to his men. "See anything suspect?"

They shook their heads. "Just supper on the stove," said one, and the other smacked his lips.

Mitchell gave a wolf grin. "Well then, I suppose we'd best be on our way to Charlottetown. But before we go, my men have traveled a great distance and would be much obliged for a little Christian charity from your stewpot."

Marilla had no desire to host these men, but if that's what it took to make them leave . . . "Certainly. Take all I have. As you see, I am alone. There's nothing I can do to stop you."

With that, she marched into the kitchen. Vegetable broth was hardly a meal, but they could have the soup *and* the pot so long as they got out of Green Gables. She put a towel around the wire handle, prepared to pick up the whole thing, when Mitchell said loudly:

"I love checkers. Who're you playing with, Miss Cuthbert? I see you've got three mugs of cocoa too."

The room bucked, then spun like a coin flipped head over tail.

"That was earlier today." Her voice was pitchy. She cleared her throat, but the tightness remained. "I was playing with . . . with . . ."

She heard their boots moving toward the stairwell.

"No!" She dropped the pot, but before she could start back down the hall, the front door opened in a bluster of cold and moonlight.

XXXIV

A FRIEND CLOSER
THAN A BROTHER

John. Once again, and always, he was there. Marilla had never been happier to see anyone in her life. He held a rifle, cocked and loaded, under his arm.

"Sirs, may I ask your business with Miss Cuthbert?"

The bounty hunter by Mitchell's side took a hostile step forward and the others gathered behind him, but Mitchell put out a firm hand. None of the men had their guns ready, giving John the advantage. Despite being outnumbered, he would get at least one lethal shot before they had the chance to return fire.

"Let's all calm down," said Mitchell. "We don't want trouble with you, sir."

"Your actions speak to the alternative." John pointed his gun squarely at Mitchell's chest. "You obviously aren't from around here, so perhaps you aren't aware. Trespassing at night is a violation of our criminal code. I have every right to shoot you and your men for no more reason than where you stand."

"Well now, are you Mr. Cuthbert? Because if not, then from where I *stand,* this is not your property, so shooting us would be a kind of murder."

"Not if Miss Cuthbert gives me her permission."

"I do." Marilla didn't wait a beat.

Mitchell put up his hands again, higher.

"We apologize for inconveniencing Miss Cuthbert. We're only

here looking for fugitive slaves on behalf of Mr. Laurens of Cottage Point Plantation in South Carolina. We're simple men upholding the law, just as you are."

"I told you, there's no one here but me," said Marilla.

"You heard her." John nodded the rifle. "It's time you take your leave of Green Gables—and Avonlea."

Mitchell tugged the brim of his hat respectfully. "Well then, we best be on our way to Charlottetown, where Miss Cuthbert says her aunt has gone. See if her slave has any information to share."

"He's a free man—her shop assistant and butler," corrected Marilla.

Mitchell smirked. "Black is black, Miss Cuthbert. No paper can change that."

It sent a chill down her back.

John motioned with the gun. "Get on."

The men filed out the front door, down the porch steps, and onto their horses, with John moving the gun steadily from man to man.

"A pleasure meeting you, Miss Cuthbert," Mitchell hollered, then gave his horse such a kick that it brayed in pain and shot off at a gallop. The four men followed.

John and Marilla stood on the porch long after the hoofbeats had receded, the cold night air creeping over them. The sweat of their brows shimmered a-frost in the clear winter's night. Marilla didn't realize she was shaking until John put an arm around her to steer her back into the house. Only then did she let down her guard. She curled into his chest. His head leaned onto hers, and he wrapped his arms around her. She pressed her ear to his heart and listened to the soft, fixed beating. No memory of the past. No worries of the future. Just the stroke of the seconds: now, now, now.

"It's all right," he whispered. His breath fanned across her forehead. "Come on, let's get you inside before you catch ill."

She moved only because he moved, her body tethered to his.

"H-How did you know to come?" Her teeth chattered.

John pulled her close to the fire and rubbed her arms until her skin kindled.

"Rachel. She saw the strangers ride past her farm to Green Gables. Thomas is away in Spencervale, so she sent Robert over to get me. This time of night, she knew whoever they were, they meant trouble."

Marilla nodded, still wrapped in his arms. She might not have ever moved if she hadn't remembered . . .

"The lads!"

She took the stairs as fast as her legs could carry her. John followed. In the West Gable sewing room, she threw open the horsehair trunk.

"Abraham! Al!"

From beneath the swaths of fabric rose two spindly, dark bodies and two sets of the most beaming beautiful eyes she'd ever seen. Marilla threw her arms about them, heads knocking into hers painlessly.

John stood alongside and marveled.

"This is Mr. John Blythe," she told them. "He fought off the bad men."

Tears streaked Al's face. "Are they gone?"

John put a hand on his shoulder. "Yes, son, they're gone."

Abraham looked to the rifle John still carried. "Will you stay with us?"

"Yes."

Then Abraham pulled his little brother to him, and they clung together like two links of a chain.

The boys wouldn't sleep without Marilla and John close by, and truth be told, neither could Marilla without the three of them. She brought pillows and blankets to the sewing room. It was the safest place if the men returned. The boys could hide quickly.

"I can't sleep," Al whispered to his brother. "Momma tells us story-tales when Sandman won't come."

Abraham put a hand on his brother's back. "I can't think of any right now."

Al sighed. "Miss Marilla, do you know any?"

"Well now, I don't know if I could think one up afresh . . ." Marilla's stomach dipped at the sight of Al's tired, tearful eyes. "Miss Izzy used to read me rhymes when I was younger. They were happy stories that helped pass the time. Would you like to hear one?"

Both boys nodded.

She hadn't thought of the nursery rhymes in years.

"My favorite was called 'The Star.'" She cleared her throat. "'Twinkle, twinkle, little star, how I wonder what you are. Up above the world so high' . . ." She paused, struggling to recall the next part.

"Like a diamond in the sky," said John.

"Do you know it, Mr. Blythe?" whispered Al.

"That I do," said John.

With his help, by the time they'd finished the poem, the boys had drifted off to steady breathing. Al curled kittenlike in the crook of John's arm. Abraham's head fell into Marilla's lap with his mouth opened wide as a snow moon. She thought how much like baby Hughie he looked. Times ten years, of course. She tucked the downy blanket under his chin, and when she looked up, John was watching her. He smiled. She smiled. It seemed a slipstream between them, driving her mind back to wonder: Could it have been like this? Our own family?

The imagining made her feel as if she'd dropped over the edge of an unseen cliff and was falling down and flying up all at the same time.

"Thank you, John," she whispered.

His eyes glimmered unspoken thoughts, and she knew she might never have the chance to speak hers again. But words of love were not the Cuthbert way.

"You have been the truest . . . the *dearest* friend of my life."

John didn't blink. His gaze shone brighter.

"And you of mine."

The gravity was too great. She gave over to sleep with the rhythm of the story following her through the darkness:

When the blazing sun is gone,
When he nothing shines upon,
Then you show your little light,
Twinkle, twinkle all the night.

XXXV.

MORNING REVELATION

Marilla awoke to the startle of a horse's neigh. She shot up on her feet before realizing that she was the only one in the room. What she'd thought was Abraham was, in fact, a pillow under her arm. John and the boys were gone. In alarm, she went out on the upper landing, smelling coffee and hearing the murmur of voices below.

"John?" she called.

No answer. She went across the hall to Izzy's room, the East Gable, so she could look out through the bare boughs of the cherry tree to the road. There stood John beside their horse and buggy, with Matthew, Izzy, and Mr. Meachum aboard.

Marilla put a hand to the light-washed window, so grateful for morning. The pane of glass dewed at her touch, and her eyes followed suit. She wiped them dry and smoothed her hair back into her bun before going downstairs.

"Our operative received word of the slave hunters on their way to Green Gables," explained Izzy. "Matthew drove all night to avoid them in Charlottetown and get back to you."

John had cleaned the spilled pot in the kitchen and made breakfast while Marilla slept. The boys ate steaming bowls of oatmeal porridge. She hadn't eaten since the morning before, but still had no appetite. Coffee was as much as she could stomach, and thankfully, John had brewed a good kettle. Izzy and Marilla sat at the wooden table with the boys while the men sentineled round.

"You saved my grandsons. I'm forever in your debt," said Mr. Meachum.

John shook his head. "No debt. We live by a different creed than our neighbors to the south. *Abegweit*—that's the original name of this place. A wise woman once called it 'a land of new birth where all colors of men and beast are free to live their brightest.' I never forgot that."

Her words, so long ago penned, seemed leaden with all the years and regrets in between. They were a reminder that she'd once had a voice and still had a choice in her future.

"*Abegweit*," Mr. Meachum repeated. "It has a beautiful sound to it." He turned to Abraham and Al. "Starting now, when we speak of Green Gables, we call it *Abegweit*."

"A secret name—like Canaan?" asked Abraham.

"Canaan is Underground Railroad talk for Canada," explained Mr. Meachum.

"Miss Cuthbert be a shepherd on the Gospel train?" asked Al.

"Of a kind, yes."

Al *thunked* his porridge spoon. "I knew it the minute I come. Miss Marilla's house *is* a dream station."

Marilla had to smile too. It was a pretty thought, if only in dreaming.

Then came a rapping at the front door, and all of them jumped up from the table.

"Miss Cuthbert—Marilla? John?"

It was Kitty, dressed in riding skirt and boots. Her horse was tied to the fence post, snorting puffs of exasperation into the morning air. Marilla had to admire her pluck. She opened the door.

"Praise be!" Kitty embraced her. "I didn't sleep a wink."

Seeing her husband in the foyer, she released Marilla and threw her arms around his neck in a kiss. Marilla felt the part of her that had come loose overnight suddenly stitch up.

"Husband!" Kitty's relief was palpable.

"I'm fine. Glad I came over when I did."

Keeping one arm around John's waist, she turned to face them. "When Robert Lynde said there were men on horseback going to Green Gables, I told John, 'That's wickedness. You must go this instant. Marilla needs you!' But I couldn't stay at the farm another hour. I came as soon as there was light—worried sick. After all, we need you too." She put a hand to her belly.

John looked her over a moment. "We?"

She nodded.

He shook his head. "So soon?"

"We've been man and wife going on two months." She blushed. "These things don't take much time."

Didn't they? thought Marilla.

The room pinwheeled, with Kitty and John at the center. The rest was an incidental blur. John picked up his wife, then set her down so carefully, it was as if her feet were made of flower petals. The floor slipped away from Marilla, but she dared not sit or she might never be able to stand again. A child. His child. Their child. This was what she'd prayed for all these years. She wanted life for him.

Marilla looked round at the faces surrounding her in the house her father and mother had built. In each pock and pit, she saw the choices that had shaped her and led her to this moment. She couldn't change one without affecting the whole.

"Marilla." Matthew called her from her thoughts. "Mr. Meachum's carriage is loaded. The posse's headed to Charlottetown, but it won't take long for them to catch the trail. The agent is waiting for the boys on the coast. They need to go now."

While Mr. Meachum tucked the boys safely into the carriage, John helped Kitty onto her horse.

"Is it safe for you to ride?"

"Being with child doesn't make a woman frail, John," said Kitty.

Marilla felt her knee pop with a step. Her back twinged from lying on the hard floor all night. Kitty was younger and strong. Their child would be the embodiment of everything new and good. Kitty would love John the way he deserved.

"Thank you, Kitty," said Marilla. "For John—sending him and everything."

Kitty smiled. John bowed. Then they turned their horses together and set off toward the Blythe homestead.

Dressed again in her blue cloak for the journey, Izzy came to Marilla's side. She understood the pain of loving at arm's length. Such a short distance, yet it might as well be an ocean to the heart. The two women watched as the riders quickly grew small. The sun arced high above the snowy pasture rutted in hoof prints and paw prints and boot prints alike.

"Look," Izzy pointed.

Just shy of the woods stood a doe, as sepia smooth as she was graceful. Her fawn nibbled the needles of a white pine nearby. She watched them watching her.

"Nature's tracks don't deceive. They lead to life. Where there are hearts beating, there is love. Keep yourself open to unexpected blessings, dear."

Izzy looped her arm through Marilla's. Like a rosette stitch, it knit them together. The fragrance of her lilac powder bloomed through the mineral tang of the snow, and it brought Marilla comfort. She couldn't honestly remember what Clara had smelled like anymore. She'd only known her for thirteen years. She'd known Izzy for double that. Twin sisters, cut from the same cloth. Marilla wondered if their spirit had been too much for the world. So great it had split during creation and then condensed back to one. In that way, her mother was there in Izzy and always had been.

John's and Kitty's figures finally dipped out of sight, like the last line of a fairy tale. Marilla had never thought about what came after.

Izzy reached down and scooped up two pieces of sandy rose quartz from the yard.

"It isn't Hope River, but it'll do." She closed her eyes a beat, then flung one of the rocks into the white pasture. It slid across the snow and stood like a dot of ink from a paused pen.

She handed Marilla the second stone. "Make a wish."

Marilla took it, smoothing it between her fingers before finally speaking her heart aloud. She'd been silent too long.

"It would be nice to know the love of a child one day."

Izzy kissed her cheek. "And so you shall."

Then Marilla pitched the stone into the pasture with all her might.

AUTHOR'S NOTE

I wrote this novel with no grand ambition. Instead, I started with the cryptic un-telling—a mystery woven into *Anne of Green Gables*, Chapter XXXVII:

> *"What a nice-looking fellow he is," said Marilla absently. "I saw him in church last Sunday and he seemed so tall and manly. He looks a lot like his father did at the same age. **John Blythe was a nice boy. We used to be real good friends, he and I. People called him my beau.**"*
>
> *Anne looked up with swift interest.*
>
> *"Oh, Marilla—and what happened?"*

Anne's question echoed in my heart my whole life: *Oh, Marilla, what happened?* This novel is my answer to that. It is my invention of Marilla Cuthbert and the foundation of Green Gables before Anne Shirley arrived with her whimsical free spirit.

This novel is unusual in that we already know the ending. Lucy Maud Montgomery provided us with the Cuthberts' finale in glorious dénouement. We're working backward in the storytelling loop, connecting the journey's end to the start. Imagine it like an infinity symbol, weaving around and through time and place, real and fictional, season upon season. Art imitating life.

I lay myself plainly before you: I am not Lucy Maud Montgomery. The esteemed, beloved works we have by her are all there are in the world and all there ever will be. This is a novel by me, Sarah McCoy. I wrote from a place of grateful reverence to a fictional landscape that has given me much scope for imagination. I wrote praying each hour that I would honor that world and add to it in a way that would make its creator proud. And now I write again with the hope that readers will understand Marilla for who she is as a woman unto herself . . . as I am unto mine.

To do Marilla justice, I rigorously studied the *Anne of Green Gables* book series. In addition, I researched as much about Lucy Maud Montgomery's life as possible, including a trip to Prince Edward Island, Canada. I walked in her real-life footsteps: down the pasture paths she took; through the balsam and "haunted" woods; and across the yards of her childhood home with her grandparents the MacNeills; her cousin's home next door, now Green Gables Heritage Place; and her favorite aunt Annie Campbell's farm, Silver Bush. I watched the island turn red as fire from Cavendish Beach and shielded my eyes from the sparkle of the Lake of Shining Waters. I met and spent happy hours talking with her family relations who still live on the island and run the Anne of Green Gables Museum. I touched her birthplace and her grave, spoke promises to her bones, and said prayers to her spirit. I did all of this so that my Green Gables story world would be suffused with hers. I wanted her blessing, yes. Just as she so earnestly sought the blessings of her readers, I seek the same.

Technical notes regarding the research and writing:

I bowed to the vernacular of the period, which would've been Marilla's lexicon, for the spellings and names of many people, places, and things. These were sanctioned by a key set of Canadian Cultural Accuracy Readers to whom I am ever appreciative. Still, we must remember that this is Lucy Maud Montgomery's fictitious rendering of Canada, Prince Edward Island, and the world at large, which I have now expounded upon through my own authorial lens.

Avonlea and the surrounding villages never existed except for here
on the page.

Below is a list of resources that I turned to time and time again
during the writing process. I'm ever grateful to the authors, all
Green Gables kindreds.

- The *Anne* series by Lucy Maud Montgomery:
  Anne of Green Gables
  Anne of Avonlea
  Anne of the Island
  Anne of Windy Poplars
  Anne's House of Dreams
  Anne of Ingleside
  Rainbow Valley
  Rilla of Ingleside
- *The Annotated Anne of Green Gables*, by L. M. Montgomery, ed-
  ited by Wendy Elizabeth Barry, Margaret Anne Doody, and
  Mary E. Doody Jones
- *Anne's World, Maud's World: The Sacred Sites of L.M. Montgom-
  ery*, by Nancy Rootland
- *In Armageddon's Shadow: The Civil War and Canada's Maritime
  Provinces*, by Greg Marquis
- *Black Islanders*, by Jim Hornby
- *Blacks on the Border: The Black Refugees in British North America,
  1815–1860*, by Harvey Amani Whitfield
- *A Desperate Road to Freedom (Dear Canada)*, by Karleen Bradford
- *Finding Anne on Prince Edward Island*, by Kathleen I. Hamilton
  and Sibyl Frei
- *L.M. Montgomery Online*, edited by Dr. Benjamin Lefebvre
- *North to Bondage: Loyalist Slavery in the Maritimes*, by Harvey
  Amani Whitfield
- *Provincial Freeman Paper, 1854–1857*, by Mary Ann Shadd Carey

- *Rhymes for the Nursery,* by Jane Taylor and Ann Taylor, first published in 1806
- *Spirit of Place: Lucy Maud Montgomery and Prince Edward Island,* by Francis W. P. Bolger, Wayne Barrett, and Anne MacKay
- "Slave Life and Slave Law in Colonial Prince Edward Island, 1769–1825," by Harvey Amani Whitfield and Barry Cahill, *Acadiensis Vol. 38,* No. 2 (Summer/Autumn-Été/Automne 2009): 29–51, https://www.jstor.org/stable/41501737?seq=1#page_scan_tab_contents
- *The African Canadian Legal Odyssey: Historical Essays,* edited by Barrington Walker
- *The History of New Brunswick and the Other Maritime Provinces,* by John Murdoch Harper
- *The Lucy Maud Montgomery Album,* by Kevin McCabe, edited by Alexandra Heilbron
- *The Selected Journals of L.M. Montgomery, Vol. 1: 1889–1910,* edited by Mary Rubio and Elizabeth Waterston

ACKNOWLEDGMENTS

The writing of any book is a journey of mind and heart. I'm infinitely grateful to many people who came alongside me to help make this book all that it could be:

Rachel Kahan, I never knew the author-editor relationship could be one that transforms a person's life . . . until I met you. Thank you for having faith in me before I knew what story seeds lay buried within. A believer in divine intervention, I'm confident that every past road was leading me to you, a kindred and bosom friend. Thank you also to MJ, A, and Taylor for the countless moments of video joy during the creative process of this novel.

Jennifer Hart, Kelly Rudolph, Amelia Wood, Alivia Lopez, and the superlative team at HarperCollins for being champions of this book. Also, Cynthia Buck, my eagle-eyed copyeditor.

Mollie Glick, my agent and literary spouse. Forged by fire, we've come through bolder, sharper, and more united than ever. Thank you for fighting for me and never leaving my side. My love to the mini Gs who are growing up to be Blythe-hearted gentlemen.

Emily Westcott for being the unsung hero of every day. Joy Fowlkes for your *joy*-full enthusiasm. Jamie Stockton for leading the charge around the globe and the rest of my CAA family for your great support.

Suman Seewat and Melissa Brooks, this novel's Canadian fairy godparents. Thank you for your expert editorial eyes. Your time and approval meant everything.

George Campbell, Pamela Campbell, the Anne Society of Prince Edward Island, and the Anne of Green Gables Museum. Thank you for welcoming me into Maud's world like family. Your generous love exceeded my every hope and expectation. I'm honored to have your blessing on this novel and your friendship in my life. This is just the beginning. I pray one day we can bring even more Green Gables to the world.

Green Gables Heritage Place docents for answering all my questions and letting me stay past closing when there was no one left but me, my mom, and Maud's memory on the porch. Thank you to Jacqueline and Emily at The Gables of PEI for going above and beyond as my hostesses while ensconced on the island.

Eternal gratitude to author friends who compassionately listened, encouraged me through the challenges, and shared the joys of this writing life. You are my tribe:

Sue Monk Kidd, for graciously reading the unedited manuscript; Susanna Kearsley, my emergency historian responder of Canadian politics; Paula McLain, Mc-Soul Sister, for spinning love like an everlasting Ferris wheel; Pepper Sister Jenna Blum, for being beautifully you; Melanie Benjamin, my yearlong bestie in Chicago; M.J. Rose and Fuzzle joys; Lisa Wingate, dragonflies forever; and Daren Wang, my Marilla man. I'm also grateful to friends who buoyed me on with laughter, tea, and endless support: Christina Baker Kline, Jane Green, Caroline Leavitt, Sandra Scofield, Therese Walsh, Karen White, and Alli Pataki, to name a few.

I'm nothing without the legions of bookstores, book clubs, and readers to whom I am appreciatively devoted. For going above and beyond during the writing of this novel, I must thank: Carol Schmiedecke, a truest kindred and L. M. Montgomery virtuoso; divine Jennifer O'Regan of Confessions of a Bookaholic; my honorary family at Reading with Robin, Robin Kall, and Emily Homonoff; Bookmarks NC bookstore beauties, Beth Buss, Ginger Hendricks, and Jamie Southern; Susan McBeth and Kenna Jones of Adventures by the Book; my WSNC radio family and Jim Steele, for being the jazzy big brother I never had—our "Bookmarked with Sarah Mc-Coy" shows are one of my favorite hours of the month.

My Person Christy Fore, her Person JC Fore, and my honorary nieces Kelsey Grace and Lainey Faith. I have a piece of you lock-et-ed in my heart always.

My First Best Friend Forever (FBFF) Andrea Hughes and dar-lings Abigail and Alice Hughes. I made a promise to you girls over teacups one June day. I keep my word. I hope you enjoy finding a little piece of yourselves forever a part of Green Gables.

Dr. Eleane Norat McCoy, to whom this book is dedicated and to whom I owe the most. Marilla's story would not be if not for you. As a child you introduced me to Maud's Green Gables world. You walked beside me through the imaginary time and places of the *Anne of Green Gables* series to the real ones of Prince Edward Island. Our sojourn together in October 2017 exceeded my every hope and dream. Your insightful musings, keen first-reader eye, and shared kindred allegiance to the true spirit of Maud's creation were in-valuable to Marilla's development. You inspire me in everything you do.

My McCoy men, Curtis, Jason, and Dr. Andrew McCoy, thank you for fiercely loving the women of our family, respecting us with your unyielding support, and honoring our passions as if they were your own. Andrew, you lived with me while I was in the writ-ing trenches (Chicago), so I must thank you specifically for giving me laughter and encouragement, even when the air-conditioning died, the basement flooded, and life seemed so uncertain that I couldn't hold in the tears. In an age when we desperately need more men of grace and vision, thank you three for being my white knights—or USMA black, as is the case!

To my abuelitos Maria and Wilfredo Norat, your legacy is a bas-tion of love. *Te amo con todo mi corazón y alma. Bendiciones y besitos por siempre.*

Titi Ivonne Tennent and Aunt Gloria O'Brien, to write a novel about one of the greatest "aunties" in literature, I had to know the love of women who raised me like their daughter. Thank you both for showing me the miraculous and boundless nature of mothers' hearts. I am who I am today because of your gracious hands on my life, never doubt it.

My husband Brian Waterman (aka Doc B), you didn't even know who Marilla Cuthbert or Anne Shirley was when I started writing this book. Yet you enthusiastically waved banners of support, trumpeted "head, not the tail" encouragement, and kept absolute faith during the dark hours when my own faltered. You even sat beside me through all of the 1985/87 *Anne of Green Gables* television miniseries—and *enjoyed it*. That's a real man. I wouldn't change one iota of the life we've created. The struggles and remodeling of dreams over the years have only made me love you more than I ever could've foreseen at seventeen.